Love and Music Will Endure

A novel based on the life of Màiri Mhòr nan Òran

Liz MacRae Shaw

The Islands Book Trust

CHAPTER I

Skeabost House, Isle of Skye, 1891

Is it the fox? Is it about the fox's stink? She wondered. She knew that the neighbours would have been complaining to him about it, grumbles sneaking out of the corners of their mouths. She strained to follow the scent. Why had the summons come now? Her mind scavenged for clues. She jabbed the tip of her umbrella between the stones as she strode along the driveway sweeping beside the river towards the loch.

'Walk tall, like Finn McCoul. Pound the earth beneath your feet.' That's what Pappa would say.

'Well I've done that often enough and enjoyed seeing my enemies tremble but it's hard to keep roaring now I'm old and battle scarred', she imagined replying to him. He had only known her when she was young with a high tide surging through her. How her Mamma used to shake her head at that strong current, the vigour within her that flooded over the banks of womanly behaviour.

'You've been trouble right from the start. What a hard time I had bringing you into the world. You had to be contrary even then, ripping your way out backwards. And afterwards you were always famished and suckled like a ravening beast.'

She stopped to catch her breath, looking down to check her shoes for mud. Those wretched corsets, nipping her as she bent. She lifted each of her heavy men's brogues in turn, grunting with the effort and scrubbed them through a clump of grass. When she was a child her mother had complained about how fast she grew. Màiri felt like a bumbling giant as she snagged her skirt on brambles or her raw boned frame burst the seams of her blouse yet again. To Mamma she was a boisterous heifer erupting from the winter byre with green meadow memories in her nostrils and trampling everything in her path.

There was the big house looming ahead, still looking raw and new laid against the dun coloured, muted winter landscape. The tower stabbed upwards, a thick accusing finger. What was she to be accused of? As a young woman when blame had struck her like a lightning bolt she had tried to flow quietly and not let the torrents spill over. But what use had meekness been when she had to fend for herself later on? Frowning she turned down the side wall leading to the back of the house. She kicked a loose stone, sending it skidding down the slope. Then she hauled out a glowing white handkerchief to swab her dripping face before heading towards the back entrance, the one used by servants, tradesmen and tenants. She had waited often enough at similar doors with Pappa when he came to pay his rent. Most of the men would shuffle in when it was their turn, caps crushed in their hands. A few sauntered in, hands plunged in pockets. Most commented on the weather, some enquired after the landlord's health, others ventured a joke. All of them though, bar one or two who were ostentatiously pious, accepted a dram, smacking their lips as the welcome heat slid down their throats. What did Pappa do? He held himself as steady as the Old Man of Storr himself and marched in with dignity – a nod but no smile.

'I'm not a supplicant,' He would say. And neither was she. All those years she had spent on platforms, the audience tight-packed as seabirds on a cliff, their cheers swirling around her. Had it been a mistake to return home? It was true that a prophet was without honour in his own land. She had done the neighbourly thing, calling on folk with a basket of warm bannocks on her arm. But people had changed their ways. They didn't want to be shown how to spin a strong woollen thread or how to cook herring the old way, straight on the peats. The lairds and their ladies were welcoming enough but they expected her to sing for her supper. Was that all she was now, an entertaining character? What about everything she had fought for? The Land League was fading from people's memories as if it had never been, just like the mighty Cuillin itself could be so smothered in mist that it disappeared from sight. We're all old now, our fine, fresh hopes curdled, she thought.

Taking a deep breath she swayed, broad-beamed, around the corner, the wind plucking at the edges of her plaid cape, making it billow out behind her. She looked over the calm sweep of Loch Snizort. The wind twitched the shimmering water, creasing its satin surface and splashing beads of rainbow light. She sucked in the moist air and let her lips stretch into a smile. The land was constant; it would always succour her. She had lived through terrors: the night-time thud on the door, the rough grasp on her arm, the shame of the prison cell. After all of that she could surely face up to a disapproving landlord?

She looked back towards the house and suddenly she realised that she could see right in through the window. She sidled closer. There was a small table there, holding a brass tray. Shiny enough but it would be the better for more elbow grease. She could make out strange, curved figures carved on it. He must have brought it back from India. What were they? Beasts of some kind? No, the legs surely belonged to people. Some sort of heathen gods? But four legs tangled together? Surely not? They wouldn't show that, a man and a woman coupled together? She chuckled out loud. Then with a jolt she saw Mr MacDonald himself heading towards the window. She stayed stock still, hardly daring to breathe. His fine, thin, face looked stern, his lips pressed together but – thank goodness – he was looking down at the table, not out of the window. His fingers reached out to a decanter and suddenly leapt back as if they had been burnt. Stiffly he walked back to a chair and sat down, putting his face in his hands. Now her own hands were shaking so much that she had to squeeze them together. He must be brooding about how he would tell her to leave. Had her neighbours come to moan about her? Where would she rest her head if she was turned out? Her children were scattered seed and her old friend Mairead back in Australia. Plenty would say that it served her right for getting above herself. Widows are expected to stay at home, Bible and knitting to hand. 'Crowing hens and whistling women are an abomination to the Lord,' as Mamma would say.

She wandered nearer to the shore and willed the calm water to flow through her. I won't leave the island I love for a second time, she vowed as she stood still, gasping in the moist air. Finally, she tramped up to the door and knocked hard. She could hear shuffling before it was opened. It was himself, adjusting a frown into a smile.

'Welcome, Mistress MacPherson. Will you not sit down?'

She levered herself into a chair. Her nervous eyes flickered around the room, quick as a fox's snout.

'You've not been in the estate office before? I was just finishing looking over some papers but I confess I expected you to use the front entrance, as before.'

'But you wanted to see me about the cottage. That's why I came round the back. The fox has run off you know. I've no man to share my life and now not even a male animal. I don't know what people are saying …' She blundered on but staggered to a halt when she saw how baffled he looked.

'I don't understand what your house – or indeed other people – have to do with our meeting. The house is yours for as long as you want it.'

4

She made a sort of sobbing laugh and stifled it in her handkerchief.

'And I'm grateful although there are Land Leaguers who still condemn me for accepting it.'

'They think that you fawn on the gentry?'

She snorted.

'They wanted me at the big meetings on Skye but did any of them offer me a roof over my head?' She gave him an appraising look. 'Do you know that during all those years of the troubles you were the only landlord who could go about in a pony and trap?'

He looked puzzled.

'All the others had to ride in a closed carriage for fear of having mud, stones or worse thrown at them,' she whooped, slapping her thigh.

'I'm relieved no-one disliked me enough to hurl things at me. Now if you'll excuse me for a moment.' He stood up and limped to the door.

'What a silly *cailleach* he must think me, blethering on about the fox. So why did he summon me?' she muttered to herself.

He came back, a boyish grin on his face and his hands clasped behind his back. He thrust one arm forward. 'I wanted you to see this.' His hand cradled something small, oblong and vividly red.

She took it, bracing her arms as if it was heavy. She squinted at it and turned it over before pressing it against her cheek. What did it smell of? Did it smell of a warm cow's flank or of a crisp winter's day that turned your breath to trails of smoke? It should smell of the countryside that had made it. Mamma used to say how parched she used to feel when they stayed in Glasgow, longing to gulp down Highland air.

'Do open it,' he coaxed.

She sighed and nestled it tenderly on her lap. Her fingers rummaged inside the bodice of her best dark purple gown, stumbling over the tiny buttons. He looked a little alarmed but smiled when he saw her pulling out a pearl handled magnifying glass. Her fingers buzzed and blundered backwards and forwards through the leaves. Then she reddened as she turned the book the right way round. Her eyes were too misted to fix on the bird tracks of the letters.

'I can't take it in. These were all stored away in my head for so long and now they're here. It was like waiting for my children to be born. I wondered what each of them would be like but I still couldn't believe it when a new stranger appeared.'

He nodded.

'Yet birth reminds me of death too. One of my daughters died young.'

He shuddered. 'Do you like the printing?'

'So many words. It took me so long to sing them all. I don't know how I managed it.'

'Well, if you recollect Mr White travelled up from Inverness and spent many hours writing them down at your dictation.'

'I can write a fair English hand but I never learnt to write Gaelic properly. I wouldn't want scholars to find mistakes.' She was pleased to see that he looked a little uncomfortable at her reproach.

'No, indeed. What do you think of the photographs of you preparing the tweed?'

She decided to be gracious. 'Very good. Of course I was brought up to learn all the household skills, not like young women today who expect to buy everything from shops.' She sniffed.

'There'll be a more formal presentation later but I thought you should see it first, hot from the press. It's a record of all those words that inspired your fellow Highlanders fighting for justice.'

'It's good that no-one can be thrown off the land anymore and have their homes torn down around them. But there are still so many hungry for land. I used to imagine that the wheel would turn and bring back the descendants of the folk driven from the island. I believed that the *Bugha Mòr* would ring again to children's voices and the shouts of young men playing shinty.'

A silence fell between them. He broke it first.

'Whatever the rights and wrongs of the Land Wars, the publication of your poetry is a cause for celebration. When my tenants come in here I offer them a wee dram although I know the minister disapproves. Perhaps a glass of wine would be more suitable today.'

She laughed. 'No, I'm happy to take a dram. It warms the heart and belly much better than your thin foreign stuff.'

'You don't adhere to the temperance rules, then?' he said with a grin as he struggled to his feet and hobbled over to the table. 'Forgive me for toasting you with water. This wretched gout is plaguing me at the moment.'

'I've always followed the Church's teachings, especially about keeping the Sabbath day holy. But I'll never understand how folk can be so peculiar that gloom becomes the food they eat. Song, shinty and the water of life all bring joy to our lives.'

'I couldn't agree with you more. I propose a toast to the success of your book and to all of us exiles returned to our native island.'

She downed her drink in one swallow and sighed in appreciation. He rose from his seat as if he was about to usher her out. Not so quickly, she thought. After all, his summons had caused her all that worry which was not good for a woman of her years. It was time for her to call the tune. She tapped the cover of the book and stood up.

'Before I go we should sing one of my songs. What about, "Farewell to the Island of Mists"?'

'Well, there're a lot of verses and my voice is rather scratchy these days.'

'Seventeen in total, I believe. I have them by heart but you may borrow the wee book of words if you wish,' she said, digging him in the ribs with an elbow.

He knew when he was beaten. So they sang together. His voice was true if a little croaky, she thought. She wished that he wouldn't sing with his hands in his pockets as so many men did. They stood side by side looking out at the loch held in the folds of the low hills. Sky and water seeped and smudged together, like colours painted on silk.

> Farewell to the place I grew up
> To the mountains topped with clouds
> Rose coloured skies of morning
> Sweeping out of the darkness
> Lighting up the Storr.
>
> Sights more beautiful the eye could never see
> Cattle out grazing on a peaceful sunny morning
> The lark on the wing singing confidently her music
> The mist surrounding Beinn Tianabhaig
> And the mountain under dew.

CHAPTER 2

Skeabost House, Isle of Skye, 1891

When Màiri left, Lachlan Macdonald hobbled over to the table. He reached over to the decanter standing sentinel on the polished tray. He had decided that he was going to have a drink even if the pain pounced again and sank its claws into his flesh. It seemed to toy with him, loosening its grip and leaving him whimpering with relief. But it stalked him and would return to savage him again weeks later. It seemed to wax strong in the damp climate. If he had remained in India would the heat have sapped its strength?

But he had yearned to return to the native island he had left as a young man and he loved this house he had built, adorned over the entrance with his own and Wilhemina's intertwined initials. A visitor who had drunk too much port one evening had told him how Henry the Eighth had used the same idea at Hampton Court. Later on the king had been obliged to bring in stonemasons to change the letters each time he had changed wives.

'That won't happen here,' Lachlan had replied tersely.

Yes, both he and Màiri, daughter of Fair Iain, had opened their infant eyes on the same beloved island. That was why he helped and defended her against her critics. She had already reached the allotted three score years and ten and although he was more than a decade younger she had left him feeling frail and limp in comparison. She was a force of nature, like a standing stone that had hoisted up its skirts to rampage across the land.

He poured himself a mean measure and sipped it, clinging gratefully to each drop. It seemed so unjust that he, a man of moderate habits, should be forced into abstinence by this damned gout. How long ago was it since he had first met her? He had long known of her powerful presence at the hustings and Land League meetings. John Murdoch had encouraged her of course. With his radical views he had assumed that Lachlan was a traditional laird, stiff with dignity rather than a younger son who had made his own way as an indigo planter.

It must have been ten years ago when John had arrived unannounced, as was his way, rosy faced and wild bearded. Lachlan had wished that he had been out shooting when John and his entourage arrived but it was a day of torrents and floods. So he had been sitting in front of a glowing fire reading the latest batch of letters and accounts from India when they had arrived. He welcomed John and his pack in for refreshment, including that fellow from London, he couldn't remember his name but he had the predatory stare of a fanatic.

'Is this your first visit to Skye?' Lachlan had asked him as they all sat at table.

'It is, and I'm horrified at what little effort the landowners have made to improve conditions for their tenants.' He paused to chew a piece of venison stew and banged the table with his fork.

'Of course, as we all know, property ownership is merely legalised theft. The solution is to nationalise all the estates in Scotland and give them to the tenants.' As he spoke he sprayed fragments of food in front of him.

He's shooting the enemy with his own hospitality, Lachlan thought, suppressing a grin as he caught John's apologetic eye. Later on there was a lull between showers. He and John left the Englishman savouring one of his host's cigars and strolled down to the loch.

'I've a favour to ask,' John had said. 'I wondered if you might be able to help Màiri. She's had to stay in Greenock to earn her living but she would dearly love to return here.'

'What does she need?'

'A house with a low rent. All the travelling is tiring and expensive for her although she's too proud to complain. She would be so useful here too – the fight has moved out of the cities to the islands.'

'As long as she's not as ferocious as your London friend. I think he would like to murder me in my bed, after he's eaten me out of house and home.'

'I do apologise about him'. John frowned but when Lachlan laughed he joined in. The matter was arranged easily enough. Lachlan offered her Wood End Cottage rent free.

'You would be doing me an honour if you accepted. It's a pleasant house and I don't want it to stand empty.'

So she had moved in. He didn't see a great deal of her from day to day but he did hear about her activities from his tenants, especially in recent years when the Land League activity had quietened down.

'Always gallivanting around the countryside, demanding a seat on a cart, appearing at people's doors and staying for hours.' That was old Mrs Beaton, prodding the ground with a stick in time with each grievance. 'What an appetite! Still at least she brings her own provisions. But she will insist that her herrings are put straight onto the hot peats, as if we didn't have proper pans in the house.' That was Mrs MacLeod adding grace notes to the criticism.

What a relief that the old ladies hadn't heard about the fox or the refrain of grumbles would never have ended. He knew too well the snags of envy that caught the successful returning Gael. She was free to treat the house as her own. He didn't want her to feel indebted but she hadn't even thanked him for getting her poems published. He remembered how she had held court in his library like a maharani while the eminent Gaelic scholar scratched away frantically to keep pace with her warbling cascade of words. Then sometimes she would halt suddenly and frown before singing out loud in a surprisingly girlish voice, very different from the confident boom of her speaking tones.

'The music guides the words like a faithful horse carries his rider when he forgets his way,' she had explained.

He had not intended to be sharp with her – that was discourteous – but she had shaken him when she had spoken about her daughter. He had felt a clammy touch on the back of his neck, the touch of his own long dead child, never spoken about and rarely brought to mind. She had been the child of his youth, born when he was struggling to build up his indigo estate. Those days were exciting but lonely too. His servant's daughter was so lithe and slender, her skin a warm brown and her eyes glowing with laughter. When their daughter was born she had the same dark velvet eyes as her mother and the baby's feathery tufts of hair were deep black. Her skin though was pale and he could see in her face a miniature copy of his own mouth and chin. He made plans for her future as he watched her grow old enough to totter about, chuckling to herself. But she caught the fever that dulled her eyes until they shrivelled and shrank back into her skull. She died so suddenly, another small victim of the harsh heat of India. Damn the woman, he thought angrily. How dare she surprise him like that so that his heart floundered again after so long?

He reached out for the decanter but stayed his hand. No, he had to starve the demon gout. He had made the mistake of giving Màiri too generous a measure and she had downed it so quickly. Is that why she had started smirking at him and digging him in the ribs? The whisky must have gone straight to her head. Good Heavens! Was she flirting with him? It was like being cornered by an elephant in must. He had heard the jokes about her craving for male company, a need that seemed to have grown rather than diminished over the years. Still, he had escaped lightly with a brief duet. He had taken care to ram his hands into his pockets to stop her seizing them.

His eye was caught by a movement outside. It was one of the farm cats, a scrawny tabby, crouching down, one foreleg raised in slow motion, its eyes fixed on its prey. Suddenly he remembered the mongoose that used to live near his Indian bungalow. Half tame, it would hover around the kitchen quarters. The servants tolerated it because it killed snakes. One time he had seen it feinting and darting around an infuriated cobra. Màiri made him feel like that bamboozled snake, constantly swivelling his head to see where she would strike next. What a holy terror she was.

CHAPTER 3

Isle of Skye, 1810

'Look there she is', Iain pointed, his voice trembling.

'Aye', replied Flòraidh breathlessly, looking at the square-rigged ship sailing into the harbour at Portree. They had come down the hill from the Sluggans, the open ground at the edge of the village where the travelling people stayed all summer mending pots and living in their strange tents with a chimney sticking out of one end. They had been to the cattle sale there. Iain was pleased with the price he had got for his beasts and kept fingering the weight of the coins through the piece of cloth knotted around his waist. His plans were working out. There was enough money for a night at MacNab's inn rather than having to stay with his wife's relatives.

'We can look around her before she sails,' he said, quickening his pace and forcing her to lengthen her usual shuffle. They hurried down to the harbour to see the *Phoenix*. She had a battered grace, awkward as a heron among the small, bobbing craft that jostled her. Iain stared in amazement. He had never seen such a large vessel, a good ninety feet long. She must be able to carry two hundred people, he reckoned. A crowd had already gathered, some carrying belongings, others to gawp. A small boat was being lowered from the ship's side with two men aboard. As they drew it up on the shore Iain caught a sailor's eye and called out, 'Did you have a good journey from Greenock?' The man looked blank and sneered. Iain frowned. The other sailor spoke to him.

'You're wasting your time with most of the crew. They've only got the English.'

'See Iain, there are families aboard already', said Flòraidh, drawing his attention to some figures sitting huddled together in the stern.

'We're going back to the ship in a moment, Mistress. Why don't you come with us and get a proper look?' the sailor suggested.

She turned to Iain who nodded in agreement but once she had been rowed over she gazed up at the ship in horror and bewilderment. How was she to get aboard? Small boats she was used to, clambering over the side into waiting arms. But the swinging rope ladder dangling from the sheer cliff face of this vessel terrified her, especially now that her pregnancy had made her body unwieldy. She imagined herself slipping and hurtling down into the sea that would drown both her and the tender life curled within.

She turned to look for Iain but he was already striding away to check that their belongings were safe at the inn. A hand reached out to grip her arm. It was the sailor guiding her hands and feet onto the swaying ladder. She gritted her teeth as she inched upwards. He stood behind her, steadying it until she staggered aboard and stumbled over shards of timber left over from the ship's last cargo.

Meanwhile, as Iain climbed the brae to the inn he could feel a lightness in his step. He would soon be his own man, master of his own land with no-one telling him what to do. Still, he felt rage when he remembered what had brought them here. They had not planned to emigrate. Only last year they were newly married and settled into a decent sized croft with sweet grazing nearby. They were harvesting their first crop of oats and barley. They were half way through by the Saturday and the weather was holding up well.

Then he woke early on the Sabbath to see the clouds moving in, dark battalions from the west. He hurried out to finish the job, ignoring Flòraidh's protests, cutting and stacking the crop, a good thing too because ferocious wind and rain savaged the land the next day and for the whole of the following week. But of course some pious busybody, jealous of his good fortune, had tattled to the minister. There he came hopping up to their door with his beaky red nose and crow black plumage.

'I hear you've broken the commandment to keep the Sabbath Day holy', he said.

'I had no choice. Would the Good Lord think it right for me to leave us short of meal next spring?'

'It's not for you, Iain MacDonald, an unlettered man, to questions God's commands.'

'Maybe not, but didn't the Saviour himself love and forgive sinners? He would understand that poor men like me have to work so that we don't starve. We can't be like the fowls of the air that neither sow nor reap.'

Hearing her husband's raised voice, Flòraidh had rushed out, wringing her hands. 'Please forgive Iain, Sir. I'm sure he regrets the error of his ways.' She grasped her husband's arm but he shook her hand off.

'I want to hear the sinner himself repent.'

Iain stood motionless, towering over the slender figure of the minister. The silence lengthened like an afternoon shadow. Eventually the minister sniffed away a dewdrop and, gathering his dignity, turned away.

But the damage was done. The other women of Skeabost shunned Flòraidh or whispered behind her back while the men gave Iain sidelong glances. She was much grieved by this and Iain himself now felt unsettled on the land that had given him so much satisfaction to work. He carried on, his anger still rumbling within him until the day came for him to pay his rent to the factor, James MacDonald, a hard faced man with shrewd eyes. He was called *Seumas an Sionnach,* but not to his face.

'What's this I hear about you taunting the minister, *Iain Bàn*? It won't be forgotten. You're a marked man now.' He grinned wolfishly.

Iain glared at him through fierce blue eyes, under thick sandy eyebrows.

'Don't you long to be free of people meddling in your life? Aren't you tired of being a bull pulled along by the ring through his nose?'

Iain grunted.

'Wouldn't you rather be free of all that canting interference?

'Of course I would but I don't see how.'

'What about going to the colonies? You would be free there.'

Iain clenched his jaw, 'I won't be driven from my native land.'

'No, but you better yourself by going on your own terms. You'll have heard of Lord Selkirk who arranged for lots of Skye folk to sail to Prince Edward Island? They've thrived there. Now a good friend of mine, a lawyer in Glasgow, is at this very moment chartering a vessel to give the same chance to other emigrants.' He raised his hand as he saw Iain was about to protest. 'No, hear me out. It's not for paupers but for men with minds of their own. Men who can go to Canada, clear the forest and claim it for themselves.'

'And what do you get from it?'

James laughed harshly. 'Nothing except getting rid of the more thrawn tenants and making my job easier, and I do get a small consideration for my trouble. I have to be careful because Lord MacDonald doesn't want to lose his more active crofters.' He shrugged, 'Well, I can see my proposal is falling on deaf ears. Of course you need to be an exceptional man to undertake such an adventure. It's not for the faint hearted.'

The conversation ended there but the idea smouldered in Iain's mind like a peat fire damped down overnight. The more he thought about it the more the flames bloomed. He did have a choice. He didn't have to stay pawing the earth like a tethered bull. He could be free.

He stood brooding in the doorway of the inn until he felt his arm nudged.

'Why not come in and have a dram to drown your sorrows?'

It was the sailor who had spoken to him earlier. They went in and sat down at a bench.

'Are you having second thoughts about going?'

'I can't afford to have second thoughts. I've burnt my boats; sold my cattle and ended the lease on the croft. I've been thinking about going for weeks but now I've seen the ship it's hit me that I'll never see my home again. It's different for you, I suppose. You spend your life sailing the oceans.'

'Aye.' The sailor swirled his drink around in the glass. 'What do you know about Canada?'

'Not much. The factor told me about it. He said how well Lord Selkirk's settlement went and how there's plenty of land still for the taking.'

His companion screwed up his face and slurped his drink down as he rose to his feet. 'I'd best get back to the ship.'

Iain grabbed the man's scrawny arm in his beefy hand, 'Wait a moment. What aren't you telling me?'

The sailor prised off Iain's fingers and muttered, 'I can't talk here. I don't want to end up overboard. Wait a moment and then follow me out.'

'What's up? Is there something wrong with the ship?' Iain hissed once they had found an empty corner near the midden at the back of the inn.

'It's not too bad. It's old and overfull but you can survive that. It's what happens afterwards.'

'Spit it out man.'

The sailor sneaked a glance around them before continuing, 'Selkirk did the job properly. He victualled the ships and when they landed he lent money to the settlers. This time you'll have to manage on your own.'

'I'm not afraid of hard work. I can turn my hand to anything.'

'I'm sure you can my friend – when you're here. But over there it's very different; bitter cold and feet of snow on the ground from October to May. The moment you arrive you'll have to set to cutting down a forest so you can clear the land and build a cabin. Have you ever built a log house? You'll arrive too late in the season to plant for the next year. Have you money to tide you over?' His words spilt out in a rush. Iain shook his head slowly.

'The other thing you should know is that all the best land near the sea has already gone. The backlands aren't so fertile and too far away from the shore for fishing. Have you relatives out there already who could help you?'

'No, but whatever your warnings, I won't turn back now. I would look a fool.'

'Well, better a live fool than a dead one. If you don't take heed for yourself think of your poor wee wife. She looks delicate. The harsh life there takes a terrible toll on women and children.'

Iain was scowling and biting his thumb, 'So you're saying we've been duped. But it can't be that cold. The factor spread out a map and showed me that Prince Edward Island is due west from here.'

'Right enough but he didn't see fit to tell you how much colder it is in winter. Anyway, you must make up your own mind.' His voice trickled away to silence and then he was gone.

Iain walked back down to the shore in turmoil. Surely it was too late now to turn back without losing face? He wouldn't get his old croft back, it was rented out to someone else now. His hopes of independence were crumbling away. Flòraidh, back on dry land, waved to him. Her face looked strained and the skin under her eyes was bruised with tiredness. She begged him to take her back to their room at MacNab's so that she could lie down.

Once inside their room she sank back on the bed and began to sob. All her fears came pouring out. She had spoken to the women who had come from Greenock and inspected the living accommodation for herself. She saw that there was a rough pine bunk for each family, with barely two feet of space from top to bottom. There were a few fish oil lamps hanging from the bulkheads and filthy lidded wooden buckets for the passengers to relieve themselves. Even worse than the dark cramped quarters was the stench of vomit and urine, mingled with the reek of the soaking briny timbers. The wood was so rotten that she could pick off slices of it with her fingernails.

'I'm terrified of dying down there, Iain,' she cried, 'What if the ship goes down in a storm or we catch a fever? What if the baby comes early and I have to give birth in that hell-hole?'

He tried to comfort her but she was inconsolable. The women had told her about the bad smell coming from the barrels of meal and salted meat carried aboard. What scared her more than anything though was the story one of the sailors had told her about an earlier emigrant ship.

'It left from Ullapool but before it sailed one of the passengers was out looking after his cattle one evening. He noticed a small creature, hopping like a rabbit from cow to cow and suckling milk from each of them. He tried to shoot the creature without success. Then he took a silver sixpence from his pocket and used it as a bullet. This time he wounded the beast and it limped away leaving a trail of blood. He asked in the village if there was anyone who had been injured and was told that an old woman had been hurt. Her neighbour heard her say that the ship would never reach America. The passenger was worried enough to ask for the *cailleach* to be kept confined in her house until the ship arrived safely.' She lifted a finger to stop him interrupting.

'Anyway, they made a safe crossing and when they docked they met another ship returning to Ullapool. Word was sent back with this boat that they could set the old woman free. What do you think happened next, Iain?'

'Some terrible disaster, no doubt,' he said sarcastically.

'Barely had the passengers got ashore when for no reason the ship sank to the bottom of the sea. It was the witch who did it!'

'Did anyone drown?'

'No but they almost did. Next time the spell might work earlier when the ship's still out at sea.'

'Well, she wasn't much good with her spells. I bet that after the people went ashore and lightened the vessel the crew took the ballast out too quickly and she toppled over.'

But no words of his could clear the haunted expression from her fine-boned face, 'I don't want to disobey you but I don't believe that I can force myself aboard that cursed ship.'

He stared at her, frowning while she gulped back her tears. Then she bent forwards, her face in her hands. He waited a moment and put an arm around her shaking shoulders.

'Hush now. You don't have to go. I've heard things too. Not silly stories about witches and their spells but about us being tricked by that devil *Seumas,* may God rot his soul in Hell.'

So the ship sailed without them aboard. The coins wrapped in the piece of cloth paid instead for them to travel down to Glasgow and start a new life there.

A few weeks later Flòraidh lay awake while her husband twitched restlessly in his sleep. When Iain had said that they must emigrate she had closed her mind to thoughts of home but now that they were still in Scotland she allowed herself to throw open the shutters. She pictured the wandering Snizort River, unravelling itself through its shallow dished valley. The encircling hills could appear stark but to her they were cupped hands holding the glen safely. She imagined herself among the trees down by the water, their roots coiled like corded veins, their branches bowing to the rhythm of the wind. The minister would say that it was God's hands that were holding the glen and the people who lived there, but she couldn't help believing too that the river, the wind, the trees and all the living creatures each had their own different spirit that gave them being. She couldn't return there now. For the time being they would have to stay in this room in a dingy close where the walls seeped damp, in a city where the air was sour and the Clyde greasy and lifeless.

Never mind baby, she whispered, stroking the mound of her belly. At least you won't be born in a distant country, an exile for ever. You'll be born in Scotland and one day we'll return to Skye.

CHAPTER 4

Skeabost, Isle of Skye, 1830s

As a child Màiri loved to hear Pappa's stories about the ship that nearly took him and Mamma to Canada, long before she was born. She shivered when she thought about how her own life was decided by a sudden turn of fate. What would it be like living in that land across the sea? It was full of dark, devouring forests. Not like here at Skeabost where her eye could soar out in the open, an eagle in flight and watch the Old Man of Storr rise up from the darkness. What more could you wish for?

'What do you know about anything? You've never been anywhere else,' Seonag sneered. She was her elder sister, raised in Glasgow before their parents returned to Skye. Màiri and her elder brother Murdo were both born later on the island. Seonag was staying with them for a short visit and how Màiri wished her far enough away.

'If Glasgow's so wonderful why don't you stay there? And why couldn't Pappa and Mamma wait to leave it?'

Seonag jabbed her sister in the ribs. 'Stop blethering and look for some eggs. I'm not wasting my time arguing with a wee fool.'

It's living in that stinking city that makes her so bad-tempered, Màiri thought as she flounced out of the door. Ah, there's Mairead. The sight of her friend coming to see her made her smile but something was wrong. Mairead was shuffling her feet instead of scampering along as she usually did.

'Come and help me find some eggs,' Màiri called.

The girls walked into the byre attached to the house. It still held the musty smell of their dun cow, *Blarach*, and her calf, even though the animals had been let outside to snuffle the moist spring growth. They rifled through the straw and Màiri plucked out two warm eggs. She made a nest for them in her basket.

'I won't be helping you do this anymore.' Mairead rubbed her eyes with her sleeve.

'Why ever not?'

'We're leaving for Australia. Do you think they'll have hens there?'

'How would I know?' Shock made Màiri's voice sharp, 'You can't go.'

'My Pappa says he can't endure it here any longer. He works so hard and bad weather spoils it all.'

'Let him go then if he wants to. You can stay with us, we've plenty of room. Lady Seonag will be away again soon. We'll tuck up nice and warm in my bed with the curtain pulled tight.'

'I have to go.' This time she didn't stem the flow of tears streaking down her face. 'It's so far away we'll never see each other again in this life.'

'Well, what you must do is look at everything here so closely that you can't ever forget it. So when you're far away you can picture it all in your head.'

She seized her friend's hand and together they ran up towards the common pasture where everyone kept their beasts. Prickly gorse tugged at their skirts. When they reached the top of the rise they flung themselves down, breathless, their faces nuzzling the neat buttons of primroses. After they had stopped gasping they played at rolling down the hill, spinning ever faster, hearts in mouths, crushing the new grass beneath them. Then they trudged further up the hill to a hideaway they had made the summer before. It was beside a lochan, hidden in a dip. They had woven a roof of branches in the gap between some rocks. Màiri's stomach began to rumble. She groped in her pocket and found a piece of crumbled bannock. She broke off half for Mairead, who remembered where they had hidden an old cracked plate and two battered wooden cups. She pulled them out from under some dried heather branches, spat on them and wiped them on her skirt. They filled the cups from the lochan. The water was teeth-jangling cold. Màiri was still hungry. She offered one of the eggs to Mairead who shook her head, screwing up her delicate features. Màiri cracked open the top of each egg in turn before tipping her head back and letting the raw liquid slither down her throat. She smacked her lips, laughing as she belched.

'Oh, we better hurry back. We'll have to tell the others your news.'

Mamma was busy kneading the morning bannocks to put on the girdle. She looked up with a frown as the children appeared in the doorway. There was Màiri with her skirt stained green and was that part of the hem hanging loose? The size of her, only ten years old, yet as tall as a woman already. And always leading with her chin. She was as ungainly as a young deerhound with big feet that promised plenty more growing. She tutted.

'Behold the dreamer cometh. Where are those eggs? I want to warm them in milk for Seonag. She needs building up.'

'We couldn't find any,' Màiri said, licking the corners of her mouth in case any tell-tale yellow was smeared there.

'Well, she'll have to have the milk on its own, then.' Her tone was reproachful.

'Mairead's leaving for Australia with all her family.'

Flòraidh smiled gravely at the child, 'I shall miss you *isean*. You're such a sweet, polite lassie.' She gave her daughter a sideways glare. 'May God's blessing be on you.'

'What about us? Are we going on that ship too?' Màiri demanded.

The door swung open and Pappa dipped his head to enter.

'We are not. I left once and never again. I shall only leave here feet first.' He grinned as he sat down heavily on a stool, taking off his cap.

Flòraidh watched as her daughter rushed over to hug him. Sometimes she shuddered, wondering if Màiri was a changeling, a fairy child smuggled into the cradle to replace the human baby. She was so different that she could hardly believe that Màiri was her own flesh, quite unlike her eldest with her deft, nimble ways. Iain looked up and ruffled Màiri's hair, coarse and strong as his own although he was fairer. They had the same jutting jaws and heavy brows. No, she was no changeling, but she was no beauty either. Iain had indulged their youngest, letting her run in the hills like a savage. She needed breaking in, Flòraidh decided.

As the days began to stretch out Màiri missed the quiet presence of Mairead, who had always been her audience and accomplice. She didn't have much time to think about her loss though for Mamma was determined to keep her busy.

'Idle hands are the Devil's playground,' she would say.

If Màiri wasn't being slapped for having a heavy hand with the bannocks she was practising how to produce a fine, even thread with the spinning wheel. She was sent out to scrape crotal from the rocks to make the red dye for the wool. Her fingers swelled with the cold as she squelched through boggy ground to dig out iris roots. It seemed so strange that a plant whose flower shone like spilt sunshine should yield such a sombre grey-blue dye. There was plenty of heavy labour too; carrying creels of seaweed to fertilise the fields or stacking and turning peats to dry them. But no amount of work could tire her furious energy. When she swept the beaten earth of the floor she wielded the broom like a weapon. It banged into the lime-washed walls, knocking down clouds of sticky, black dust from the encrusted rafters, a coating settled there from generations of peat fires. Finally, in the evenings while her father went to the cèilidh house, sometimes taking Murdo with him, she had to stay at home cutting down Pappa's old clothes to fit her brother. She hacked through the fabric as if it was an enemy hide and one time cut her finger to the bone. Mamma was angry about the blood stains seeping through the cloth. That task was bad enough but even worse was having to knit a shawl for her sister. To Màiri's relief Seonag had returned to Glasgow. As a parting challenge she announced that she hoped to be betrothed soon, after all, she had a whole herd of men keen to marry her. Kenneth, the chosen one, worked in Glasgow too, but his father would soon come over from Kintail on the mainland and speak to Pappa about the wedding. And both her parents nodded and smiled, even though they knew this was not the way of doing things. Kenneth should come himself to ask for their daughter's hand.

'It's different in the city,' was all her mother would say in explanation. So they had to make new clothes for her wedding. The knitting pins rebelled against Màiri's fingers, slipping and dropping stitches. She felt her life closing in; those imagined Canadian forests growing tall around her so that she couldn't see beyond them. They were bars squeezing out the light and swallowing her up in their shadows. The endless sky, the soaring mountains and the shifting tides had all vanished from sight.

But now it was May at last and they were going up to the shieling with the other women and children from the village. She had overheard Mamma and Seonag talking about it before her sister left.

'I shall be more at ease this year with only the younger two. They're not of an age yet to be a worry.'

'Oh, Mamma, did you used to worry about me then?' asked her sister, giggling.

'Of course I did – a pretty girl like you and those lads prowling around like foxes outside the hen house. I'm so pleased that you're to be married soon.'

'Well, I doubt you'll have to worry about Màiri on that score, even when she grows up.'

'That's not a kind thing to say about your wee sister.' But there wasn't much conviction in her mother's voice.

But nothing could quell her excitement as they finally loaded up their old horse *Dileas* with kegs, churns and casks, blankets slung over his back and a spinning wheel teetering on top so that he looked like a tinker's beast. When they were small, Màiri and Murdo used to be lifted aboard him for the journey, their short legs splayed across his broad back. Now they walked alongside, helping to herd the cattle up to the fresh summer pastures where they would meet the other women and children from the village. Before they left they had filled the churns with cream. Drops trickled out as they travelled and the calves were allowed to lick the spills as it stopped them from wandering off. It kept the children trotting on too because they knew that the cream would have turned into butter by the time they arrived and they would be allowed to spread some on their bannocks.

Their small party headed the few miles to *Bealach a'Chaoil-reidh*, the narrow path leading to the hill where the bothies lay. No-one knew when they had first been built, but each year they were repaired and re-thatched. Milking the beasts, churning the butter and making the cheese kept the women and girls busy. Once the evening milking was done people and beasts could lie back on the mossy grass, studded with ladies mantle and campion. *Blarach* was so calm up there that she didn't need to have a rope tied around her back legs when she was being milked. Seonag should have one of those, Màiri thought, to stop her lashing out.

Everyone sang at their tasks. The cows gave a better yield when they heard a familiar song. The hard work at the churn was lighter if you sang. Best of all were the songs in the evening as they all sat around a fire outside in the glowing light that lasted most of the night; songs about the old heroes, about courtship and love.

They had marching songs too this year. Murdo was in a sulk. He was desperate to go off to the fishing with Pappa but he had been told to spend a last unwilling summer at the shieling. He planned to become a soldier and amused himself by getting the younger boys drilling with staves held over their shoulders. Màiri joined in as she enjoyed strutting up and down, finding that her clumsiness disappeared when she had a rhythm to follow. After a few days of the drilling Murdo scowled when she arrived to join them, brows pulled together and eyes spitting sparks, looking very like Seonag, she thought.

'You're not marching with us anymore. You're making a mockery of it. Only men can be soldiers,' he snarled as the other lads grinned.

She strode silently up to him and stood close, staring. Suddenly she thrust her staff down thumping the ground right by his feet. Instinct made him leap back.

'I'm just as tall and strong as you are.'

'But you're still a lassie, even if you're a big one. You've no place here.'

She looked down her nose and, head held high, turned sharply and marched away.

When they returned home in July the long white nights were shrinking and she too had to shrink back to life at home. Still, there was the harvest to look forward to, the hectic cutting down of the oats before the weather turned its tricks on them. Then down to the mill with *Dileas* hauling a full load. The feast afterwards was so tasty, the usual bannocks but with silky butter spread on them, butter that held the memory of the summer pastures. Rowan jelly too and soft crowdie cheese with its clean, salty tang; herrings and tatties baked in the embers of the peats. And afterwards, the singing; songs of joy and celebration. She loved the turning wheel of the seasons. But she longed for something more … if only she could put a name to it.

CHAPTER 5

Skeabost, Isle of Skye, 1830s

She fell asleep picturing the harvest feast but woke suddenly, her heart pounding. Was it a dream that had roused her? No, she could hear muffled shouting coming from outside.

She swung her legs out of the box bed and peeped round the curtain to see Pappa groping around in the dark, searching for his boots. Quietly she pulled on her shawl and skirt over her shift.

She crept outside, following Pappa but keeping her distance. He tilted his head to listen as the noise started up again. It didn't sound like someone shouting in pain or fear, more a sort of bellowing. He hurried towards the house of their neighbour, Donald MacKinnon. At first glance his home looked much like their own, crouching down into the earth, but as they came closer they could see the ragged line of the turfs on the roof, the lopsided peat stack and the muddle of tools by the door. There was his black cow, shaggy head lowered, treading backwards and forwards in front of the byre. She was lowing in distress, stamping her feet and banging her horns against the door. A strange crooning came from inside.

Màiri stood back in the shadows as her father whispered to the beast. 'What's the matter, old girl?' He half turned and out of the corner of his eye he saw Màiri move.

'What are you doing here, lassie? Well you can make yourself useful calming her down while I see what's going on.'

She inched forwards, singing her own cow's favourite tune. The animal turned her big mournful eyes towards Màiri, dark pools fringed with eyelashes thick as reeds. While her father slipped inside the door she found a piece of rope snaking among the abandoned pots and nets. After tethering the beast to a tree she put her head round the door. Her mouth fell open. A young red calf stood there, stumbling on its neat little hooves. Clinging to its neck and slobbering into its face was a strange creature with a pale back, scrawny legs and sagging buttocks. Pappa was pulling the creature off the calf. It turned, arms flailing and she recognised the blotched red face of old Donald. What drew her eye though was the purplish worm nosing out from the undergrowth between his legs. She gasped in surprise making her father spin round.

'Go into the house and bring some clothes for him.'

She hurried back with a long shirt. Together they pushed the old man's protesting arms through the sleeves.

'Come on now Donald, we need to take the wee beast back to her mother before she curdles her milk with worry.' Between them they half led, half lifted him inside to his bed. He muttered and groaned in protest but soon he was snoring and dead to the world.

Màiri felt pleased that her father had not ordered her back home but let her help him. There were so many things she was told she couldn't do; fishing, playing shinty, drilling like a soldier and going to the cèilidh house. The night's events must be some sort of omen, she decided. It was as if she had climbed up one of those tall Canadian trees that barred her way. Now she could see the way ahead.

During the next week she hurried to finish all the mending jobs her mother had given her, even completed the hated shawl for her sister. She was all quiet diligence, no complaining or making faces. The other unusual change her mother noticed was that Màiri often had a faraway expression on her face and her lips moved silently. Well, she's growing up and maybe she's even learning the consolation of prayer, Flòraidh thought.

That evening Màiri said, 'I thought I'd go out and take the air, it's such a fine evening.'

'A good idea.' Flòraidh ignored the whisper of suspicion in her mind. Instead she smiled and patted Màiri's arm.

Once out of the door she ran to Alasdair Dubh's house. He was renowned as the best storyteller in the village so the cèilidhs were held in his house. Most of the local men and boys came to listen to tales and riddles, exchange news and gossip and sing a few songs. Màiri crept in and stood at the back, unnoticed in the deep shadows thrown by the candlelight. Her lips moved as she readied herself. Alasdair himself was preparing to tell a story. He put down his clay pipe and wet his lips.

'I thought, my friends, that you might like to hear another of the adventures of the old fool, although some folk called him a wise man.' There was a murmur of approval.

'One night when the rain was heavy enough to drown in the fool knocked at the door of the big house belonging to the minister. He could hear heavy footsteps approaching until at last the door creaked open. There was the minister himself in his nightshirt, a candlestick in his hand. He glared at the fool.

"Please, kind Sir, it's a terrible night and I'm soaked to the skin. Will you give me a bed for the night?"

"No, I've no room."

"But you must have plenty of rooms in such a big house."

"No, I haven't."

"But I can't stay outside in this storm."

The minister frowned at the fool's miserable expression. "Very well then, but it's most inconvenient. All I can give you is the loft. Follow me."

So the fool trudged behind the flickering light, along echoing corridors and up staircases, each narrower than the one before. Eventually they came to a dusty ladder leading up to a trapdoor.

"There you are. Climb up and sleep in the loft but you must be gone at first light."

The fool cried out, beside himself. "You're very kind Sir, but I can't go up there."

"Why on earth not?"

"I'm scared of heights and I'm so tired after my long walk that I haven't the strength to lift up the trapdoor."

"What a useless fellow you are," the minister snorted. "Here – hold the candle while I open the trapdoor." He huffed and puffed his way up the ladder for he was a heavy man. He pushed at the trapdoor until it gave way. Finally he heaved himself up into the loft.

"There you are," he shouted down. "I hope you're grateful for the trouble you've caused me."

No answer.

"Did you hear me, you insolent rogue?"

Still no answer.

"I'm coming down and when I do I shall put you out of the house for your rudeness."

This time he could hear a cackle. Furious now, the minister lowered himself down on the edge of the opening and stretched out a leg to reach the top rung. It dangled in the air. He peered down into the darkness. The man had gone and so had the ladder.

The fool picked the choicest food from the kitchen; venison, beef and wheaten bread. He found beer in a barrel and a bottle of whisky. When he was as full as an egg he looked in every room and lay down on every bed until he found the best one. He slept the sleep of the just on a down mattress with fine linen sheets, waking refreshed at the crack of dawn. Then he packed some provisions for his breakfast and skipped off like a goat into the hills.'

'And what about the minister?' one of the lads asked.

'Oh, he shivered all night, shouting in vain for help.'
The audience laughed and clapped.
'What about a cheery song now,' a voice called out.
'I've got one, a new one.' Màiri wriggled and dodged her way
to the front. 'You'll have to listen hard to find out who it's about.'
Before anyone had time to comment she started to sing.

> Save me from meddling women,
> Cried out the mean old hermit.
> Leave me at peace in my home
> With all my stuff where I left it
> I can see it there around me
> While I sit and have a wee dram.

> Save me from meddling women
> It's grand with my things all together
> My pots, pans, nets and tools
> All I own piled up in a heap
> I can find at once what I need
> While I sit and have a wee dram.

She paused for a moment, looking around her to see if she had
their attention. Most faces looked surprised, a few of them
suspicious but they were listening. Relieved, she unfolded her tale,

> Save me from meddling women,
> Like my sister out from Portree,
> Stalking up hill and over moor
> Itching to get her hands on my stuff
> And tidy it all out of sight
> Oh, I need to have another wee dram.

> Save me from meddling women
> Back she tramps over hill and moor
> I'm lost without my things around me

And sit with my head in my hands
My heart fills up with despair
Oh, I need to have another wee dram.

There were chuckles now and people joining in the repeated
lines.

Save me from meddling women
I hunt for all my treasures
My pots, pans, nets and tools
One by one I find my precious store
And pile them up in a heap
Oh, I need to have another wee dram.

Save me from meddling women
Dog tired I go to my bed
My eyes shut, I drift away
What wonderful dreams I have
I'm young again and with my love
Oh, I need to have another wee dram.

Save me from meddling women
Morag my love comes to me
With her red curls and deep soft eyes
I cradle her head and kiss her
Her lips so moist and what a long tongue
Oh, I need to have another wee dram.

Save me from meddling women
Who is it who shouts in my ear?
"Stop kissing her poor hairy face
Take the calf back to her mother
Go and soak yourself in the loch
No, you can't have another wee dram.

'Go on lass, sing it again,' a voice called out,
And so she did until they all knew the words.

'Well Iain Bàn, I had no idea you had this young bard in your house. She's got a gift although she's a wee bit rough round the edges yet,' said Alasdair Dubh. There was pride mingled with doubt on her father's face. As they strolled home together he said, 'Well that wasn't bad at all. But I don't know what your mother will say. Just as long as you don't get above yourself and think you can be a story teller like Alasdair Dubh'.

But Màiri wasn't listening. She had escaped the stifling forest and was striding on her way.

CHAPTER 6

Skeabost, Isle of Skye, early 1840s

Màiri became the village bard. She wrote funny, mocking verse but only about outsiders. Her lines on Donald MacKinnon were allowed because he was too unsociable ever to appear at cèilidhs and get to hear them. She was often asked to sing about the bride and groom at weddings, taking care to praise them and all their forbears of course. She was skilful at knitting the words into patterns with tunes she knew. It was the words that were more important and a good number of verses were expected.

Sometimes she composed more personal poetry that she kept to herself, verses about the world around her and about their animals. She created verses about *Blarach* the milk cow, but especially about *Dileas*. The hardworking grey horse had been there for the whole of her life. When she was very young she would play underneath his belly, pretending his legs were the corners of a house. He moved his big feathered feet as daintily as a dancer around her. He never kicked, unlike the cattle. She used to puzzle in her mind why it was that the cut peats were called 'little feet' when they were stacked up to dry. Three would be put on end together in a tent shape and a fourth one laid flat on top. They looked more like a crooked house than a foot, she thought. Then one day she watched him lifting his hooves gently around her and she saw that the triangular shape of the peat stacks was like a hoof. Both she and Murdo had learned to ride bareback on his warm, rolling back, clinging onto his rough mane.

Dileas was getting older and slower now but was as willing as ever. He swished his tail and nuzzled her ear when she recited her verses to him. One day a few months after her triumph at the cèilidh house her father left home early.

'He's business to do in Portree,' her mother said before sending Màiri off to collect plants for the dye pot. When she came in for her dinner she noticed what a wonderful smell was coming from the cooking pot.

'I've made a sausage from lights and liver,' her mother said, ladling out slices. It was delicious. Meat was a rare treat. They only tasted it if a beast had died suddenly or they were given a piece of venison from a neighbour. No questions would be asked about how they had come by it. She looked up from her plate to see her mother watching her intently while her father concentrated on cutting up his slice.

She leapt to her feet, sending her stool flying and ran out, haring up to the pasture. No sign of him. She trudged back inside again.

'I hope you're not turning your nose up at that good meat,' her mother said.

Her father looked up, his eyes moist. 'He was getting past working and still eating his head off.'

She picked up her knife, thinking it would be wrong to reject her old friend's last gift but the sausage had turned into slime in her mouth. She pushed it down her reluctant throat, willing herself not to gag. Later she honoured his life in verses in the style of the old praise songs for the Fiann or for a renowned clan chief. It began 'Valiant big hearted beast with strong limbs that never tired.' She kept the words tucked up safe inside her head and only sang them when she was alone in one of the horse's favourite grazing places.

Màiri grew taller and her brother left home to try his luck in Glasgow. Her mother kept saying how much she missed him, but Màiri was delighted to be the only child left at home. Flòraidh's low spirits meant that she slackened the reins on her daughter and Màiri could now spend more time outside climbing the hills or rowing on the lochan.

Suddenly the light broke through again in her mother's face. She started to sing once more as she worked. And all because of the letter.

'Seonag's coming home to be married to Kenneth. Isn't that wonderful? My first-born's getting married. The minister repeated the letter for me three times so I would be sure to remember it all.'

She smoothed out the paper, her reverent fingers tracing the words that held the magic news. Anyone would think it was Moses' tablets, sent down from Heaven, Màiri thought to herself.

'We must clean everything in the house and there's so much cooking to do. You'll have to help me Màiri.'

So it's the king and queen coming now, with all their nobles, she sneered inwardly.

'Oh, and you can make a special song for them. Kenneth is a MacRae from Kintail – so you'll have to include his family.'

I knew that making that wretched shawl wouldn't be the end of it, she thought. Still she did what was asked of her, although finding warm words was like dragging a plough through rocks.

The wedding day dawned bright and all went as planned. Kenneth was a modest, easy going young man, just as well, married to Seonag, she thought. The weather held, there was a fine spread of food and enough whisky for the toasts. Pappa spoke about how happy he was with his new son-in-law, even though he wasn't a Skyeman. He turned to his younger daughter and smiled. She sang her new song with gusto. She was pleased with its rousing end:

The wild land of Kintail
Holds the wild MacRaes
And one of them, Kenneth
Has claimed a Skye maiden.
The eldest of her family, like
The first of the Seven Sisters
But she's not waited in vain
As did they, for her love to return
He has a strong arm to wield
A long, firm, hard blade
Matched by the long, hard blade
Of his wife's powerful tongue.

There was plenty of applause at the end although Màiri wondered about why the laughter suddenly surged when she spoke of his fine blade, not that men had swords these days but she thought it sounded heroic. Everyone started to clear things away ready for the dancing. She seized the chance to slip away and find somewhere quiet to relieve herself. Dancing along and humming, she had just turned around the corner of the byre when she felt something thud into her back, winding her. Before she could recover her balance she was spun round so that her shoulders scraped against the jagged surface of the wall.

'You, I might have known you would spoil things'.

Her sister's thin face was so close that Màiri could see the flecks of spittle bubbling on her lips.

'Making a fool of us both. Wild MacRaes indeed, and then that stuff about my tongue.'

Màiri found her own tongue again, 'But everyone seemed to enjoy it.'

'You wee fool. Of course they like to get their own back and don't you act the innocent. You did it deliberately to show me up. It's a good job you weren't the oldest of the seven sisters. Who would want to be your suitor, you big, ugly beast? All of them would have been left as spinsters.'

'Isn't that what happened anyway? They asked to be turned into mountains when none of the brothers came back to marry them.'

'Don't you answer me back.' Her hand lashed out, slapping Màiri's cheek. Her own cheeks were a hectic red and she started to cough. With a final glare she turned away.

Màiri shrugged and pulled the collar of her new white blouse straight. Thank goodness Seonag would soon be going back to Glasgow.

CHAPTER 7

Skeabost, Isle of Skye, early 1840s

After her sister left with her new husband life went back to the usual pattern for Màiri, but as the months passed Mamma became more fretful.

'Why haven't we had any news from Seonag? I'm sure she would get word to me if she was expecting.'

Murdo and Màiri made faces behind their mother's back. Later when they were alone she said, 'So our wonderful, blessed sister can't get herself pregnant.'

Her brother laughed. 'She and Kenneth need to go up to the Old Man of Storr and lie together there.'

Màiri looked puzzled.

'Come on, surely you've worked out what happens between a man and a woman?'

She shook her head and her face reddened.

'We take the cow to the bull and put the ram in among the ewes and make sure the male beast does his duty.'

She nodded, giggling.

'It's the same thing for people although we keep it secret. Now if poor Kenneth is a bit limp the Storr should give him the idea.'

She was so surprised that she was left speechless. Murdo laughed at her astonished face.

'Don't you believe me?'

Well she did. Although his information had startled her it felt as if he was telling her something that she had always known but never put into words. Mind you, she couldn't imagine Seonag losing her dignity enough to do such a thing. When she sat in church the next Sunday she found herself imagining the solemn people there coupling; sour old widow Beaton who always had her nose in the air and the pious elder who looked as if his face would split like a rock if he ever laughed.

During the short, wind-lashed days of winter another letter came. Màiri rushed inside when she heard the terrible keening sound in a voice she couldn't recognise. She found her mother on her knees trying to rend her clothes while the Reverend MacLeod knelt beside her, begging her to pray. Pappa hurtled in when he heard her wailing and tried to hold her close. She pulled herself away and glared at Màiri, making her freeze.

'My first born gone, dead before me,' she kept howling.

The minister told them what the letter said. Seonag's health had started to fail while she was expecting a child. She took a fever and couldn't eat properly. The growing child seemed to sap her strength. When she began to cough up blood she had to take to her bed and she died before her child could be born.

For the first weeks Flòraidh's grief was unabating. An unlatched gate in a storm, she swung madly, trying to tear herself free from her hinges. In the end her flayed throat could shriek no more and instead she moaned ceaselessly like the wind trapped in a chimney or a cow desperate to be milked. Eventually she quietened but that was almost worse. At least while she protested Màiri knew that she was still alive. The silence made her keep searching for her to make sure that her mother was still there. The unspoken grief became a laden creel on her mother's back, bending her double, a weight that she could never put down.

Pappa tried to comfort her. 'We've lost our eldest child but we still have other children.'

But that only seemed to inflame her. She would pull away from him and glower at Màiri in a way that made her shudder. She hadn't wanted her sister to die, but she couldn't pretend to herself that she missed her. How could she miss a closeness she had never felt? They had been seeds that fell too close to the tree and as they grew into saplings they reached out to the light, scraping and scratching their branches together. But guilt, like the smell of tainted milk, hung around her.

She did what she could by taking on all the household tasks and helping her father with the outside work. He didn't complain but like *Dileas* before him he was slowing down, his back stiff and his joints swollen. Màiri's life beat to a fixed rhythm while other girls her age were going to weddings, dancing to new steps and being visited by suitors.

Life was becoming harder; the talk at the cattle markets was all about lower prices and rising rents. Mamma turned to religion for consolation. She had always been devout but now she was inspired by the fiery conviction of the missionaries. Pappa, as always, kept his distance, attending church just enough to avoid censure. However, he was impressed by the strength of the newer breed of minister. Some landowners, Lord MacDonald among them, refused the new sort of spirited ministers land to build a church and they held outdoor meetings instead. Even though their own minister, Maighstir MacLeod, had a spacious church to preach in he spent much of his time giving sermons in the open air, whatever the weather, drawing huge crowds to hear him.

'Do you know that one time when he preached at Uig it started to snow so heavily that he told me that he could hardly tell the congregation apart from the ground where they were sitting. Only their faces showed where they were,' Mamma said, her voice trembling with wonder at such a display of piety.

'No doubt their faces glowed like beacons of righteousness,' Pappa muttered.

A large meeting was planned to take place at the Fairy Bridge, a remote spot where three streams met. It had a fearsome

reputation. Evil spirits were said to gather there and no-one
wanted to cross the bridge after nightfall. Horses would shy as
they approached it, lathering and quivering, their eyes rolling in
terror.

'The Reverend MacLeod is a godly man and he will banish the
evil from there if any living soul can,' her mother declared. It was
intended that all of them would walk there, including Murdo,
who was back home on a visit. However, when the day came,
Mamma had one of her turns. She was pale and shaky, saying
that she was too ill to go. Pappa was determined to stay with her.
Màiri suspected that he was relieved to have a respectable reason
not to go. So she and Murdo were to uphold the family honour
by attending. She rose early for the long walk but found that her
brother had already left with his friends.

'He said that they could go faster without you', Mamma said.

She grunted, wondering what Murdo was up to. 'I can make
my own way there easily enough.'

'Take care. Look out for other folk you can walk with.'

Màiri sighed. Mamma was usually so cold towards her and
at other times she would fuss over her, like a broody foster hen
clucking in alarm as the ducklings she's raised take to the water.
So she set off alone, happy to stride freely. She met scores of
people, all surging towards the bridge; men, women, skipping
children, babies carried in shawls, as unstoppable as the three
streams themselves. She had never seen so many folk all together.
She could hear the voices of yet more, singing psalms as they
came over the hills. They sounded like Fairy voices coming from
deep within the earth. As the groups mingled together they
flooded over the hill. That is how it must have been when Our
Lord was preaching, she thought.

Although most of the worshippers came on foot, some arrived
on horseback. They tethered their beasts at a group of trees.

Màiri's eye was caught by a dappled horse. Her heart lurched. He looked so much like *Dileas* that she had to go over for a closer look. It was a different animal of course, smaller and a mare. As she turned away to join the people who were settling themselves for the service she felt Murdo's hand on her arm.

'Ah, there you are. What are you doing?'

His hazel eyes, so like their mother's, narrowed and gleamed.

'We thought we'd wait here and have some fun while the minister's talking,' he replied, his eyes challenging her, but she only shrugged. He was his own man now. She wasn't going to interfere. She went to join some families from the village. They smiled and made space for her beside them. As there were so many people in the congregation Reverend Macleod couldn't stand in front of them all at once and hope to be heard. Instead he toured the crowd on horseback, repeating his words to each group. He was a fine upright man with a wide brow and glowing eyes that seemed to probe into the very depths of your soul. His voice would change in an instant from a clarion call down to the soft whisper of a mother to her baby.

His text was from the Book of Isaiah, "Wash you, make you clean, put away the evil of your doings from before mine eyes: cease to do evil, learn to do well." He proclaimed that even if your sins were scarlet red they would become white as the driven snow if you obeyed God's commands. Màiri clenched her eyes shut, feeling again the clammy guilt that smothered her whenever she remembered her sister. She could hear sobs and groans all around her. She opened her eyes to see people swaying and shaking, clapping their hands and reaching out their arms. Some fell insensible to the ground as if in a faint while others spoke in tongues, uttering words that made no sense to her.

'No matter how mired you are in sin, reach out your foul, black leprous hand and God will receive you.'

Now more folk were groaning, swooning and writhing on the ground. I'm a true believer, she thought, so why is the Holy Spirit not entering me? She stood, a lonely observer, excluded from the ecstasy of those whom the Lord had chosen, those who could see beyond the vale of tears towards the joys of Heaven.

The minister had finished circling the crowds. He sat on horseback still, his hands raised as the congregation bowed their heads in prayer. Did that mean that the service would soon be over? What about Murdo among the horses? Did he realise?

She slipped away, creeping around the back of the crowd and then running hard as she neared the trees. As she suspected Murdo was there with several other young men riding bareback on the galloping horses, crouched low over their necks. She smiled when she saw that her brother had chosen the dappled mare.

'Hurry and tie them up again. The service is finishing'.

They slowed down and jumped off, laughing. Men and horses tossed their heads. She knew most of the young men but one of the riders was a stranger. He didn't rush like the others but sat proudly, sinewy thighs pressed against the horse's flanks, fingers plaited through its mane. So entwined were horse and rider that they seemed like one creature. He whispered to the animal, stroking its ears. Then he turned and smiled at her. It was as if a rainbow had suddenly appeared, a dazzling arc across the sky. He slithered off his mount in a swoop of limbs and rubbed his face against the horse's cheek. How she envied that dumb beast. For once, she who was never lost for words found her tongue stuck to the roof of her mouth. All was confusion as they rushed to calm the animals and tie them up again.

'Their owners will wonder why they're so tired and sweaty,' the fair young man said grinning.

Before she could answer they were all waving and running off and she was left as breathless as the horses.

CHAPTER 8

Skeabost, Isle of Skye, early 1840s

'That was a near escape.' said Murdo later on.

Màiri smiled. 'You all got safely away then? That tall young man, I've never seen him before. Is he from round here?'

'Ah, you mean Anndra'.

'That's an unusual name.'

'Aye. He's from the south of the island. His family were thrown off their land.'

'And where does he stay now?'

Murdo grinned, 'So many questions. Why do all young women want to know about him? He's in Portree at the moment, living on a poor bit of land and doing some fishing.'

Her thoughts were already flying far off like migrating swallows. It wouldn't matter if he didn't have any money or land. He could live here, on their croft. They would manage, even if they had a nest full of children. That would be a small price to pay for having him in her bed, warming her body inside and out.

Murdo laughed, 'You should see your face'.

'How do you mean?' She frowned.

'Standing there licking your lips and your eyes all dreamy like a dog having its belly rubbed. I'm in your debt, so I'll see what more I can find out. But I imagine he's got a sweetheart already.'

She bristled at the edge of pity in his voice, 'I was just curious.'

A few nights later she heard a thud outside, followed by muttered swearing. She hurried out to find her brother, who had tripped over in the dark. He was swaying on his feet and she hustled him away from the house towards the well.

'We can't have Mamma seeing you in that state,' she hissed. 'Walk up and down while I get you some water to drink.' She lowered the bucket.

'We've had a wee dram or two to celebrate. I'm not going back to Glasgow. I'm going to Fort Augustus.'

'I'm not surprised. It's what you've always wanted. The army's better than emigrating, but Mamma will take it hard.'

'Aye. That reminds me…' He put his hand to his mouth, grimacing.

'Reminds you of what?'

'N… nothing.'

She shook his collar, 'What won't you tell me?'

He sighed. 'Anndra's going too.'

'As a soldier?' She could feel her heart sinking, but still he would come back one day.

He wouldn't meet her gaze. 'No.'

'What's he doing then? Spit it out.' Her fingers clenched on the handle of the bucket.

'Australia. He's emigrating.'

Murdo lurched to one side but he was too slow to avoid the swing of the bucket. He howled as the cold water struck him. She hurled the bucket down, tears glinting in her eyes and overflowing down her cheeks. 'That'll sober you up,' she screamed.

The rainbow had vanished in the instant she had glimpsed it. Everyone's life seemed to be changing, except hers. Anndra gone for ever. Murdo in the army. All the young women of her age away working in the Lowlands. If not working they were married, with several youngsters around their skirts and another in the belly. As Màiri grew into her twenties Mamma became more tight-lipped about her refusal to consider the few offers of marriage that came her way.

'You should be more modest, not making up verses. That's not fitting for a woman wishing to marry. Mind you, I've heard that George Beaton is looking for a wife. He's a godly man and a hard worker. You could do worse.'

Màiri had been horrified. George Beaton indeed! He was at least twice her age and bandy legged. She had caught him gobbling her up with his greedy, parched eyes. She knew well enough that she was no beauty, her features were too strong, her body too broad and tall. Even her feet didn't fit a ladylike pattern; they were so large that only men's brogues would fit them.

'How come that men, no matter how ill-favoured they might be, imagine that they could be a suitable match for a young woman?'

'A woman needs to marry and she can't always be too choosy. When God told Noah to build the Ark He commanded him to bring aboard a male and female of every creature. A woman on her own is against nature.'

The anxious creases on her mother's face made her hold back an angry retort. Instead she paused before laughing and saying, 'You'd marry me off to that grubby old bachelor, Donald MacKinnon?'

'No, indeed, there are limits even to my matchmaking.'

At least I made her smile, Màiri thought, and that happens all too rarely these days. But despite her joking she felt uncertain about her future. She was determined to stay a spinster rather than settle for an old man. There were plenty of songs that warned about sad young girls betrothed to greybeards. The thought of a wizened *bodach* sniffing around her, then thrashing and gasping on top of her in bed, like a fish caught on a hook, it was unbearable. Imagine being expected to kiss a putrid mouth full of blackened stumps of teeth. No, she would rather endure the neighbours' pity for her unwed state. If only Anndra had not gone away.

What was the answer? Her parents hadn't pressed her to go down to the Lowlands to work and she was grateful for that. She knew that her help on the croft made life easier for both of them. She knew too that Mamma was terrified of her last child sickening and dying in a damp, grimy tenement.

One summer evening she went outside where her father was watching the sun's lifeblood staining the sky. Seeing him there, unaware of her presence, made her heart jolt. His back was bowed and he leant heavily on a stick. Was this her Pappa who used to rail against injustice and was so fearless of authority?

'Mamma thinks I'm not docile enough to find a husband. Do you think I frighten men away with my opinions and my verses?'

He threw his head back and laughed his old confident rumble. He was silent for a time before replying.

'Do you remember the story about the MacCrimmond piper and the Fairy Bridge?'

She nodded. It was one of her favourites.

'Well, when the piper found his way to the Fairies' underground kingdom through the cave at Harlosh he met a beautiful woman there. Some say she was the Queen of the Fairies herself. He was enchanted by her and stayed there for what he thought was a short time. But as you know Fairy time is different from ours and in truth he was away from his people for many days. When he was ready to leave she offered him a present of his own choosing. He wanted a silver chanter. She gave him a magic one that made his fingers move like quicksilver when he played it. He stirred the hearts of everyone who heard the music he made on it. She told him, "When you dance everyone will dance with you and when you play a lament the whole island will lament with you."

'But, as always, when we have dealings with the Fairies there's a reckoning to be made. She told him the day and the time when he would have to return through the cave to her and never leave her again. That time was some years ahead and MacCrimmond, being young, believed that the day would never dawn. So he agreed to her terms, returned home and became the most famous piper of his day. His sons and grandsons followed him as pipers for MacLeod of MacLeod, although it's said that none of them had fingers as nimble as his own.

'Eventually the day arrived that had been marked for his return. He bade his wife and children a last farewell and with a few companions walked back to the cave. Then he turned his back on all human kind and, playing his chanter, walked alone into the darkness without a backward glance. His wee dog, though, trotted in to follow his master. Everyone else waited silently at the cave's mouth and strained their ears to catch his playing. They could hear both the chanter and the dog's barks rising up from below the earth. At a spot near the Fairy Bridge the chanter fell silent but they could still hear barking. Suddenly the dog shot out from the cave with his hair all black and singed.'

Màiri waited but he said no more. 'I always enjoy the old tales but why have you told me this one now?'

He smiled, 'Like me, you're impatient to change the world. We both protest like the wee dog. As you know barking at the minister got me singed in my youth. I was nearly exiled across the seas and had to pay a penance of living in Glasgow. I lost a good croft and had to settle for poorer land when we came back.'

'So you're advising me to do what's expected and become a dutiful wife, even if it makes my heart shrivel within me?'

'No. At least, not yet. You're the Benjamin of my old age. I don't want to lose you and Heaven forbid I'm no minister to preach to you about your duty. Maybe you're MacCrimmond in the story, rather than the wee dog.'

'How so?'

He drew on his clay pipe while he considered his answer, 'No doubt the minister would disagree but I believe the Fairies are the spirits of the old folk who lived in the hills before our people came here. You can't refuse a gift from the Fairies or they will turn against you. MacCrimmond had to take the silver chanter, whatever the cost to him. Now you've the gift of poetry. You have to use it. You shouldn't become as pious as those miserable folk who've been converted and stop singing. That would be spurning their gift.'

He laughed and tapped her arm. 'Anyway, we'd better go inside or your mother will believe we are plotting something.'

CHAPTER 9

Skeabost and Carbost, Isle of Skye, 1844

At first Màiri was heartened by her father's words but the seasons marched on. Now well into her twenties, she felt as if she were standing drilling on the same spot, like those days long ago when she had tried to join in her brother's soldier games. It was harder than ever to eke out a living on the family croft. They grew few oats now and no barley at all. The soil was exhausted, even with all the seaweed dragged up from the shore to improve it. Without a horse it was draining work using the breast plough. So, like their neighbours, they turned to the bountiful potato and bought their overpriced oatmeal from the factor with money from selling the cattle.

Her mother had finally struggled ashore from the shipwreck of grief after Seonag's death. Her sadness had become a shawl draped around her shoulders rather than a backbreaking load. Now it was her father's spirit that seemed to drain away, leaving him morose, gazing into a clear sky and expecting storms. As a child Màiri had seen him as unchanging as the landscape, an upright pillar like the Old Man of Storr. But rock could crumble, gnawed silently away by wind and rain. The tide was running against him and she must tackle him again about the future.

They had finished planting the potatoes and were sitting with their backs against the wall of the house, enjoying some spring sunshine.

'Let's hope for a good harvest,' she said.

'Aye. But I heard a fellow say that the tatties failed in some places on the mainland last year. First the stored ones turned into a reeking mush and then the ones still in the ground went bad.'

'They've always done well for us though, haven't they?'

He shook his head. 'I don't know what will happen to us Gaels. So many have left already. How can we cling on?'

She held back a sigh. 'Surely the worst is over now. Those who have stayed have good big families to follow them.'

'That's part of the problem. There's not enough land so they slice it up to give everyone a piece. Then no-one has enough to live on.'

She took a deep breath, 'Well that needn't happen here. I can take over. If a widow can be a tenant why not a daughter?'

Pappa's troubled blue eyes had looked distant but now he turned to face her.

'But Murdo will leave the army one day. I must hold this land in trust for him and any son he might have. I will not divide it.'

He saw the look of flayed hurt in her eyes and dropped his gaze. She stood, looking down at him.

'So what life would I have if I stayed, except as a poor relative in someone else's house?'

He shaded his eyes to look up at her, 'You're still young. You could marry and have your own home. That would be for the best.'

'Well, I shall have to think about what I must do.' She turned on her heel and strode off before her father could see the tears scalding down her face, but she knew that the jagged splinters of her voice had pierced him.

In the following days Màiri carried out her tasks with a savage energy. She stormed up the hills, forcing the bemused cattle to canter ahead of her. Bad enough to live the tough life of a crofter but for a woman, she thought, it seemed doubly harsh to be a beast of burden and a bearer of numberless children. Only a loving husband could make that bearable. She would only agree to marry if there was love, or at least kindness, between them. She would never accept the stale leavings of more favoured women even if she faced disapproval for being too fussy. But if she refused the only offers that had come her way from ugly and selfish old men she would have no land or independence. Perhaps she could brace herself to marry an old man who would die soon and then she could take over his tenancy? But the idea of being caressed by gnarled old hands, roughened like tree bark, brought bitter bile to her throat. There was only one answer. She must leave Skye and earn her own living. Like an otter caught in a trap she would have to gnaw off a limb so that she could escape. And maybe one day she would have enough money to return and live in style. That would show everyone. She had heard the whispers:

'She's a strong lass but it's a pity she's so big and plain.'

'And brazen too. But her father's always been full of himself.'

She ran headlong all the way to the shore, heart hammering in her ears and hair streaming behind her. She tossed her thoughts from hand to hand and then skimmed them out to sea. Bending down, she chose a stone, one with a streaked pattern waving across it, blew away the sand clinging to it and traced its sea smoothed surface. But there was no answer from the world around her except the one she didn't want to hear.

She would have to leave. But where would she go? She didn't want to go to Glasgow as so many islanders had done. Pappa had told her often enough of the city bleached of live colours, the horses kept in dark stables and slipping on slimy cobblestones, never seeing a blade of grass. Even the mighty Clyde was sick and smelt of decay. The city had sucked out the life of her sister. No, she couldn't go there.

What about Inverness, smaller and nearer? She broached the idea with Mamma. Màiri had expected a protest but instead her mother considered the question calmly.

'The air would be fresher right enough but how would you get there? There's no regular steamer boat and it wouldn't be right for a young woman to travel all that way alone by cart. And what about the expense of it all?'

Màiri though had made up her mind to go and set about finding a way. She spoke to the minister's wife who listened, hiding her surprise. She couldn't remember any of that proud family ever asking for help. A few weeks later she called Màiri over after morning service.

'I've the very thing for you. Reverend Carmichael in Carbost has a wife who is awaiting the birth of her first child. She wants to travel to her family home near Inverness. You could accompany her.'

So it was settled. Her father insisted on walking the twenty-five miles with her to the manse.

'I'm not in my grave yet and I can have a rest before I go back. I can even take a wheelbarrow to push you if you get tired,' he joked.

She was surprised how he seemed to have recovered his spirits. So they trudged to Sligachan, hugging the coast as the Cuillin loomed ever closer. Then they turned towards Carbost and found the neat, square house overlooking Loch Harport. They were given a grave welcome by the minister, a sharp featured, earnest man and his placid wife. Pappa was anxious to return home and made the return journey after two nights' rest. It was the first time she had ever travelled so far from her home. Part of her looked back over her shoulder, missing her familiar surroundings, like a puppy sent to a new family.

During the day the minister was either out visiting his flock or writing sermons in the small front parlour. A scrawny wee girl came in to do the rough work while the minister's wife sat sewing baby clothes. Màiri had her own small room up in the eaves. She enjoyed the novelty of climbing stairs and feeling so high up that she could look the hills in the eye. She had to duck to climb into her small bed but once she was in it that first night she felt a fluttering excitement too, an eagle chick flexing and flapping its wings, lurching on the edge of the nest, looking at the long leap below.

CHAPTER 10

Carbost and beyond, 1844

Her eyes snapped open and she jerked herself upright. The room was full of brooding shadows. She shuddered and clenched her hands on the blanket. There was a sound from below her window, a door being unlatched. She remembered where she was and sighed. Something had woken her, something from outside caught in the net of her dreams, rocking her as it was hauled aboard. She had been dreaming about that night when old Donald MacKinnon was shouting and singing to the bewildered calf.

But there were real voices now coming from inside the house. She could hear Mrs Carmichael summoning her, but Màiri was already stumbling down the stairs. Her employers were looking out of the window, pointing at plumes of grey smoke to the south.

'Ah. There you are Màiri. You must help me load food and blankets onto my husband's horse.'

'What's happening?'

'Hurry up girl, there's no time to explain.'

What disaster has happened? She wondered. There must be a fire but she was too unfamiliar with this western part of Skye to know where it might be. The minister was as tight lipped and urgent as his wife so she concentrated on helping him lift the provisions onto the horse.

'If only I could carry more,' he muttered.

'Excuse me Sir, have you any more beasts?'

'I could get hold of another one or two but what use is that when there is only one of me?'

'I was just wondering, you see. I learnt to ride as a child. I don't know what disaster has happened but if we both rode we could lead another pack horse and carry much more.' She spoke softly and looked down when she had finished.

He frowned. 'I don't know what to expect when we arrive. It might be dangerous.'

'I understand, but if there are women and children in difficulties, a second pair of hands might be useful.' Again the modest downcast look.

He stared at her and nodded. 'Very well. Needs must when the Devil drives.' Who was the Devil here, she wondered.

They set off, each on a sturdy garron with Màiri leading a smaller pony behind them. She noticed with amusement that the Reverend rode stiffly, his knuckles clenched white on the reins.

'We follow the Carbost Burn and then the Eynort River south. Then we climb over the ridge through *Bealach na Croiche*.'

'And where is it we are headed to, Sir?'

'Tuasdale, a settlement of twelve families. I've been worried for some time about them. The land is divided between two landlords, neither of whom has any care for his tenants. I fear we are too late to stop them.'

'But the smoke seems to have died down.'

He fell into a gloomy silence. Despite the circumstances of their journey she couldn't help feeling a surge of pleasure at being out on the moor on an early autumn day after being confined to the house. She felt her horse's swaying gait beneath her, the sea borne wind snatching at her hair and the salty taste on her lips. Far above their heads an eagle circled, rising to become a tiny dot. They breasted the ridge and the way ahead opened like an unclenching fist. It was a wide, green valley leading to a meeting of two streams.

'It's beautiful here, and fertile.'

'That's part of the problem,' he replied.

Everything looked as it should; houses sprouting out of the earth, the slopes on each side carved into lazybeds for potatoes, the hill pastures still green, but there were no people or animals to be seen. The village seemed to be under an evil enchantment.

'It's so silent,' she hardly dared to whisper, 'Look up the hill there, Sir. It's still smouldering. What a terrible smell. What on earth were they burning?'

They dismounted and climbed up to the cottage standing on its own. The thatch had been set alight and was still smouldering in sullen blackness. Sticky, treacly streams slithered down the walls and oozed onto the ground.

He prodded some of it with his shoe. 'I think it's the stored cheese and butter.'

'And what are you doing trespassing here?' They both jumped at the snarling voice. A group of men had appeared from behind the house with mastiffs trotting beside them, teeth bared. The man who had spoken was broad shouldered, with his cap pulled well down over his eyes. All three of them carried thick sticks.

'I'm the Reverend Carmichael, come to check on the welfare of my parishioners.' Màiri admired his courage as the slight man held himself tall and spoke out in ringing pulpit tones.

'Well, you don't need to worry about them, they're gone,' the first man barked. He turned to smirk at his companions.

'What do you mean, gone?'

'Just what I said.'

Carmichael held his ground, staring at the speaker.

'We're just doing our job. Go and speak to Mr MacCaskill or Dr Lachlan MacLean. They paid us to move the people out.' He waved his arms impatiently, making the nearest dog jump up.

One of his companions added, 'They need this land for keeping sheep.'

Still the Reverend stood glowering and implacable. The dogs circled, whimpering.

'You will have to answer for your actions to a higher authority on the day of Judgement.'

Two of them shuffled and looked away but their leader shrugged, turned his back and, whistling to the dogs, sauntered off down the hill.

Màiri could contain herself no longer, 'Where have you driven them away to?' she shouted.

'A fiery lass, is it? Like the old woman who lived in this house. She made a fuss too. Wouldn't leave until we made it too hot for her. Then she took to her heels, squawking like an old hen.'

Màiri bent down and picked up a jagged stone. Carmichael sprang forward and grabbed her wrist as she bent her arm back to aim.

'Drop it at once. You're only making things worse.'

She struggled against his grip. 'They've driven all these poor people from their homes. They must be stopped.'

'But this isn't the way to do it. "Vengeance is mine sayeth the Lord." '

'I wonder which path they took. We didn't see anyone coming up here,' Màiri said, when she had got her breath back.

'We can't ask those bailiffs now,' he replied.

She hurled the stone away.

'It was a mistake to bring you when you're so intemperate.'

She didn't seem to hear him. 'They can't be far away. They would be slow carrying all their belongings with them.'

His expression was still pinched and disapproving. 'They would have taken the shore path beside *Beinn Buidhe na Creige* towards the church.'

As they turned their horses' heads Màiri thought bitterly how the melting stores of cheese would glow as brightly as the Yellow Hill of the Sunlight itself as they poured down the walls of the burning house. As Reverend Carmichael had predicted they found the people, sitting in hunched groups inside the church, stunned and blank faced. Even the children were cowed and silent. The minister moved among them, distributing food and blankets but they seemed barely to notice him. She went outside to gather firewood and came across an older woman among the gravestones. She was sobbing as she scraped up handfuls of earth, scooping them into a small dish. Màiri knelt down beside her.

'I'm taking my last memory of the land. I'll never return to live and be buried with my forbears here.'

Màiri touched her arm. She could find no words. After she had lit a fire to warm them she found the old woman whose stores had been destroyed. She stared blindly in front of her, her lips mumbling and her hands plucking at her shawl like the scrabbling claws of a trapped bird.

'All that good food wasted. They even used my basins of milk to douse the fireplace. How will I live?' Rivers of tears poured down the crevices of her cheeks. She brushed her hand across to stem the flow. 'What use are tears? I've shed more tears already than all the milk my cow ever gave me.'

There was no time to think while Màiri and the minister did what they could to help. Some families were already setting out to the homes of relatives. They shouldered clattering pots and pans, held drag-footed children by the hand and coaxed along lowing cattle. One of the men complained that they had not been allowed time to lift down any of the roof timbers. She gasped, the wood was so precious. It was never left to waste. How would they be able to build a new house? They put the weakest among them on the horses; a new mother and her tiny, bleating baby, the bewildered old woman and two small children stumbling with fear and exhaustion. As they led the sad, bedraggled group back to Carbost Màiri's head teemed with questions.

'Why've they been treated like this?'

'Greed. The landowners don't need people any more. They say there are too many of them. Sheep, the big English sheep, are more profitable.'

'I know times are hard but the land here is good.'

'That's why the landlords wanted it, to make more money in rent. This time they didn't even offer them inferior plots in exchange, or a passage on a ship.'

'Maighstir Ruaridh doesn't agree with emigration. He says folk should be given enough land to live on.'

'Hmm, but emigration and the chance of a new life might be better than what these people face scraping a living on a relative's plot.'

Màiri thought about what her father always said, "If it's such a land of milk and honey abroad why aren't the landlords falling over each other to buy a berth for themselves on a sailing ship?" Aloud she said, 'Can nothing be done to stop the cruelty we saw today? The landowners and their bailiffs should be stopped.'

'Indeed they should but how is that to be done? Not by violent methods like throwing stones. We must look to the Bible for guidance. Think about the parable of the tares, Màiri. Remember how the servants wanted to pull out the tares growing among the wheat? Like you wanting to throw a stone? But the Lord said, "Nay, lest while you gather up the tares, ye root out also the wheat with them. Let both grow together until the harvest; and in the time of harvest I will say to the reapers, Gather ye together first the tares, and bind them in bundles to burn them; but gather the wheat into my barn. The reapers are God's angels who on the Day of Judgement will throw the sinners into the fiery furnace." How does it continue?'

'There shall be wailing and gnashing of teeth. Then shall the righteous shine forth as the sun in the kingdom of their Father.'

He nodded. 'You are well versed in the Good Book, but beware the sin of pride, Màiri. Judge not that you be not judged. What is the state of your own soul? Will you be among the wheat or the tares?'

She winced. He had touched a sore place. She remembered as a small child sitting on Pappa's lap and tracing the lines on his palm with her fingers. She found a silvery scar and curious, pressed it. He winced and took his hand away, 'That's an old wound from a gutting knife. It healed but I always know it's there.'

Her sister's death was Màiri's scar. Seonag had been so angry and upset over Màiri's poem, saying it had blighted her wedding day. Mamma had never blamed her in so many words but the accusation was there in her eyes. Seonag was so delicate, unlike her younger sister and should be treated gently. Had her verses hammered themselves like nails into Seonag's coffin? Did Mamma believe in her heart that the wrong daughter had died? Those were questions that could never be asked or answered. Pappa had told her that being a bard was a gift that she couldn't refuse, but was it a cursed gift? Did her guilt mean that she couldn't condemn anyone else's actions? Mamma, like the Reverend, would quote Scripture, "How wilt thou say to thy brother, Let me pull out the mote out of thine eye; and behold a beam is in thine own eye?"

Pappa, though, would argue with Mamma about religion. Like boats moored side by side in a choppy sea their hulls would scrape and grate. What would Pappa say to the Reverend Carmichael? "I don't see the oppressors seeking forgiveness for their sins and crying out for salvation. It's the godly folk who end up in tenements in the city or disappear across the seas."

'Don't look so troubled, Màiri.' The Minister's voice interrupted her thoughts, 'You were intemperate earlier but you have been a good Samaritan today to these suffering souls. We must make haste to Carbost now. Tomorrow you can help the women gather more supplies while I organise the men to carry them to those in need.'

So she wouldn't be given a chance to protest again. Màiri didn't know whether to feel angry or relieved.

'Will this be the end of it Sir?'

'I wish I knew. The Assyrians have attacked but I fear the Babylonians have yet to come.'

'So this is only the beginning?'

'Maybe so. We must follow God's commandments and pray for his guidance.'

Inverness, 1844

The next few days passed in a blur of activity as Màiri worked herself to a standstill, making enough bannocks to feed a hungry regiment, stacking them in towers and wrapping them in cloths. The congregation had been generous in giving oatmeal, potatoes and bedding and no-one was left without a roof over their heads. Those who didn't have relatives to go to were taken in by families in Carbost. Màiri shared her room and her bed with two girls in their early teens. They blundered behind her wherever she went, like hand reared lambs. During the day she kept them busy helping her in the kitchen but they were fretful in the night, muttering in their sleep and thrashing their limbs about. So to stop herself getting vexed with them she bedded down in the kitchen. She walked to the evicted families who were staying close by, carrying a deep basket piled with food. Going to visit them reminded her of the times when she had walked with Pappa the six miles to Portree to sell cattle. Some of the waiting animals bellowed in protest while others froze, too shocked to move or make a sound. It was the same with these people, driven away from everything that was familiar and dear to them.

The minister and his wife worked without sparing themselves. Màiri had to be firm, almost ordering her mistress to rest for the sake of herself and her unborn child. When she finally set off on the steamer to Fort William with Elizabeth Carmichael she felt glad that she had been so busy that she had not had time to dwell on the journey and what would happen afterwards. She had never been on a ship, only small boats. This vessel had no sail, only a funnel whose bellow shuddered through its decks. It sliced through the waves too fast, leaving the land shrinking behind them, the hills swaddled in mist. She was on her way, it was too late to turn back. Like the lobster that blunders into the pot she had no way of turning round.

After docking at Fort William they travelled by carriage to her mistress's family home on the Inverness road. She left the next day on a cart that would take her the rest of the way. She climbed up and settled down in the back, leaning against the sacks of meal. She felt for the small bag tied around her waist. The coins clinked together and the folded paper crackled. Mamma had been anxious to unearth a Skye connection in Inverness to smooth her arrival there and ease her own worries about her last child leaving home. She had identified another Flòraidh, a distant cousin who was married to Iain MacPherson, a hemp weaver in the town. Even more promising, she smiled, the couple had an unmarried son living with them. In a lather of excitement she had scurried to the manse to ask for Maighstir Ruaridh Macleod's help. She returned, eyes gleaming, waving the letter in triumph.

'You must keep this safe and hand it to the minister at Inverness Gaelic Chapel. It says that you come from a God-fearing family and asks him to introduce you to the MacPhersons.'

Màiri sat on the cart, straight-backed and grim faced, hoping that the carter and the other passengers couldn't see how terrified she was. As they neared the town surprise drove away her fear. She gazed open-mouthed. Everything seemed so big, as if made for giants. The river was so wide, straight and full of boats. She was used to humble bridges like the Fairy Bridge, crouching down under the hills, but the bridge over the Ness soared upwards on its seven arches, rising like a crown above the river. There was the massive castle brooding on its hill, but what most impressed her was the Tolbooth spire jabbing at the sky. It seemed as tall as the Tower of Babel.

She noticed a group of women on the other side of the river beyond the bridge. They were all barefoot, sleeves rolled up and skirts hitched up above their white knees. They pummelled the washing in the water, soap suds floating around them like flakes of snow. Her heart lifted as she watched them. It was like washing days at home, she and her sister splashing each other while they pounded the clothes until the water was dyed grey-black. Then they would haul out the sodden clothes, heavy as a net full of fish. Once hung out on a rope to dry the sleeves and legs would fill with wind, wriggling and writhing to free themselves. All those people in the fine houses needed to have their clothes washed, she thought. There's bound to be work.

She asked the carter to stop and leapt off the cart without a backward glance. Groping inside the bag she found the minister's letter and tore it into shreds, laughing aloud as the scraps scattered, falling like feathers. She ran after the washerwomen who had shouldered their tubs and were trudging up the hill. They called to each other, sounding as friendly as gulls telling each other where the fish could be found. She followed them into a street lined by tall houses with sharply angled roofs and castellated eaves. Then they stopped in a square. There was a large stone set in the middle of the road and the women dumped their tubs there, straightening and rubbing their backs. Behind them was the solid bulk of the Town House. Màiri craned her neck to look up at the arched doorways and the two floors of long windows above. Was it some sort of palace?

'Are you looking for someone?' a voice called out in Gaelic.

She turned towards the wiry, middle-aged woman with her reddened arms. 'Aye, I'm looking for a position.'

'Well you've come to the right place. This is the Clachnacuddin stone. All of Inverness stops here for a gossip.'

'I'm Màiri. I've just arrived from Skye.'

'I think we might have guessed that my dear, what with your accent and ruddy complexion.' She laughed but not unkindly.

'To say nothing about the clothes,' added a younger woman with gleaming eyes and curly hair sprawling over her shoulders.

Màiri smiled uncertainly, suddenly uncomfortable in her hairy tweed skirt and faded shawl.

'And take a look at those boots. What giant did you get those from? Are they Finn McCoul's cast-offs? They must breed big folk on Skye. Big and hairy like the cattle.' The younger woman made a loud 'moo' and hooted with laughter.

Màiri glowered and clenched her fists.

'Take no notice of that *banshee* Jeannie. She can't stop herself from being rude,' said the older woman. 'I'm Morag. You can stop with us for the time being until you find your feet. It's no palace but I dare say you're used to sharing a bed.'

'Not for years, since my sister, Seonag, left but I can happily squeeze into a small corner,' Màiri accepted gratefully.

She ended up staying with them for weeks. She had work, a bed and company. And what work! She considered herself to be hardy but the laundry work was exhausting, pounding clothes in the river and carrying sodden heavy bundles to the drying green. She spent her sparse free time resting and couldn't rouse herself early enough on the Sabbath to go to church. What would Mamma think? The longer she left it the harder it became to go and make herself known at the Gaelic chapel.

'Only the well-off have time to be religious,' Jeannie laughed, tossing her bubbling head of curls.

'You sound like my Pappa,' Màiri laughed, but she secretly worried about how shocked Mamma would be by her behaviour.

One fresh day they were sitting, legs outstretched on the Clach. She closed her eyes, glad of the rest.

'Good day to you ladies. How are you all?' a deep voice rumbled above her. She opened her eyes to see a burly man of her own age, a little taller than herself.

'Well enough, Isaac. How about yourself? I've not seen you around for a long time,' Morag replied.

'You won't have met Màiri,' added Jeannie. 'She's from Skye and still has heather sprouting out of her ears.'

'I hope you've not been tormenting her,' he growled with a half-smile on his face. 'Have you forgotten I'm from Skye myself?' He turned to Màiri and grinned broadly, showing strong teeth. Her face lit up at the reminder of home.

'You're bound to be related then,' chuckled Jeannie, glancing at Isaac under her lashes, but his attention was fixed on Màiri who hadn't spoken.

Morag, thinking her tongue-tied and wanting to help, touched her arm, 'Isaac could help you. He's a shoemaker and keeps all of Inverness shod. He would know who might need a servant girl. It would be easier work than washing.'

'I can do any job around the house, Mamma taught me well. I'm used to hard work,' she spluttered.

Still staring at her he tilted his cap back and scratched his head, 'Pick up one of those tubs and hold it at arm's length until I tell you to stop,' he told her.

She did as he asked, balancing one of the tubs that was weighted down with soaking clothes. She looked him straight in the eye as she gnawed her lip with the effort. The women watched silently as she struggled to stop her arms from trembling. After a long minute he told her to put it down. She did so, slowly and carefully.

'You're certainly strong and you've got spirit. Walk down the road with me and we'll call at a house where I know the mistress is looking for a willing worker.'

He turned away from the gawping washerwomen. Màiri followed, head held high and Jeannie winked at her behind Isaac's back.

CHAPTER 12

Inverness, February 1846

'Have you heard any news from Skye at all?' Morag asked Màiri when they bumped into each other by the Clachnacuddin.

Màiri shook her head.

'What about Isaac? Has he heard anything?'

'He's had no news either. One of his customers let him read his *Courier* after he had finished with it.'

'And?'

'He got into a lather. "How dare they compare us to bog Irishmen, saying we eat nothing but potatoes."' Màiri mimicked Isaac's actions, slapping her thigh with an imaginary newspaper before scrunching it up and trampling on it.

'Aye, he's a man of strong opinions,' laughed Morag.

'And how's my favourite Skye heifer today?' shrieked Jeannie as she joined them, throwing a sinewy arm around Màiri's waist and pinching hard.

'Och, stop tormenting the poor lass,' chided Morag, 'She's worried about her family back home.'

'Do you know what I heard just now down at the harbour?' She put her hands on her slender hips and smiled.

'Is this something you heard from Angus, your fancy man?' mocked Morag.

The younger woman pouted in mock indignation, 'Well it's true enough. There are two boats down there, waiting to be loaded for London. Guess what the cargo is?'

'Tatties,' chorused the others.

'But that can't be right,' protested Màiri, 'There's not enough to feed people here and yet they're taking supplies away to London.'

Jeannie shrugged, 'Well that's the way of the world isn't it? The rich only think about themselves.'

'Something should be done to stop it,' Màiri cried, 'Pappa always says you should speak out against injustice.'

'Aye, and what happens then? The poor are punished and nothing changes,' muttered Morag.

'Well, something's being planned,' Jeannie said.

'Come on then. Tell us,' urged Màiri.

'You're just itching for a fight. Look at that jaw of yours, jutting out like the prow of a ship,' teased Jeannie. She seized Màiri's hands, 'And I bet those big fists of yours are clenched, ready for action. Well, there's lads watching the warehouse where the tatties are stored. When they see the carts being loaded they'll send out wee boys as runners and a big crowd will hurry down to Thornbush Pier and block their way.'

'And who will do that?' asked Morag.

'Lots of folk. Men, women and boys, too many for the constables to get through and arrest anyone. Some of the men are dressing up as women to confuse them. They won't be as likely to take a swipe at a woman.'

'Those constables have itchy fingers. They like an excuse to lash out,' said Morag.

Jeannie ignored her and turned to Màiri, 'Are you with us then? You Skye folk are fighters aren't you?'

'Indeed we are. There are lots of tales about the bloody battles between MacLeods and ...'declared Màiri, but she hesitated, all her indignation skidding to a halt.

'Come on Màiri, surely you're not running scared?' Jeannie goaded, 'I expected you to be up at the front, swinging your claymore.'

'I'm keen to come right enough but what would Isaac say? He doesn't approve of fighting. He says that you have to be canny; play them at their own game and stay within the law.'

'Well, we're not going to be fighting, we're only going to stop the carts,' insisted Jeannie.

'Aye, but he would say that should be up to the men.'

Jeannie grunted in derision while Màiri frowned, 'It's like being pulled between my parents again. Mamma's so careful in what she says and does while Pappa stands his ground. He even argued with the Minister about working on the Sabbath. That was how they ended up in Glasgow for years.'

'And here was me expecting that a big, brawny lassie like yourself would have some fire in her belly,' sneered Jeannie.

'I have,' Màiri cried out, clutching her head in distress.

'Come on, Màiri, how will Isaac even find out? He works all the hours God sends,' Jeannie declared, grabbing Màiri's wrists in her wiry fingers, 'we'll have some sport, you'll see. When I get the word I'll come down your road and tap twice on the back door. Don't worry, your mistress won't hear.' She stretched up on tiptoes to lift up Màiri's downturned chin, then skipped off, whooping, her shawl unfurling at the edges like a banner.

Later, when Jeannie came for her, they scurried together down the road, arms linked, joining other small groups in the darkness, parting and sidestepping to make way for the newcomers, then forming a line and stepping out. It's like being back at home setting out to go to a dance or a wedding, she thought, my feet slipping on shiny rocks and springy heather. She felt a flurry of fear, like a cuddy fish tossed into a basin. Her heart skittered as she thought how here she was sliding on broken, slimy cobbles and surrounded by the grim faces of strangers. There was a whiff of danger, like the scent of a fox. She shivered but then chided herself, "I'm as free as a wave of the sea, one lost among the swell of many others."

'Why are you grinning like a wild woman?' Jeannie's voice jolted her.

'Because I feel full of life,' she shouted.

A man's voice roared, 'There are the carts up ahead.'

The crowd heaved and juddered before surging forward. Now we're like a flock of gulls, Màiri thought, swooping and swinging behind a fishing boat. Gulls feel no shame or guilt. They just do what they need to do.

The throng slowed as it neared the carts. The horses jostled and fidgeted. Looking over her shoulder Màiri could see some of the constables at the edges of the crowd, trying to push their way through with their clubs. They were being forced back by shoulders, fists and feet. It seemed to her that the constables too were doing what they had to do, even though it seemed wrong. She had hated it when her father went out with the other men to hunt seals. To her their deep-pooled eyes were human; she believed the tales about the selkies, the seal folk who could shed their skins and become people. But her father had taken the furious young Màiri onto his knee and explained how the seals ate through the fishing nets and took the food out of the family's mouths, 'They do what they have to do to live and so do we.'

People, like animals, had to follow their destiny. Màiri smiled to herself. How scandalised the Minister would be if he knew that she was comparing animals to human beings, "Man was given an immortal soul. We are not mere beasts driven by instinct," he would declaim.

Looking around she could see elation in some faces, fierce anger or apprehension in others. The horses were very fretful now, rolling their eyes and squirming. One of them started to rear up on its hind legs. The flustered carters began to turn their charges and the crowd shifted back to give them space. The carts set off back to the warehouses while cheers and yells burst in the air like fireworks.

'We've done it. We've beaten them,' cried Màiri, flinging her arms around Jeannie's neck.

Jeannie looked at her pityingly, 'You don't imagine that's the end of it, do you, lassie?'

CHAPTER 13

Inverness, 1846

'Oh, my poor head hurts. It feels as if it's been used as a shinty ball,' Màiri groaned, 'and I'm black and blue all down my side. I don't know how I kept working this morning at all. Thank Goodness it's the Sabbath tomorrow and I can have a rest.' She slumped down heavily by the Clachnacuddin stone.

'You poor *isean*,' commiserated Morag, 'That pig of a constable gave you a real thumping. I suppose with you being so tall he must have thought that you were a man disguised in women's clothes.'

'He must have been half blind or just seen your back,' hooted Jeannie, 'If he'd seen yon big lumps on you he would have known you could never be a man.'

Morag glared at her. Jeannie continued, 'Anyway it's not just the constable's stick that gave you a sore head. Don't you remember all the wee drams you had when the bottles were passed back and forth? That's what gave you the courage to say your piece.'

'What piece?' Màiri asked.

'You certainly gave as good as you got,' smiled Morag, 'It was when they were tipping the cart into the harbour. It was quiet for a moment and you called out, "That'll serve them right for keeping tatties from the starving Skye folk." Then a man shouted out, "Well, you're not a starving *Sgitheaneach* yourself, lassie, that's for sure." So what did you do? You turned your back on him, slapped your rump, hoisted your skirt up and called out, "They breed us good and sturdy on Skye." And everyone cheered.'

'Did I really say that?' asked Màiri, blushing.

'Aye, but I wouldn't worry. Just make sure that he doesn't get to hear about it,' muttered Morag who had seen Isaac approaching.

'Come on, you,' she told Jeannie, hauling her to her feet, 'we'll let them have a few words in peace.'

'Just look at the state of you!' Isaac exclaimed, peering at Màiri's half closed eye and mottled bruises. Did your master or mistress do this to you?' She shook her head.

'Well, Isaac, now folk will think you've been taking your fists to her,' cackled Jeannie over her shoulder. Morag gave her a furious cuff over the ears and pushed her on her way.

He put his hands on her shoulders and stared, 'You were involved in that business last night, weren't you, with that Jeannie? You're lucky that you haven't broken any bones or been locked up,' he continued, frowning and shaking her slightly.

'Don't take on so, Isaac. How were we to know that it would turn nasty? For three nights running we turned those wagons back. Two nights ago one of them even ended up in the water. What a splash!' Her eyes danced.

'It wasn't just a bit of harmless fun though, was it? Some of the mob broke windows at the Provost's house and I heard that the Provost himself was struck by a stone.'

'Aye, but what about the constables lashing out at everyone with their sticks? They gave me a beating and I wasn't throwing anything.'

Isaac sighed and pulled her closer, 'Well thank the Lord that you weren't badly hurt or arrested. You risked being turned out of your job without a character.'

'Why are you talking as if I was the one in the wrong? What about the wrong done by those rich people making money from high potato prices while poor folk go hungry? They're the ones you should blame. Three nights running we stopped them. Maybe they've learnt their lesson now.'

Isaac shook his head and spoke more gently, 'You've not heard then? Early this morning eight loads were taken down to the pier under armed guard and stowed aboard. They're on their way south as we speak.' He took Màiri's hand, 'Don't look so crestfallen. It was bound to happen. What am I always saying about the way forward for working men? We must stand together but stay within the law.' His rallying cry did nothing to raise Màiri's spirits.

Isaac lifted Màiri to her feet, 'Come on, let's walk a little way. Anyway, I've heard some better news from Skye. The disease has struck hard there but no-one is starving. Lord MacDonald has been giving out meal to the worst afflicted.'

'That's something. But as Pappa would say, no doubt they'll have to be properly grateful for any charity.' She sighed, 'It'll mean more people leaving the island.'

'Well we have to face up to the truth,' Isaac declared, tucking Màiri's arm through his own and steering her past horse manure strewn across the cobbles, 'The future lies here in the towns and cities. I make shoes for everyone but I'm building up my business with the people who run Inverness; the merchants, the magistrates and especially their ladies who want the new London fashions. I smile at their whims and take their silver. When I've saved enough I'll have apprentices and rent a fancy shop. Then I'll get a seat on the council. That mob, you see Màiri, is like a flooded river. It destroys everything in its way but then it shrinks back again to nothing.' He stopped and turned to her, 'But I'm the burn that keeps on flowing onwards, gradually gaining strength, deepening and widening my influence as I go.' He looked into her peat brown eyes that were nearly level with his own, 'You could be part of that life.'

'But I want to go back home. I don't want to spend all my life here.'

'Maybe we could afford to go back one day.'

'But how would I ever earn enough money to do that?'

Isaac laughed, 'You're not listening to me. I've had it in mind to marry you from the first time we spoke and you held out that heavy basket even though your arms were trembling. You're strong and hardworking, not like those vain young women who imagine that they can snare me with their simpering faces. But you must keep away from riots and stay peaceably at home .We suit each other well enough, don't we?'

As he squeezed her hand, Màiri felt his controlled strength. Yes, she could gladly share a warm bed with this man, enjoy the deft touch of his fingers and the weight of him on top of her. And his family was from Skye too.

'But will you promise me that one day we will return to live in Skye? I want cattle to tend. I want to wake early and see the Old Man of Storr standing stark against the sky with clouds bearding his face. And what of our children? They must know where they came from and see their homeland for themselves.'

'You're jumping ahead. You're talking about children and you haven't even said whether you will marry me. Are you a wicked woman who is thinking of having children out of wedlock?' he whispered in her ear, the scrape of his dark beard making her tremble with desire.

'No, indeed. I shall be happy to spend the rest of my life with you and I shall learn how to be a respectable lady.'

CHAPTER 14

Inverness and Skye, 1862

The cottage smelt of warm bannocks, bubbling soup and drying clothes. Màiri tucked her youngest under her arm and shouted out to the other four playing on the Green. Then she turned to her husband, 'No, Isaac. This is my father. I must go this time. I missed Mamma's wake and I won't leave it to relatives and neighbours this time. Flora will look after the others. I know your mother won't like it but she'll survive until I get back. Maybe she'll even miss me a little when I'm not there to wait on her.'

Isaac opened his mouth but shut it again. He could see that she was determined and he didn't have the strength to argue. His new work as a chimney sweep seemed to have eaten away at his sinews and the sour smell of soot was always in his nostrils. Meanwhile Màiri crackled like burning heather despite having five children and an aged mother-in-law to care for.

So for the first time since their marriage she left their cramped cottage in the Maggat, overlooking the Green, to travel away from Inverness. When they first came there to live Isaac had told her that the house was near the river. It would surely remind her of her home, near the Snizort on Skye. She had smiled and squeezed his hand, not wanting to disappoint him by saying that this river couldn't be more different from the Snizort. The Ness was so wide, surrounded by buildings and where were the mountains? He carried on, telling her the story of the local strongman, Jock on the Maggat who had once carried the Clach na Cudainn all the way up to the Old Jail steps.

'I was grateful for that stone many times when I rested my heavy tubs of washing on it.'

'I would hope you would be even more grateful to the stone for meeting me there,' he had growled in mock anger, pressing her close to him.

She had resolved to make the best of her new life. Like Ruth she had said, "Whither thou goest, I will go; and where thou lodgest, I will lodge; thy people will be my people." At least she had said that to Isaac, unlike Ruth she had not felt able to speak such words to her mother-in-law. And she had grown to like Inverness. She thought of its people with affection as *'Clann na Cloiche'* for it was true that the stone had brought Isaac to her. The town was a good foster mother to her, although it couldn't replace her birthplace.

And so she returned to Skye where the blustery autumn weather lifted her skirts and carried her into the new house. It was a strange homecoming because she had never set foot in this house. Her parents had moved there when they had to leave the old township after the landlord had sold the land for a sheep run. It didn't look so different from her old home, a low lying, round cornered black house, its stones moulded into the landscape but the house still smelt raw to her. It wasn't steeped in years of peat fires and memories like the old home.

Iain Bàn had been as hale as ever, so they had told her. No-one had ever known him to take to his bed with illness, even for a day.

'But I knew someone would need my services,' the gravedigger told her. 'The night before, my tools began to rattle against each other where they leant on the wall of the byre. Sure enough, the next morning your father's neighbour noticed that he hadn't come out to smoke his pipe as usual.'

'And she found him still in bed. He had slipped away during the night,' Màiri replied.

How she hated the idea that his neighbours, not his family, had lifted his still-warm body, laid him out on an old door suspended over barrels and covered him with a sheet. They had remembered to put salt on his belly and turn the mirror to the wall to deter evil spirits. But he would have wanted familiar hands to prepare him for his final journey.

She had surprised herself during the wake. While the voices around her murmured and rumbled she had started to rock backwards and forwards on her stool near the fire. She started to chant, a cascade of words about her father, how he could quieten a fractious beast, plough tirelessly all day and know by instinct where the shoals of fish would be lurking. She recounted the tale of how he fell foul of the minister and nearly ended up in Canada and of how when he returned to Skye he knew exactly the best place to dig his well. Her words gained power and speed, a waterfall of sound, praising his life and keening over its ending. Maybe some of the folk there disapproved of what they saw as an old heathen custom but she knew that Pappa would have been pleased.

On the morning of the funeral she looked around the house for the last time.

'What have you done with the mirror?' Her father's voice echoed behind her. She almost expected to see him reach out to turn the old mirror's speckled face outwards.

When they all lived in the old house he would duck down in front of it to make sure his cap was on straight before rushing to the door, flinging it open and rubbing his hands together, ready for the day ahead. Now she plodded to the door, her head drooping, but as she eased it open she straightened her shoulders and strode out towards the church. When she arrived she was greeted by kind looks, firm handgrips and soft voices, but something was askew, out of kilter. Sitting down on the hard bench she closed her eyes for an instant while she wondered what was amiss. The thought struck her, a chill gust that seeped into her bones. She had become a guest, a visitor in her native place, when she left tomorrow the door would close, sealing her on the outside.

Reverend MacLeod conducted the service. He was old now, his face swathed in a cloud of snowy hair but his voice was still powerful. But to Màiri his words were sounds without meaning, beating waves and howling winds. She was an orphan now. The frayed rope anchoring her to home had ripped free and the storms were hurling her out to sea. Listing and low in the water she kept herself afloat for the rest of the day until she could sink exhausted into bed.

To her surprise she awoke the next morning to find the storm within her abated, but she had a terrible thirst that could only be quenched by a drink from the well by the old house. As she plodded up to it she could feel the spate of words from the wake still swirling through her, surging down the waterfall and pouring out to the sea. They formed rows of waves, pulling out into the ocean, urging her to plunge into their songs as she had done in her youth.

> The hills have changed, the marshes
> Even the clouds in the sky
> Where once there were warm-hearted people
> Now there are sheep.
>
> When I came to my old home
> Where my people lived
> I was welcomed bitterly
> By barking dogs.
>
> Tears ran from my eyes
> As I stood there
> Remembering my people
> Now sleeping in the grave.

> I looked for the spot by the fire
> Where my mother once sat
> Giving us lasting joy
> With her love and pride in us.

The old house was deceptive. From a distance it looked unscathed, but as she came closer she could see that the thatch was mangy. She put her shoulder to the swollen wood of the door until it lolled open. In the corpse chill within she found the dark part of the floor where the hearth had been. As she kicked the blackened petals of ashes they released the smells buried deep in the stones; the reek of drying fish, the damp hay breath of cattle and the sharp red burst of rowans bubbling into jam.

Sobbing, she ran out, not stopping until she was up in the hill pastures. She knelt down to ease her racing heart and noticed a scrap of cloth snagged on thistles. It fluttered, a frail tattered flag, and for a wild moment she wondered if it was a fragment from her own torn shift all those years ago. She shook her head at her silliness. No, it must belong to a present day child, escaped with her friends to play among the silent houses. Would this child, like her young self, have gone back home tired but exultant to be scolded about her rough, boyish antics?

And all too soon it was time to return to Inverness. Her memories of her return to Skye had to be tucked away while she dragged her thoughts towards what would await her at home. The girls would have coped well she was sure but no doubt the *cailleach*, that bed-bound brooding presence, would punish Màiri for daring to escape.

'What a wonder she is, almost one hundred now, as old as Methusalah,' Màiri's neighbour would declare, shaking her head in amazement while Màiri grimaced, thinking her great age more a curse than a wonder. Although the old woman was slowly sinking she still seemed to be immortal. No matter how much her body weakened, that complaining voice never lost its strength, resounding through the house and throbbing in her ears. How unjust it seemed that this old hag was called Flòraidh, the same given name as Mamma, dead now for some years, such an anxious soul who had tried to tread carefully through life. Now that she was older herself, Màiri could understand how trampled Mamma had been both by herself and Pappa, big heedless beasts who churned up her hopes and plans. Now, mother-in-law Flòraidh was a different matter. She caused trouble deliberately, using her tongue as a bludgeoning sword. When Isaac had first introduced them she had snorted, 'So this is the lassie from Skye who thought herself above calling on us when she arrived.'

'Well Mother, there's no harm done. We met each other in our own time.'

But the harridan wouldn't be silenced. 'She's no beauty and she'll need to be broken to the bridle. Still she looks as strong as a mare. She should breed healthy children.'

When Màiri felt her first child quicken within her she knew that she could not endure having this woman near her when her time came.

'I know you want to go back to Skye to have the first baby,' Isaac said, 'but it's too far. You can't travel on your own when you're near your time and I can't afford to lose you. Surely my mother will be enough help for you. She's had plenty children and knows what it's about.'

How like a man to imagine that any woman would do as a support, as if helping with a birth was only about knowledge rather than trust and affection. Her fears had swelled alongside the growing baby and in the end she confided in Morag, who listened quietly and then asked, 'Would your mother be able to come down if you got word to her?'

'I'm sure she would but how can I get a message to her? I would need Isaac to write it and give it to someone travelling to Skye. I don't think he would be willing to do that. He would be afraid of what the old witch his mother would say.' Màiri felt disheartened.

'So we'll have to get someone else to write it.'

'But who can we get to do that?'

Morag smiled shyly, 'I could write it for you.'

'You can write, and read too?' Màiri gawped as her friend nodded.

'I'm rusty but I've never forgotten. My parents sent me to the church school. I was the only one of their children left alive and they wanted me to have more chances than they did. I learnt to read Gaelic first so that I could read the Bible to them. Then I started to learn English too.'

'So why are you just a washerwoman? I'm as ignorant of learning as a bird on the wing but you …'

'It all came to an end when my Pappa died suddenly. I was ten years old and my mother had no money. She sent me to my aunt in the town to earn my living. How I railed against my poor mother. I'd loved the school and I didn't notice how thin my mother was getting. She died within a year, poor soul, and by then I was a kitchen skivvy.'

'Did anyone know that you could read and write?'

'No. I kept it secret. Masters don't like servants who know too much.'

The message was safely delivered and so was she. Her mother had coaxed and cajoled her through the ordeal of Flora's birth.

'How did you know when to come for Màiri's lying-in?' Isaac asked her.

'Now you're descended from Skye folk. You shouldn't need to ask that question.'

'Second sight?'

'Of course,' she had replied with a twinkle in her eye.

And what a blessing it was that Mamma and mother-in-law shared their Christian name. Isaac's ferocious old mother thought that the baby was named after her and not after her other gentler grandmother. But who would have thought that the *cailleach* would live for ever?

*

'Thank goodness you're back. My mother's been asking for you all the time.'

Looking at his gaunt face, Màiri thought how he seemed to have aged ten years while she had been gone. Well, maybe he would understand better what she had to endure with the old woman. She braced herself to go in to see her. Now that she had lost both her parents she couldn't stop herself from loathing this woman who lived on while they had died. She eased the door open to find Flòraidh asleep. Only her head was visible. Her shrivelled body barely disturbed the bed clothes and the flesh had been scraped from her skull. She clearly had only a thin-shelled hold on life. Màiri was shocked by the speed of her decline but she could also sense the familiar anger, padding beside her like a wolf on a leash. She sat down on the chair beside the bed, looking with a horrified curiosity at the bluish, crinkled eyelids which were as transparent as the skin of a newly hatched bird. She steeled herself to grasp her hand. It was as clammy as a frog's skin.

The eyes snapped open, revealing accusing blue shards.

'You've come back at last,' Floraidh sneered.

Màiri heard the rumble of the wolf's growl. She pulled the rope tighter. 'I came back as soon as I could.'

'You shouldn't have left me.'

The wolf lay down, submissive but poised to spring.

'I didn't know you were getting worse.'

A dismissive snort came from the bed. Màiri felt her throat tighten and stayed silent. The wolf slumped down and closed its eyes.

'I'm sorry I've been such a burden.'

The wolf's ears twitched at the unexpected words. Its suspicious lips curled back on glistening teeth as it prepared to snarl. She gently pressed the animal's head down.

'I know you are. Don't let it concern you,' she whispered, gently opening up the clawed fingers as they scrabbled on the sheet. The old woman closed her eyes again. The wolf whimpered and curled up like a cub.

'Stay with me.'

So Màiri stayed until the faint breathing faded away completely.

CHAPTER 15

Inverness, 1871

Màiri sat motionless on a hard chair in the darkened room, the rough bark of her fingers rubbing together. The house had never seemed so empty. The wake, with all the stories and songs, had briefly conjured up life like *Na Fir Chlis* who swirled and swooped across the heavens. They disappeared as suddenly as they had come and left the sky doubly dark. How strange it was to sit here so idle. She spread out her blotched hands with their swollen joints. For so many years she had been so busy, filling every moment. That busyness had stolen her life away, as it did for people who had spent time with the Fairies. Their time with them would seem to pass in a flash but when they returned home they found that years had gone by and everyone had grown old and grey.

When she looked back at her life it seemed like a river. For the first part before she left Skye it wandered like the Snizort, winding down to the sea. Those early days spent under the cloud-wrapped hills, tending the crops and the animals, seemed to stretch back as far as her eye could see. Her life since she came to Inverness had drawn her along the current of the broad River Ness, its waters swelling and teeming as she spent years carrying the cargoes of husband and family.

Now the children were grown, especially Flora, a brisk and calm young woman who had come up to Inverness to scoop up the stunned and silent Effie and take her back to Glasgow. Poor Effie, she was the only one who wasn't full grown, not much older than Morag had been when she had lost both her parents and … no, she mustn't let her thoughts stray near the cliff edge. Effie was not going to be an orphan like Morag. No, Màiri thought, I will recover. It was only that she felt so completely lost and abandoned. She was like the weaned calf taken from its mother too soon, wandering in circles and lowing inconsolably, hungry but refusing the bucket of milk. But like the calf she would bow her head in time, accept sustenance and live with what was left, in spite of all that had gone.

Time, it would take time. And there was her son Iain, working with time, learning to be a watchmaker. He was safe enough living at his master's house. She didn't have to fret about him. How strange it was that in measuring time, counting it out in small change on a clock face, men could think that they had trapped it. Time for her had stopped. She was a clock beyond repair.

Still, she must count her blessings. But it was so hard to swim against the tide of despair. She had five healthy children, all well grown. It was only her third born, the first wee Màiri, who had died. That was the only birth that had left her ill. She had been feverish for days and weak as water. It was the only time in her life when her strength had failed her and she had feared that she might die. But her fear had nested in the wrong place. She had begun to recover. That spring morning the hopeful light had woken her and she had turned to the cradle beside her bed, but she knew at once that the baby's soul had fled her body. She held the tiny cold corpse in her arms, fragile as a dead bird. The worst of it was knowing that she had died alone in the depths of the night without a warm breast to comfort her. But no, even worse was the gnawing fear that her death could have been avoided.

When her labour was under way Isaac had hurried to fetch Anna MacDonald, the wise midwife who had helped at Mairead's birth. Unfortunately Anna had been stricken down with a looseness of the bowels and could not attend this time. Isaac had been terrified of going back home empty handed. He was feeling guilty, too, for this baby had been conceived when Mairead was only four months old. He was given the name of another woman, a stranger with sour breath and broken, dirty finger nails.

She it was who, like an evil fairy, had tainted Màiri and stricken the baby mortally. She shivered and drew her shawl closer around her. How it hurt to press old scars but her mind shied away from touching the new raw wound. She stood up and opened the door to gulp down the cold outside air. How she missed Isaac. Sometimes she would sleep so heavily, in a deathly trance sinking to the black depths of the ocean. Then dawn summoned her back to the surface. She would lie back with the waves gently lapping her face, looking about her like a curious seal, wondering about the day ahead. Her hand would touch the cold sheets beside her, she would remember and the net would tighten, dragging her down, her lungs bursting for breath. Desperately she would bite through the tangled ropes and burst back to the surface exhausted.

The evenings were cruel too. She would hear his slow footsteps and the rasp of the cough that had dogged him ever since he started cleaning chimneys. The acid soot had bored through mouth, eyes and skin, sucking out his strength. The bones of his broad shoulders protruded like scoured rock and he lacked the strength to fight the terrible headaches and fever that felled him. For two weeks he lay in the darkened bedroom, groaning and retching in torment. It had been a blessing when delirium released him from pain. And she was so helpless. All she could do was nurse him, damping him down with wet cloths and soothing him.

It was odd, really, how she had gained a reputation as a nurse when she didn't believe in fussing and clucking over patients. Maybe it was that steadiness she had; people trusted her to cope.

She was often asked to lay out the dead or to sit with the gravely ill and dying. She supposed that her gift was that she could hold them safe, as she had done all those years ago with the basket of sodden laundry. Earning some money had been useful too but what was she to do now? How could she bear to nurse anyone, when all she could see was the torment in his sunken eyes and thrashing limbs? How could she help others hold on? Yet what else was there? Taking in washing paid so little and would wear out her ageing body. How could he have left her in such straits? All those fine dreams of his dissolved away.

She had dreamt of him last night, upright and sturdy, in his prime. He had called out, "Look at that rainbow. It's so bright and I can see where it comes to earth." By the time she turned her head to see it was already beginning to fade and soon there was nothing left at all. He had worked so hard crafting beautiful shoes and cultivating the gentry. He had even taken on that lad Ruaridh, chirpy as a wagtail, for an apprentice, but changing times overtook him. He condemned the crofters for clinging to old ways but then he did the same thing himself.

By the time Effie was born Baillie Simpson was opening his shoe factory. The machines could cut and sew the leather tirelessly. So what did Isaac do but work longer and longer hours to keep pace, barely sleeping. To no avail as his shoes still cost more to make than the factory ones. She would wake in the night and feel the cold space beside her. Shuffling downstairs she would find him slumped asleep over his lasts, like a worn out horse drooping between the shafts. Soon they were living on little more than potatoes and onions. The children's faces were china white.

It was she who had insisted that he pocket his pride and ask for work at the factory. For so long she had acted the dutiful wife, quiet as a parrot in a covered cage, but now she squawked loudly and wouldn't be silenced. At first things improved; he had regular wages although he hated the loss of his freedom. Then the Baillie showed that he was as black-hearted as the landlords who kept tightening the noose on the crofters. The landowners raised the rents while the Baillie's treachery was to shrink the wages. Isaac thought he had the answer, 'We working men must stick together and use the law to help us.'

So he started a union and told Baillie Simpson that he must increase their wages or face a strike. Again they were back to near starvation for weeks until the Baillie agreed a small rise in the wages if the union was disbanded. So the shoemakers returned to work, but Isaac was stopped at the door and turned away. And did any of his workmates stand by him? Not them, too scared of losing their own livelihood. There is no worse betrayal than that of a friend.

Isaac pulled himself up again, 'I shall work for myself and then no-one can turn against me,' he used to joke when he started to clean chimneys but after that he never had the same spirit. He was clogged up with all the disappointments until he seized up altogether. He couldn't be taken apart, cleaned and put together again like one of Iain's clocks.

He said that he was the captain of our family's ship, thought Màiri, but he couldn't read the waters. I rage at him for letting our boat hit the rocks and losing the cargo of our dreams. I rage at all the men who treat us Gaels so wrongly. I shall never believe again that men should act while women keep silent. But I feel so sad for that young man I met, vivid and bright as a rainbow in a lowering sky.

For the first time Màiri allowed herself to weep at the death of Isaac and all their hopes, splintered on the rocks and scattered on the ocean.

CHAPTER 16

Inverness, 1872

'Don't just sit there lass. Go and finish the cleaning,' scolded Màiri.

'Why? They're all away at the funeral, thank the Lord. Then they'll have the cold meats. The master won't be back for a long time and do you think he'll notice a bit of dust?' replied the girl, flicking a greasy strand of hair that had sneaked its way from under her cap.

Màiri shook her fist, 'Don't you use the Lord's name in vain, you slovenly wretch. Show some respect for that poor bereaved gentleman.' She glowered at the girl and stalked off into one of the bedrooms. Kate grimaced at Màiri's broad back, held stiff with indignation.

'Who does she think she is, ordering me around?' she muttered.

Màiri's shoulders sank as she closed the door behind her. She slumped into the bedside chair. If only it were Flora helping her, hardworking and capable Flora instead of this impudent young miss who mocked her behind her back. She smoothed the bedcovers distractedly. There was no imprint left behind of that poor lady who had sweated and shivered her life away. It was hard to believe that she was no more. She had been so ill and so scared, clinging to Màiri, her eyes tormented like a child awoken by night terrors.

'Tell me I'm not going to die,' she had pleaded.

And she was far too young to die, only a little older than her own Flora. When the Captain opened the door he would be so alarmed by his wife's distress that he hung back in the doorway, not knowing what to say or do. He was a frightened boy, his fine uniform only a dressing up costume. So Mrs Turner, poor soul, had no-one to talk to but Màiri. With her sparse English she struggled to understand her patient's delirious mutterings. So she tried to comfort her as she would a sick child. She stroked her hair and sang her lullabies. The words were foreign to her but the music seemed to give her some solace, helping her slip into a restless sleep.

She had tended her charge well, mopping her with cool cloths and cleaning up the stinking fluids that gushed from her trembling body. However, the singing, cleaning and soothing had not been enough. Mrs Turner had died, and less than a year after Isaac. Màiri felt a crushing weight around her heart when he went but this woman was virtually a stranger. It wasn't the same but she still felt a heavy sadness at the waste of a young life. She reminded herself that she had nursed Mrs Turner well and eased her passing. There was nothing to reproach herself for. She had kept her mind fixed on the task and like a soldier under fire she didn't allow fear to unravel her. She had gained a reputation for being calm and reliable. That was why Captain Bolland had recommended her to care for his friend's suffering wife. Not many women would nurse those who had the signs of high fever and agonising loose bowels. They were afraid of being infected themselves and carrying the contagion back to their own families. No one knew how the deadly illness spread but Màiri believed that keeping herself and her patient spotlessly clean would give them both a better chance of surviving.

'More clean linen today, you're as fussy as the gentry,' that slatternly lass had mocked. Màiri had lashed her with her tongue so that now the wretched girl only muttered under her breath. This time, of course, cleanliness had not been enough to save her patient although maybe it had protected Màiri herself. Did saving her own life matter? She was still uncertain about that. The pall of Isaac's death still hung over her and today she felt exhausted. She had slept fitfully, waking, startled, by a dream of home.

She was walking along the familiar loops of the Snizort when the encircling hills started to tilt and lean as if they would fall inwards and bury her underneath their weight. Surely that was a warning of some impending trouble? No, she wouldn't brood on that. Today or tomorrow she would be paid. Then it would be back to her usual duties at the Bollands' house. She should rest now while she had the chance.

In the small hours Màiri was startled awake by a thump on the door. She called out to the girl to open up but there was no response. Grumbling, she struggled to her feet, wrapping her shawl over her nightclothes. As she unlocked the door it was flung back on its hinges by a soldier who called out to someone behind him. There was Captain Bolland looking stern and Captain Turner too, staring at her with hatred in his eyes. Before Màiri could gather her wits the first soldier pushed her aside and marched through the hallway to her room. She rushed after him, pulling at his jacket as he flung open the battered chest that held all her belongings. Shrugging her off roughly he delved inside and, triumphant as a magician, tugged out a flurry of clothes. At the top was a scarf of jade green silk. He swirled it aloft before handing it to Captain Turner. He stared at it before crumpling it against his nose and inhaling deeply. For a moment his face was screwed up in torment before he brought it back to stiff attention. Màiri gasped as she too caught the lingering traces of Harriet Turner's scent.

The two officers exchanged a glance and nodded at the soldiers. Màiri was seized and pushed roughly towards the front door. Shouting in indignation she gestured towards her nightclothes. Captain Turner nodded brusquely. She was released and allowed to return to her room to dress herself with clumsy, trembling fingers. What terrible mistake was this? Did they really imagine that she, a woman renowned for her honesty, would steal anything from her dead mistress, let alone her favourite scarf, the one she had clutched in her last agonies, twisting and winding it in her poor frenzied fingers? Màiri's thoughts scattered like rooks at the crash of gunfire. Her few words of English had been scared from their roost.

'I have done nothing wrong, I have done nothing wrong,' she mumbled to herself in Gaelic, raising her voice as she stepped into the hall and finally delivering it in a loud volley to Captain Turner. He glared at her before turning his back. The soldiers pinioned her arms and forced her outside, hauling their stumbling captive towards the prison. The few people out and about so early stopped to stare and Màiri felt her face redden. Suddenly she heard her Pappa's voice breathing in her ear, 'Step out, Màiri. Remember those long strides of yours. I always said you had the quick gait of the Fairies in covering the ground. March out now.'

So she held her head high and stepped out strongly. In a daze she trudged over slabs gleaming damply, flat as gravestones marking the death of her good name. Then the cell door clanged shut on her, final as a coffin lid.

I must not carry a burden of shame that's not mine, she thought. There is the stink of treachery here. What would my dear mother say about it? She would turn to the Bible. Betrayal. Wasn't our Saviour betrayed for money? And Joseph, of course, I have always felt drawn to him. When I daydreamed while I was churning butter or milking the cow Mamma would say, "Behold the dreamer cometh," mocking me as his brothers mocked Joseph. Then they sold him into slavery before he was betrayed a second time by Potiphar's wife. She hated him when he turned away from her lust and had him thrown into prison, just as I have been. But he wasn't abandoned. He had the second sight and his dreams came to Pharoah's ear. His predictions of famine were heeded and he saved the Egyptian people from disaster. Like him I will not lose hope. No doubt the minister would say that I have false pride to place myself on a level with Joseph. Me, a mere woman whose task is to obey and be silent. She stretched out on the hard bed, but sleep was impossible. Her thoughts writhed like eels in a net.

But have I not been obedient? I have bent like a sapling in the wind to the will of others. I was a dutiful wife to Isaac. Later I was a dutiful nurse, hiding the gashes in my heart while I tended that poor dying lady. But where has that duty and sacrifice led me? My spirit is as empty as my parents' old house, slowly fallen in on itself. The door has warped and buckled, the roof sags. Soon the stones of the walls will be spat out like decayed teeth and the undergrowth will grow a green shroud over it all. Only the gable ends will stand as dumb memorials to all my hopes when I was a girl.

But dumbness is no disgrace. I'm only dumb because I haven't the English words to proclaim my innocence. Who would want to bear false witness against me? Baillie Simpson's son is a powerful man now, a judge. Would he remember his father's anger about the strike? Would he want revenge so badly that he would pay someone to take Mrs Turner's things from her closet and hide them in my chest? I find that hard to believe. Maybe he will judge my case. If so, I pray he will be a just man, like Solomon.

What about Captain Turner? He looked at me with such hatred. Has he been turned inside out with the madness of grief and blames me for his wife's death? I don't know who has done this to me. I must take comfort from my clear conscience. When I am taken to court they will see that it is all a foolish, terrible mistake.

Màiri spread the thin, dirty blanket over herself and tried again to settle on the hard board. She remembered lying on a mattress freshly filled with heather as a child. When she couldn't sleep in the long white midsummer nights Pappa would tell her to compose a poem in her mind so that it would mingle with her dreams in the magic space between the sea and the shore. But how could she make a song out of angry words alone? They would be too jagged to make a poetic shape. Surely songs were about love, joy, sadness or exile?

CHAPTER 17

Inverness, April 1872

'Oh, Sir, do please stop. I need to speak with you.'

Rev. MacKay halted his spindly, heron legs and looked down his beaky nose at the wiry old woman, gasping as she recovered her breath.

'It's big Màiri. You know, Isaac's widow. She's been put in prison and accused of theft; of taking clothes from that poor young lady she was nursing when she had barely breathed her last and she can't understand how it's happened and she's to be tried at any moment and can't defend herself when she doesn't understand the charge that's written in English and she's in a desperate state indeed and I thought of yourself to help her and explain to the sheriff that it's all a terrible mistake and ...'

'Slow down, woman. You're gabbling. I don't recognise you. You're not one of my flock, are you?'

'No, Sir, but Màiri is. Màiri MacPherson.'

'And you say that she is innocent of any wrongdoing?'

'Of course she is. She's as honest as the day is long. Some folk might say that she is too honest in speaking her mind but no-one could accuse her of stealing and expect to be believed.'

'Yes, indeed, she isn't known for turning the other cheek,' he noted, frowning.

'But she was not the one at fault. She has been wrongly accused. She needs someone respected and fluent in English, like yourself, to help her.'

'Mmm. I shall have to ascertain what the position is. It would avail us nothing to fan the flames of discord before investigating further. Leave the matter with me.'

Morag opened her mouth to protest but her lips froze under the icy blast of the minister's gaze. Who could she ask now? She shuffled her feet while she ransacked her mind. Hadn't Jeannie's husband Angus spoken warmly about the excise superintendent? He always took time to speak to the workers in Gaelic when he came to the brewery, Duncan said. He was a thoughtful and earnest man, no drinker at all. They always teased him and tried to get him to have a wee taste but he would turn them down with a smile – not righteous at all. But where would she find him? Didn't he live out of the town, towards Clachnaharry? That was much too far to walk. No matter. She would go to the brewery and ask there about him. So she turned her protesting feet back towards the town centre.

She found Angus as ruddy and hearty as she was bloodless and pale.

'You're in luck. He was here an hour since and now he's checking out the inns. Sit yourself down while I go and find him.'

*

April 1872

Dear Mr Mackintosh,

I trust that you will not consider me importunate in writing to you. I know of your sterling work in improving the amenities of the town. However, I am appealing to you now as a fellow Gael and one of the founders of the Gaelic Society.

If I may set the scene before you: a defendant recently appeared in one of our courts, a native of our own Highland province, a woman speaking in her mother tongue, the language of the Gael. When she was called she seemed not to hear. She was called in a strange tongue and heeded it not. Bye and bye she started up and made enquiry and although she spoke the language of the country there was no-one who knew what she said or who could speak to her in terms which she could understand. The poor woman must have felt as if she were in the Tower of Babel.

The case was reported as follows in the pages of 'The Inverness Courier',

'A very painful and disgraceful case came before Baillie Simpson at the Police Court on Monday. A nurse named Mary MacPherson was engaged to attend a lady lying ill of fever. The lady, comparatively a stranger in Inverness and living with her family in lodgings, unhappily died and the nurse took advantage of her position in the house to pillage her wardrobe. While the funeral service was being read at the cathedral, she was ransacking the boxes of her deceased mistress. The charge was fully proved and the prisoner was sentenced to 40 days imprisonment.'

A friend of the accused alerted me to the trial. This lady was distraught, utterly convinced that the charge was false. She begged me to use what influence I could. After interviewing Màiri I felt confident that she was speaking the truth in protesting her innocence. So I spoke with Captain Turner, her erstwhile employer. He, poor gentleman was still so stricken by his young wife's demise that he was incapable of rational discussion. However, I did ascertain from him that Màiri's services had been offered to him by his friend and fellow officer, Captain Bolland. The latter and his wife were fulsome in their praise of Màiri's rectitude and honesty. They were at a loss to understand how her character could have changed so dramatically so as to turn her into a thief.

I arranged for the unfortunate woman to have legal representation at her trial, sadly to no avail. While the trial was in progress the young girl who had been employed by the Turners as a maid of all work suddenly left the district. It seems likely that she nursed a grievance against Màiri and had maliciously sought to incriminate her.

Màiri, not surprisingly, feels a keen sense of betrayal and insult. Baillie Simpson spoke to her when she was released, saying that he hoped that she had learnt her lesson. The only lesson she has learnt is that she can have no faith in the justice of Inverness and she is resolved to leave the town. She plans to stay with her daughter in Glasgow and hopes to secure work there as a private nurse.

Like me she is approaching the autumn of her days. She is strong and robust. She resembles a sleeping lioness as yet unaware of her power. In particular she displays a sort of indomitable courage, whether in disregarding her own danger in tending patients suffering from serious infections or in expressing her righteous anger at the injustice she has suffered. Although almost completely unlettered she has a poetic sensibility. She has composed verses about her imprisonment. Much of them furnish a mundane record of events as they unfolded. However, there are signs that she can see beyond her own immediate plight to reflect on the grievous fate of her countrymen. She writes with true sentiment of how,

> *"Now they're driven over the ocean*
> *By hard-hearted men*
> *No cattle to be heard in the pasture*
> *No herdsmen to call them home."*

She would dearly love to return to Skye but her family croft has disappeared like so many others and she would have no means to earn a livelihood.

I obtained for her from the Bollands the favourable reference which is her due. Secondly I suggested that I use my influence to secure her a position at the Royal Infirmary to train as a nurse and midwife. She could then command a more regular income and should she return to Skye she would have the knowledge to ameliorate the condition of the people there.

After reflection she was agreeable to my proposal although she was concerned about her lack of learning, especially in the English language. I was able to tell her that I had secured the offices of Reverend MacKay in this matter. He had already agreed to find her a suitable teacher in Inverness and to make enquiries for further assistance when she moves to Glasgow. He was most expeditious in this matter. Maybe, although he would never admit it, his conscience was pricking him for being so dilatory in her defence earlier.

So, as you will already have surmised, I am going to ask you, in your capacity as one of the leaders of Inverness society, to use your influence to help this woman secure a position at the Royal. Her situation has led me to think again about the plight of our people. My thoughts have tended to concentrate on Highland men as the agents for betterment of the Gaels. After all, woman's role is one centred on family duties. Yet, as with every rule, there are exceptions. A woman like Màiri, no longer young but with strong, albeit unformed, energies need no longer be confined to the purely domestic sphere. She can enrich the lives of others and inspire young women to attain a modest professional standing.

I shall retire soon from the excise service. I have already contributed articles to the Scottish and Irish press, especially on the land issue and I am keen to establish a newspaper here in Inverness which would provide a voice for Gaels. I shall become a full-time newspaper man and scourge of the 'Courier'.

Your faithful servant

John Murdoch.

CHAPTER 18

Glasgow, 1872

Flora hauled the sack of potatoes up the worn tenement stairs and through her own door. Panting, she left her burden sagging in the corner of the room. Effie was inside, scouring tears away with the back of her hand while bangs and crashes could be heard coming from the tiny scullery beyond. Flora slumped down on a chair and squeezed her younger sister's hand, 'What's wrong, *isean*?'

'Mamma's cross again,' she sobbed.

'What's it about this time?' asked Flora with a sigh.

'Oh, the usual … the *Sasannachs* and their horrible language.'

The scullery door trembled on its hinges as Màiri flung it open, 'You should only speak Gaelic at home. I can't be doing with that wretched English. It's a slovenly language that limps along shuffling its feet.' Màiri swung her head like an angry bull, 'There's no music to it. And it's devouring Gaelic speakers, even my own flesh and blood.' She jabbed an accusing finger at Effie.

The girl looked at her sister for support, 'All I said to Mamma was that we need to speak English outside so that people can understand us.'

'So that's what going to school does for you. It turns you into a traitor to your tongue and your people.'

Flora's voice was calm, 'But Mamma, none of us can stop the tide from coming in. We live in a city, we're not in a wee village on Skye. We have to talk to all sorts of people. If you try to speak Gaelic to them they look down on you and call you "daft Irish".'

'What are we coming to? Even the Gaelic chapels hold English services for those who think themselves too high and mighty to speak to God in the language they learnt at their mothers' knee. Those *Sasannachs* don't just take away our land and drive us from our homes. They are taking away our history, our stories and now plucking our very thoughts from their nests too.'

'We're not turning our backs on Gaelic, just saying that it's different for us. We don't know Skye, except through your stories. Effie and I have only ever lived in towns. We've been to school and if you remember Pappa was very keen that we should learn. We speak Gaelic at home but we learnt to read and write in English. That's the way of the world here.'

'Well the world's wrong then,' shouted Màiri, thumping the table.

Flora stood up, straightening her back and looking up at her much taller mother. She spoke slowly and carefully.

'Mamma, I know that it's been hard for you leaving Inverness and coming to Glasgow, especially when you have to sleep at the hospital so often but Effie too has had a hard time. She's lost her Pappa and her home.'

Both Màiri and Effie sat open mouthed at hearing the normally placid Flora speak so vehemently. The air bristled with tension. Màiri blew her nose thunderously, 'You sounded so like your dear father then,' she snuffled. The storm passed over. Her craggy features crumbled and melted into tears, 'I'm just a useless *cailleach*,' she sobbed.

'Come and sit down, Mamma and tell me what's really upsetting you.' Flora's voice was gentle again.

'I'll never get my nursing papers. I'll look such a fool and I'll be letting down Mr Murdoch and Mr Fraser MacKintosh after all their help.'

'Why shouldn't you get your papers? Your English is good now, even though you hate the language and you were an excellent nurse to start with.'

'I know I'm a good nurse. I can clean the ward from top to bottom and make beds shipshape. I lift patients, feed them, bring them bedpans. I sit with the dying and lay them out when they have breathed their last. I can dress stinking wounds without flinching.'

Both her daughters nodded and smiled. Màiri sat down with a groan.

'Do you know we had a dresser yesterday, a young student, delicate as a lassie. He was so overcome at seeing a big abscess being lanced under a patient's arm that he had to rush out to spew up his lunch. When he returned, pale as a corpse he straightaway swooned and fell in a dead faint.' Màiri gave a harsh laugh.

'So what's the matter? I've never seen you so overcome before,' Flora asked.

'It's the writing,' said Màiri flatly, 'You have to write notes about each patient. If I can take my time I can manage.'

'So?'

'Well, today when I was writing up my notes one of the stuck-up First Class nurses was watching me. The first I knew of it was when I heard a snigger. She was looking over my shoulder and nudging her friend so that she could come and laugh at the silly old woman who writes like a child. "Try not to hold the pen as if it's a weapon," she laughs and her friend giggles, "and do put your tongue back in. You're enough to scare the horses." Why should I have to endure their rudeness? I'm old enough to be their mother, or grandmother even. It took me back to when I was in that courtroom.'

'They should know better,' replied Flora, stroking her mother's arm,

'But surely you won't allow cheeky slips of lassies stop you from being a nurse? There must be other older nurses like yourself?'

Màiri sniffed, 'I suppose so but they're all rough Glasgow keelies or wild Irishwomen not long off the boat. There aren't any proper Gaels.'

'Does it matter where they're from?' Flora raised her hand to halt her mother's glowering protest, 'It's different in Glasgow. We have to mix with all sorts of folk.'

Màiri curled her lip in contempt while Flora rubbed her aching back. 'Well, I need to boil up some of these for our tea,' she said, dragging the sack of potatoes behind her, 'If it's all too much, why don't you leave the Royal and go back to doing private nursing?'

'What? And let yon snooty women get the better of me? Have you no faith in your mother?' Màiri shouted indignantly to Flora's retreating back. As she closed the scullery door behind her, Flora turned to wink at Effie and put her finger to her lips.

Later that evening Flora lay in bed, watching the shadows reach out across the ceiling and sighed softly.

'What is it? whispered Effie, curled up beside her.

'It's all such a struggle. No, not you, you're not any trouble but …'

'It's Mamma isn't it? She always seems to stir up a storm when she comes here.'

'I know she's had hard things to bear but when she's miserable she spreads her unhappiness around, like a disease she's brought back from the Royal.'

'I thought that nurses were meant to make people better, not worse,' Effie giggled.

Flora smiled, 'She always seems so big and sure of herself that no-one thinks she can be hurt, but her pride is wounded when people mock her. Joseph says that she's too much of a thin skinned Highlander, taking offence and pulling out her dirk when she thinks she's been slighted.'

'Pappa used to keep her calm. I know he can't come back but I wish the old Mamma would return. She used to be fun, singing while she cooked our meals and telling stories when we sat around the fire at night. Now she snarls like a cross old dog,' Effie stifled a sob.

Flora squeezed her sister's hand, 'I know, but things will get better, you'll see. When Iain comes through from Inverness next week why don't we all go to the shinty match? Joe can come too.'

'Aye, it will be something to look forward to. Maybe you and Joe will be able to sneak away for a wee cuddle.'

'You cheeky rascal! I'll tickle your feet and make you squeal like a piglet,' laughed Flora, grabbing her wriggling sister.

CHAPTER 19

Glasgow, 1873

'Probationers Buchanan, MacKay, Ross and yes, you too MacPherson, report to male surgical where you're to learn about the application of carbolic acid dressings,' Sister MacLean's voice was like a gale hurtling down a close. 'Come on now, I mean at once,' she scolded, 'Make sure your caps are straight.'

The four women hurried out of the ward. Buchanan and McKay moved with the supple grace of youth while the older two waddled along behind them. When Màiri had first arrived at the hospital she had kept craning her neck in wonder at the domed and pillared entrance, but now she scarcely noticed it and grumbled about the climb up the grand staircase.

Sister MacLean was a staunch member of the Free Church, a stickler for high standards, both moral and professional. Màiri had worked diligently and so avoided being scorched by her tongue. She was apprehensive at leaving the familiar surroundings of the chronic ward but at least Catriona Ross was coming too. She was a fellow Highlander, middle-aged and widowed like herself. Catriona's parents had been evicted from Islay. Her Gaelic sounded quaint and ill-favoured to a Skye ear but she was a quietly resolute woman who had lived in Glasgow for many years and was well informed about the ways of the Royal.

'Come on now, we'll have to put on a good show,' she told Màiri as they hurried on their way, 'It's a different set up from Sister MacKay's incurables. The surgeons have their dressers to treat their patients and they don't like nurses interfering.'

'We'll have to set them straight then,' muttered Màiri, folding her blacksmith's arms across the upholstered slab of her bosom.

'Well, let's look at the lie of the land first. This part of the hospital was very famous when Mr Lister was here. Have you heard about him? He saved a lot of lives. Well, I suppose you wouldn't as you were living in the backwater of Inverness,' she grinned. 'No? He's regarded as a saint by the folk of this city and not just by the Papists either, even though we Protestants aren't supposed to believe in saints.'

'So what did he do?'

'He saved the lives – and the limbs – of badly injured patients who in the past would have had to endure amputations and probably died from sepsis. I heard about his first case from a nurse who was there.' She paused.

'Go on, then.'

'A wee lad was brought in. Jamie Greenlees he was called. He had been run over by a cart and his leg was badly broken with a compound fracture. Other surgeons would have cut his leg off at once but Mr Lister didn't. He reset the bone. Then he used carbolic acid to wash out the wound and soaked the dressing with it. After that his leg was bandaged, splinted and left. All the doctors kept hovering around the child, sniffing the dressings when they passed his bed. When he started to cry, complaining that his leg hurt, they all shook their heads, "I said all along it wouldn't work." But there was no fever and no stink. After four days Mr Lister came to cut the dressing open himself. Everyone was holding his breath. One of the dressers knelt down beside Jamie to remove the splint and unwind the bandages. Mr Lister removed the tin foil holding everything in place and prised off the dressing. He raised it slowly to his nose before passing it around to the other doctors. It was like a miracle. There was no inflammation or suppuration, only some redness on the edge of the wound and a healthy bloody crust forming.'

'That was amazing indeed. So was it the carbolic that made his leg sore?'

Catriona nodded. She finished her story as they were arriving at Men's Surgical, 'The wee boy piped up, "So tell me, Mister will yae, if it's so much better why is mae leg so sore?" Everyone laughed and Mr Lister smiled and patted the lad's head. Then he cleaned and dressed the wound and this time left it for another five days. Wee Jamie still had no fever and he began to eat as much as the horse that ran him down. After six weeks he walked out of the hospital, fit and strong on two legs as good as they were before. And that was only the first one. Mr Lister did the same for many more poor folk.'

During the following weeks Màiri watched with interest to see how Mr Lister's new methods were used on patients who needed operations for accidents, tumours and tubercular infections of the bones. At the same time she was frustrated by how little the nurses were allowed to do. As Catriona had warned, the dressers ferociously guarded their role in tending wounds and nurses were excluded from ward rounds. Màiri observed as much as she could. She was horrified and surprised to see that some of the doctors scarcely washed their hands between patients. It seemed so different from the care that was taken over keeping wounds clean. She scowled, her lips clamped tight with the effort of not protesting. She was tormented by memories of the midwife with the black rinds of dirt under her nails, who had attended her at Màiri's birth.

For a time she reluctantly heeded Catriona's warnings about keeping quiet but one day she passed Miss Tait, the Matron, in a corridor. Bobbing in a half curtsey she spoke, keeping her voice low and calm, 'Matron, may I ask you a question?' She rushed on without waiting for a reply, 'I'm working on Men's Surgical and I cannot understand why some of the doctors don't wash their hands between patients. We nurses are very particular about cleanliness and I understand that Mr Lister …'

'Enough, Probationer MacPherson,' the Matron sucked in her withered cheeks and glared at Màiri through gimlet eyes, 'It's not for you to ask questions. We work under the direction of the medical staff.'

'But surely …'

'Don't contradict me,' she retorted, her bony wrist protruding from her dark sleeve as she waggled her index finger, 'If you continue to be insubordinate I will make sure that you do not complete your training in this hospital. You are here to watch, learn and obey instructions.'

Màiri was silenced but not cowed by this encounter. She looked out for the fair, angular young man who had fainted in the chronic ward. She saw him one day with the other dressers on male surgical and waited for a chance to speak to him.

'I see that you've changed wards too,' she observed. He flushed when he recognised her, grinned awkwardly and smoothed down his sandy hair. He looked so young that he reminded her of her son. 'I've got a stronger stomach now. The only problem here is the carbolic. I end up reeking like a chemical laboratory. And just look at my hands,' he complained, showing her fingers as grey-white and puckered as those of a drowned sailor.

'Can I ask you a question? I don't understand why it is that so much care is taken with dressing the wounds but some of the doctors don't bother to wash their hands. I've heard about how Mr Lister insisted on cleanliness in everything.'

The young man nodded, 'He was very particular in everything he did – and devoted to the care of his patients. He came in every day to check on his patients' progress, even on Sundays.'

'So why did he leave the Royal?'

He dropped his voice. 'The Hospital Board said that he cost too much money because he kept his patients in for too long. He kept them until they were completely healed, even if it took months. Then he wrote a report about how unhealthy the surgical wards were when he arrived in Glasgow. There were bodies from the cholera outbreak in '49 buried in quicklime in the foundations. The Royal never forgave him for writing that.'

'So he sticks by his beliefs.'

'Aye, he didn't try to court popularity. Mind you, all famous doctors will fight to the death over their pet theories, rather like your Highland clans.'

They were both laughing when the young man saw a doctor approaching, with a disapproving expression on his face. He suddenly remembered that he was one of the chosen medical race while this ageing woman with her roughened hands was from the servant classes. The narrow causeway that had appeared between them was abruptly swept away. He raised his voice, 'Well, Nurse, that's all I can say.' As he turned away he muttered, 'If you need to know any more you'll have to go and ask the great man himself.'

Màiri tried to silence her questions after that but they wouldn't be gagged. As a child she had been taught to respect men in authority. The Minister was a Man of God with book learning far beyond her own understanding. Then over the years she had struggled with her disillusionment as the Church preached meek submission to parishioners who were being driven from their land. Now as a nurse she was expected to venerate doctors but so many of them seemed to ignore good sense when it came to cleanliness.

The only answer was to stop brooding and take action, like that time long ago when the crowd in Inverness had tipped the potatoes into the harbour. How exciting that had been, scaring the folk in charge who were always telling the likes of her how they should conduct themselves.

CHAPTER 20

Edinburgh, 1873

A week later Màiri boarded the train to Edinburgh. She had told
no-one of her plan; not her friend Catriona who would raise
her eyes to Heaven and call her a fool, nor her sensible daughter
Flora who would try to soothe her as if she were a fractious child.

She boarded the train buoyed up with her daring, but when
she reached Edinburgh she felt weighed down by the stern, grey
city. The castle, looming over the city from its high vantage place
made her shiver. It reminded her of the last time she had seen
the castle in Inverness at the time of her trial. Did this castle also
contain a court and might she be arrested for making a nuisance
of herself? She let out a bitter laugh then looked around in
apprehension in case people in Princes Street turned to stare at her,
wondering if she had escaped from an asylum. But no-one paid
her any attention. As an older woman, dressed in her worn plaid
cloak she was anonymous, even invisible. She asked a labourer for
directions to the hospital. He was intent on his own journey and
told her, barely glancing up. Once there, she looked around until
she found a notice announcing Mr Lister's twice weekly lectures.
At that moment she blessed Flora's insistence that she persist with
learning to read and write English. Even better – what luck –
there was a lecture due to begin in an hour. She stayed on the
fringes of the crowd which milled in the dark corridor leading
to the theatre. It was mainly young boisterous men, who ignored
her. When the door was opened they spilled through.

'Come on lads,' a voice shouted out, 'Shut the door quickly
before any of Mr Lister's microbes get in.'

She slipped in under cover of the laughter and edged into a space near the back of the tiered rows. There must have been nearly two hundred people there and the air thrummed with anticipation. One group started singing,

> O there's nae germs aboot the Hoose,
> Germs, busy germs

to the tune of the Burns song, 'A man's a man for a' that.'

Màiri smiled to herself. The high spirits reminded her of Murdo and the other young men who had been racing the horses while the service was going on at the Fairy Bridge, and young Anndra of course, brave and beautiful as Finn McCoul himself. But that was so long ago.

She looked down the steep drop to the stage where there was a narrow wooden table surrounded by sawdust-filled trays to catch the spilled blood. A few upright chairs were arranged against the partition in front of the first row of seats. The scuffling feet and murmured conversations stopped as a small, solemn procession entered. It was led by a man holding aloft a covered tray of instruments. A dresser followed, carrying a bottle of chloroform and a mask to anaesthetise the patient. The third figure brought in a piece of apparatus on a tripod. Màiri could make out a lever and a bottle. So she supposed that must be the carbolic spray. Two older men followed, walking stiffly and unburdened by equipment. Last to arrive was a trim, erect figure, a man not much younger than Màiri herself. His hair was thinning at the crown but growing in thick swathes at the sides of his face where it merged with the tufts of greying side whiskers. That must be Mr Lister. More dressers followed, wearing blue overalls and bringing the patient, lying down on a trolley. Lister bent down to speak to the figure, murmuring gently. While an assistant administered the chloroform the surgeon surveyed the audience with an air of calm authority. He started to speak in a clear but soft voice, with a slight hesitancy. Everyone craned forward to listen.

'This lady has a tumour which requires a mastectomy. She is in her middle years, no longer of childbearing age but responsible for the care of a young family. As a result of this operation she may at best make a complete recovery while at worst she will have gained some extra time to continue a productive life.'

He fell silent for a moment and briefly closed his eyes as if in prayer. Màiri wondered if he was thinking about his sister Isabelle. Catriona had told her how he had operated on his sister against the advice of other surgeons. 'She lived for another three years because of his courage,' Catriona had said. But what would it feel like to slice into the living flesh of someone you loved? Màiri could imagine acting as a midwife for one of her daughters but that would be different because they would be striving together, helping a new soul into the world. Still, childbirth, like surgery, was shadowed by fear.

Lister's eyes snapped open. He stood erect and alert until everyone was completely silent before starting his lecture.

'As you know gentlemen I have long been a champion of the antiseptic method of surgery, ever since I read an account of the experiments of the esteemed French chemist, Louis Pasteur. I first encountered his work when I was not a great deal older than some of you. Often in promoting the efficacy of the antiseptic approach I have felt like poor Sisyphus condemned forever to push a heavy boulder up a steep hill. I have wished that germs were as obvious as green paint so that I would be spared the endless task of trying to convert the sceptics, both inside and outside our profession.'

He paused and smiled slightly. One of the dressers began cranking up the lever of the spray apparatus. There was a gentle hiss and a faint chemical smell began to seep through the theatre. Suddenly a clear, loud voice slashed into the Sunday service hush, 'Let us s-pray'.

A collective gasp shuddered around the building, horrified at the sacrilege. Lister gravely lifted his head to gaze in the direction of the voice and raised an eyebrow. Then he stepped forward, holding his arms out behind him. One of his assistants respectfully helped him out of his black frock coat. While Lister carefully folded back his shirt cuffs the young man held out his operating coat for him to put on. Màiri gasped. Even from her position near the back she could see that the garment was old and stiff with a rusty plumage of dried blood. She bowed her head quickly, fearing that she had drawn unwanted attention to herself.

As Lister operated he continued his lecture, his voice confident and fluent.

'Gentlemen, as surgeons you must never let theories stand in the way of your observations. There are of course different theories as to whether the removal of the lymph glands is appropriate during a mastectomy.' He inclined his head towards a young man near the front who had raised his arm. 'Yes, what is your view on the subject?' he asked, smiling gravely.

'Surely it is best to remove the glands, thus ensuring that all malignancy is destroyed.'

'That is indeed a valid argument but how does the surgeon know whether the tumour is malignant or not?'

'I don't know, Sir.'

'An honest answer. Always remember that we know so little. I don't know the answer either. Observation is not enough to make a reliable diagnosis. The surgeon should never cut more than the necessary minimum. So how shall I decide? What do I know about this patient? She's a woman who has had a hard life and is not well nourished. That would suggest that the minimum of surgery would be advised. However the tumour is extensive and has been growing for some time. I suspect that it is probably malignant. So I shall remove the glands to give her the best chance of survival.'

Màiri had been so absorbed in the drama of the operation that she had almost forgotten her reason for attending. It was only as Lister removed his gory operation coat and the audience began to shuffle to their feet that she remembered with a jolt that she would have to approach him. Most of the students scuttled out quickly like children released from school but a few people were walking down the steep central steps to approach the eminent surgeon. She hovered behind them, noticing his prominent nose below the broad furrowed forehead and the deep clefts slicing down from the corners of his mouth. When it was her turn to speak she looked directly into the deep set eyes, level with her own. His lips set into a thin, dour line and she hurried to speak before her courage shrank too much.

'Sir, I feel honoured to have watched you at work. I have come to put a question to you. I understand the importance of using carbolic in the dressings and spray. Could you tell me please why there is less attention paid to keeping everything else as clean? I have noticed at the Royal where I work that doctors are not always careful about washing their hands and,' she gulped, 'excuse me for saying this but I noticed that you wore a dirty old operation coat yourself.'

Màiri felt her cheeks ripen to a red embarrassment in the stunned silence.

'Are you a doctor, Madam?' His tone was distant.

She took a deep breath and rallied, 'No indeed, Sir. I am a nurse and a good one, as you are a good doctor. And I am a Skye woman who is not afraid to ask an important question.'

'So I see. I have visited your majestic island,' he replied with a faint smile. 'And now you must excuse me Madam.'

'We must each of us follow our own way,' she said quietly as he swept away.

Lister turned to his companions, 'How was such a person able to gain admittance? You know that I disapprove of the fairer sex attending medical lectures and she was not even a lady.'

'Shall I go and apprehend her, Sir?' enquired one of the dressers.

'No, that won't be necessary. What an extraordinary woman.'

CHAPTER 21

Glasgow, 1874

It was Sunday morning and Màiri was sitting on a hard bench with Effie, now sixteen years old, in the Gaelic chapel. She was glad of the hardness that numbed even her well-upholstered bottom. It meant that she was too uncomfortable to fall asleep, or even worse, start snoring, during the minister's lengthy sermon. It was a relief to be sitting still, whatever the discomfort. She was finding midwifery draining, much harder than the ordinary nursing had ever been. The worst part of the nursing had been the feeling that she was sinking in a sea of English, its brackish taste swilling in her mouth and making her thirst for a chill, clean stream of Gaelic. Still, by degrees it had become easier, like the light nibbling away at the edges of January darkness. She had looked forward to the midwifery training for it meant that she could work outside the hospital with its stiff rules and insist on her own standards of cleanliness. However, she had not realised what a toll it would take on her ageing body. A midwife was rightly called a '*bean-ghlùine*' for she spent so much of her time cramped on her knees, watching and waiting on the labouring woman. Màiri would either be crouching low down or more often having to clamber up to balance on the edge of a box bed set into the wall of a tenement. If all went well there was joy in welcoming a new life into the room but during the waiting period there were the louring fears, knowing how things could so suddenly go dangerously wrong. Would both souls survive the ordeal? She remembered how she had first learnt of the risks of childbirth.

She was a young girl when she had come skipping inside to find Mamma and Seonag poring over the contents of her sister's wedding chest. Curious and attracted by the smell of the dried heather and herbs nestled among the cloth she had edged her way in between the two women and reached in to finger the garments. The shifts, sheets and shawls had rustled like petals in her fingers. Then at the bottom her hand bumped against some heavier fabric. She asked what it was and saw the hesitation in Mamma's eyes while she considered her words, 'It's a shroud,' she had whispered.

'But that's for a dead person. Seonag's's much too young to die. Why would she need it?

'Well, we have to be prepared because sometimes a mother dies when she gives birth.'

Màiri snatched back her hand. Mamma reached out to her but she tore out of the house and ran without stopping until her lungs were searing. She'd flung herself down among the startled cattle, kicking and punching the ground as if it were to blame for burdening her with this terrible, unbidden knowledge.

'We are sinners from when we are inside our mothers' wombs,' the minister intoned, jolting her back to the present. Màiri couldn't believe that. How could a new baby be sinful, any more than a newborn calf or lamb?

'Then Satan collects from our childhoods a further productive crop of sins: insolence, covetousness, malice and self-conceit.'

Rather than feeling at odds with the minister she let her thoughts drift away. She imagined herself to be a selkie, one of the seal people who could pass as a human being. She would hide her seal skin so that she could return to the sea at times like this. She would lift her supple coat from its lair, smooth it over her back and glide under the water where no voices could reach her. Today though, although she could drown out the minister's voice, she couldn't rid herself of the memories of the last birth she had attended.

There was no joy to be found in that grim room. The woman was expecting her ninth child. When Màiri arrived the two youngest children, wan faced and bent-legged, were peeping around the door. She led them to a neighbour. The *cailleach* took them in with a lot of tutting. If only those children lived in the Highlands, Màiri thought, they would still be barefooted but their legs would be straight and they would have some colour in their cheeks. She greeted the groaning mother and set about her first task, evicting the husband who was lying sprawled and snoring across the box bed, next to his suffering wife.

'Go away you interfering old witch. I need my sleep,' he shouted when she shook him.

'Are you going to get out of there or do I have to haul you out myself?'

He muttered and swore but she stood her ground until he got up and stamped out. His wife managed a grin between contractions.

'You're the first midwife to get the better of him. When he sees the cape and apron he thinks it's a do-gooding lady he can frighten out of her wits.'

Again the minister's voice broke through, '"And if your right hand offend thee, cut it off and cast it from thee; for it is profitable to thee that one of thy members should perish, and not that thy whole body should be cast into Hell". What this text means is that it's not enough to say, "I did not commit murder," if you have committed murder in your thoughts or if you have wished another soul to die. Those thoughts make you a murderer because you have committed a terrible sin in your heart. Even if you only commit murder in your heart it's as if you had done the deed itself.'

His voice was becoming more insistent and beads of cold sweat were gathering on her brow. She couldn't ignore him any longer. She was swept back onto dry land and forced to take off the sealskin. She knew that she had not committed murder. She hadn't put a smothering hand over the baby's face.

She had knelt there, on that stinking bed, urging the exhausted mother to bear down, cradling the baby's head as he emerged. Then the horror of seeing the cord squeezing his neck. As she started to gently uncoil it the rest of the child emerged and she saw that poor crippled foot bent inwards. She had paused to wonder what sort of life he would have – lame, with a worn out mother and a brutal father. She stayed frozen for what seemed a lifetime before her numb hands fumbled to release the cord from the limp little body. He made no sound and she tried to rouse him, rubbing his back and then slapping it. Eventually she stopped and wrapped the tiny body gently in her apron for there was nothing else. She handed him silently to his mother who opened the covering to look at her child. Her face was tossed flotsam, thrown from grief to numbness and back again.

At last his mother spoke, in her native Gaelic, 'Maybe it's a blessing he didn't survive. What sort of life would the wee mite have?' Màiri encircled them both in her arms and the two women wept silently together.

Now she was here drenched in a guilt that she couldn't speak about. Had she hesitated in unwrapping the cord because she had wanted the baby to die? Had she murdered him by neglect?

The sermon had finally ended. Sunlight spilt through the windows. She closed her eyes but the outline of the windows was still branded on them. I shall have to throw myself on God's mercy when the Day of Judgement dawns, she thought. She was roused by Effie's small warm fingers nuzzling into her palm.

'Don't worry. I'm still here. I was only thinking about God's forgiveness and mercy.'

The girl frowned. 'But that wasn't what the minister was talking about. He was saying how terrible God's wrath is towards sinners.'

'But I know He is a forgiving Father to those who truly repent. You remember how kind your own Pappa was?'

'I still miss him every day. Every night I take out the last pair of boots he made for me.'

'I remember how I had to make you stop wearing them. You were hobbling because they became too small.'

'I didn't want to take them off, though.'

'God's mercy and love is as wide as the ocean, as strong as the wind and as high as the Cuillin, don't ever forget that.' Màiri squeezed her daughter's hand so tightly that Effie winced.

CHAPTER 22

Glasgow, February 1875

The three people walking up the aisle of the hall were a mismatched group. Leading them with his long stride was John Murdoch. Now in his late fifties, his tall broad-shouldered figure and vigorous white beard suited Highland dress. The sprouting thickets of badger hair on his sporran swung against his heavy kilt as he walked. Above it he wore an elaborate, silver buttoned jacket with a wide plaid pinned across his chest.

Close behind him was Màiri, also tall and upright, her solid trunk jutting forwards like a ship's figurehead. She looked queenly in a dignified gown which rippled in dark folds to the floor. Her round face was stern and her hair was scraped back under a tightly fitting turban topped with feathers that jiggled like a cockscomb. Her small, brightly defiant eyes warned that she had a sharp beak and claws.

Trotting along after them on his short legs was Professor John Stuart Blackie. Older than his companions, he was clean shaven with a filmy waterfall of snowy hair pouring over his shoulders. He wore a hairy shepherd's plaid and narrow tartan breeks that drew attention to his spindly shanks.

Màiri shuddered, thinking how the professor's long nose and free flowing mane made him look like a water horse caught in the act of transforming himself from human to beast. The water horse was a fearsome creature which would lure an unsuspecting person to mount it. Then it would plunge into deep water and drown its rider. John, thinking that she was nervous about the meeting, sought to reassure her, 'Don't fret. This Highland

Society is full of friends. I've said that no word of English is to be heard on stage tonight,' he whispered, his eyes gleaming.

After ushering his guests to their seats he stood up to speak. Màiri was enthralled. The only public speeches she had heard before were sermons, apart from Mr Lister's lecture. But that was like a sort of medical sermon. John's speech was a call to arms. He demanded that the landlords change their evil ways. It made an entertaining change from listening to the minister urging the congregation to repent of their sins. He spoke with conviction, ending with a demand for action:

'Where once the Highlanders of old put their shoulders together we must put our heads together. Here is work for our Highland Associations to do wholesale good by raising their voices. The voice of the country must be raised in protest, especially the voice of our Highlanders driven to the big cities. They must give forth a sound which can neither be mistaken nor resisted, demanding that our Parliament consider the state and condition of our rural population.'

In the interval afterwards she was delighted to find herself surrounded by members of the audience, talking eagerly about her Bernera poem published in the 'Highlander' and asking her what other songs she would give them that evening.

'Would you mind singing next, before the Professor speaks? It looks as if everyone is keen to hear you,' John asked.

So she stood on stage, gazing at the audience and trembling, like a dog desperate to be released to run out on the moor. So many people! Most of them strangers too and gentlefolk among them. She breathed deeply and closed her eyes, waiting for her starting note to ring out its clapper inside her skull. Then she unfurled her voice as she told the story about the men from the small island of Bernera, off the west coast of Lewis. They had been goaded beyond endurance by Sir James Matheson's factor telling them that for the second time their grazing land was to be taken from them and replaced by a barren plot. They refused to comply and so fifty eight eviction orders were sent out, one for each family. Her voice was firm and resonant as she described how they marched to speak to their landlord:

> When you went into line
> With your sticks and your coats
> Going up to the town of Stornoway
> I thought the troop was splendid;
>
> When you reached the mansion
> James Matheson asked,
> "What now has happened
> When the plunderers are after us?"
>
> One of you stood out in the camp
> With his blue bonnet in his hand
> And in hard, flawless English
> He spoke to him as he ought:
>
> "Since we and our ancestors
> Have lived in this place without debt or tribute
> And your wicked factor with his devices
> Is sending us from our homeland
>
> If you will tell us in an orderly way
> If you yourself instructed him
> We will do as you desire
> If you are a man worth your coat"

She paused before singing the next verse in a peevish tone, keeping her voice quiet so that they had to strain to hear,

> "It does not suit me to tell you today;
> I am a little frightened

Since you resemble the Fian
Who will not yield until they pursue the enemy."

She unleashed her war cry,

You people who proved your rights
My blessing be with you
For having protected the poor Gaels
From every oppression and anguish.

As she held onto the last note she stood motionless, her feet braced against the swelling tide of excitement in the hall. As the note faded the waves of applause surged around her. Now she could understand why ministers preached such long sermons. They wanted to gulp down the attention until it was sucked dry, but singing was better than sermonising. She had the joy of the applause, spilling and streaming towards the stage. Each time it ebbed a little she would move to leave the stage but then it would swoop and roar once again. She scanned the rows from front to back and from side to side; the flushed faces, the glistening eyes and the open mouths hungry for her words. So many of them – Gaels and the children of Gaels, all exiled to the clatter and grime of this big city. Shoulder to shoulder they stood, braced together like the skiltrons of spearmen waiting for the fearful English at Bannockburn.

Still they kept calling, clamouring for more songs.

'I'll sing you my new one, the one I'm still working on.' Well, why not? Hadn't she often as a child drunk milk still blood hot and bubbling rather than waiting for it to cool and settle? She felt a little shy for this new song expressed so many of her own feelings that she feared breaking down. She imagined Pappa whispering in her ear, 'Go on lass, they're eating out of your hands.'

So she sang again, her voice at first struggling to rise, like a swan's frantic flapping to get airborne:

> Though my hair has greyed with
> forgetfulness and sadness
> And the sun of my fifty years has
> Darkened under the clouds
> My thoughts are filled with a great desire
> To see the Isle of Skye, the elements
> And the mist.
>
> But who has ears and a heart which beats
> With life
> Who would not sing the song with me
> About the hardships which have befallen us?
> The thousands who were cleared
> Robbed of their belongings and their rights,
> The desires of their hearts and their thoughts
> Are on the Green Isle of the Mists.

A soughing wind rippled through the audience. She paused and allowed the currents to hold her floating in the air, wings outstretched. Then slowly beating them again she continued,

> I'll dry my cheeks, hold back my tears,
> A new springtime is with us
> Many have come through the winter
> All around new grass is sprouting
> Branches are coming back to life
> On the Green Isle of the Mists.

Her voice hung in the air until it was lifted up by gusts of applause. As they died back she landed softly again on the water, folding back her wings and dipping her head. Again the audience stamped and cheered only letting her return to her seat after she promised that she would lead them in the communal singing at the end.

John rose to introduce Stuart Blackie and the audience slumped into silence. The professor smiled, undaunted, 'I can't pretend to emulate Mrs MacPherson's display of emotion,' he began, smoothing down his straggling locks, 'To start with I don't belong to the fairer sex and ...'

'So why do you wear your hair long?' a voice called out from the back of the hall.

His eyes bulged but he swept on, 'Neither can I claim to be a Highlander by birth. I'm a proud Aberdonian. However, I can lay claim to a number of compositions, penned in English, about the beauty of the landscape.'

He paused, beaming at the audience. The same voice shot out again, 'Is that Greek he's speaking? Didn't John Murdoch say that he's a professor of Greek?'

'Shh. It's him trying to speak Gaelic but his accent's terrible, poor soul,' his companion replied in a stage whisper.

Folk began to snigger and Màiri could feel the back of her neck tingle. She knew too well the sting of mockery but at the same time she could feel bubbles of laughter in her throat. So she bent her head down to smooth the folds of her gown. The professor seemed to droop for an instant but then he bowed and spread his hands wide.

'I'm relieved Sir that you recognise my attempts at your venerable language. I fell in love with it many years ago when I first heard it spoken at Kinlochewe. I decided then that it was a worthy cause to champion. As you may know I'm raising funds to establish a new Gaelic Chair at Edinburgh University. Indeed, I travelled to Balmoral to ask the Queen herself if she would contribute,' he simpered.

'Well, I don't know why you needed a special seat but did she give you anything?' It was the first speaker again.

The small professor puffed up his feathers. 'Indeed she did. She kindly promised me £200 despite my execrable Gaelic, although the Prince of Wales found himself unable to oblige.'

There was more laughter but it sounded kinder now.

'Ladies and gentlemen, may I give you my rendition of, "The song of the Highland river?"'

He read in a high, wispy voice. To Màiri and many others in the audience it seemed strange to hear verses floating rudderless with no tune to steer them:

> Dew-fed am I
> With drops from the sky,
> Where the white cloud rests on the old grey hill;
> All green and grey,
> To the wooded ravine I wind my way,
> Dashing and foaming, and leaping with glee,
> The child of the mountain wild and free
> Under the crag where the stone crop grows
> Fringing with gold my shelvy bed,
> Where over my head,
> In fruitage of red,
> The rock-rooted rowan blushfully shows.

He stopped for effect. Not being familiar with English poetry Màiri was puzzling in her mind about the quality of the verse when John Murdoch jumped to his feet. 'Thank you indeed, Professor Blackie for speaking so warmly of the beauty of the Highlands. However, I fear we shall have to savour the rest of your poetry on another occasion. If you remember I said at the outset that tonight the Gaelic language that you champion so strongly was to be the only star in the firmament. All our proceedings must be in our native tongue and not eclipsed by English. We shall show that we have no need to stand on English stilts to express our thoughts. I shall report tonight's events in *The Highlander,* and those who cannot understand them must submit to have the account interpreted for them. Then they shall have a small taste of the inconvenience and loss to which some of our people have been subjected because they don't understand English.'

His words brought tears to Màiri's eyes. She felt they had been spoken especially for her and to her. After they had all sung some of the old songs together and the audience was spilling out into the night, John turned to her and smiled, 'They took you to their hearts tonight. I hope this is only the first of many such meetings.'

'Well, we are a race who love music. I must say that I admired the Professor's spirit even though he did look a fright with his witch's hair.'

'His wife would agree with you. One time when she could endure it no longer she took scissors to his locks while he was asleep.' He threw his head back and laughed.

'Like Delilah did to Samson. But the professor's hair grew back.'

'Aye and John didn't lose his strength either. He's an eccentric but people like to hear eccentric characters and he's a good ally in our cause. I must say how much I enjoyed your *'Eilean a cheò'*. I'll be delighted to print it. I thought it was magnificent, except for one detail.'

Her eyes glinted but she waited for him to continue.

'It's the part where you praise Lord MacDonald's new bride and ask him to incline his ear to the needs of his people.'

She gulped. 'And why would I not do that? His family have been chiefs on Skye since the beginning of time. He understands and defends us.'

'How can you say that? He's run up huge debts by living like an English lord on the backs of poor Highlanders. He clears whole villages of their people so that he can sell the land to sheep farmers.'

'No, it's the Lowlanders and the *Sasannachs* who take our land from us. He's the laird who cares for his folk,' she protested.

'I only wish that was true, my friend,' he said softly, patting her arm.

She pulled her shawl tightly over her shoulders at the sudden chill of the dank night air.

CHAPTER 23

Os, Isle of Skye, March 1875

Màiri enjoyed replaying the meeting in her mind but there were a few jarring notes that made her flinch. The first discord had sounded when she returned to her seat and a voice from behind her said, 'Was that the best John Murdoch could find? An old, illiterate woman from Skye?' Illigitterate indeed! How dare that snooty English speaker insult her family by suggesting her parents had behaved shamelessly. Her ears straining, she sat taut with the effort of not turning round.

'Well, Robbie Burns himself was only a ploughman when he was taken up by Edinburgh society.'

This time it was a cultured male voice, tinged with amusement.

'It's not the same thing at all. He might have been poor but his father had him tutored at home. Anyway you wouldn't find a proper lady disporting herself like that on stage,' the woman sniffed in disdain.

What force of will it had cost Màiri to stay still, back rigid and head proud. And what about Professor Blackie? She had been overwhelmed to learn that she would be appearing on the same stage as such a distinguished scholar. Yet, hadn't he made rather a fool of himself?

But it was John who had most perturbed her. She would always be grateful to him because he had rescued her from despair and given her a new life. She had thought they were of one mind about the sufferings of the Highlanders. So she had been so taken aback when he rounded on her about Lord MacDonald. She felt as if a good-natured beast that stayed quiet for milking had suddenly turned on her, kicking over the bucket and knocking her off her stool.

What I need, she decided, is a rest and change of air. Once the spring came she would go to Skye. She had heard from Mairead. After all those years in Australia she was returning home for good and she had invited Màiri to stay with her. What could be better?

*

Now here she was, her first night in her friend's house. She felt unsure after the first flurry of her arrival. They had been close as girls but that was so long ago. Now they were like dogs that had been separated as puppies. Meeting again there was the familiar smell of a litter mate but they didn't know whether to lick each other or growl a warning.

'Come on Màiri. Will you put those wretched things down. You don't have to pretend to be a wee Highland wifie.'

She dropped the carding brushes, narrowing her eyes.

'Well, I'm not used to sitting still. I didn't as a girl and then I was always making clothes for my children and even when I was nursing I …'

'But there's no need to do it now. You were fair hammering those brushes. Mind you, I can remember you spinning when you were a lassie; the wheel sped so fast that it nearly flew off,' she smiled. 'I think you can't settle after all that excitement in Glasgow.'

'I'm no slip of a lassie now,' Màiri chuckled as she surveyed her broad hips, straining against her corset. 'How did I get so stout? I was never a wispy wee thing but I was fair and bonny enough. Living in a town and bearing children is what ruined me. Each babe that popped out left more weight behind it.'

Mairead straightened her already erect back and smoothed her hands over her own slender lap. She clamped her lips at such indelicate conversation. Had Màiri been so coarse in the old days?

'It was exciting being at the meeting. Of course they needed me to draw in the Highlanders. I'm one of their own, not a lady idling in her parlour.'

'I expect a lady wouldn't stand up there with all those men,' Mairead sniffed.

An awkward silence settled. Màiri started to hum under her breath and then softly added words,

> Rising early on a May morning,
> Early light coming up over the hill
> The cattle lowing herded together
> Shafts of sun on the hillside hunting
> Night's dark colours into a corner
> The sweet lark singing high above
> Reminding me of when I was young.
>
> There I grew up without a care
> Wandered the moorland
> The heather tearing at my shift
> The row deer in her small hollow
> By the silent lochan.
> I as light-footed through the heather
> As the snipe in the marsh
> Hillocks, peat banks, hollows call back
> Reminding me of when I was young.
>
> My memory teams with all we did
> I can't contain it all
> Wintertime weddings, gatherings
> No lantern but a burning peat
> Young ones dancing, making music
> All gone, the glen is empty
> Andrew's ruin, so full of nettles
> Reminding me of when I was young.

Towards the end Mairead was humming and smiling. 'How do you keep all those words in your head and not lose them?'

'I don't know. Some of my poems are like hens that run away to lay their eggs in secret and there I am hunting everywhere for them.'

'You need to get someone to write them down. A sort of milkmaid, drawing off your words. You know how it is with a house cow, the more you milk her the more she yields.'

'So, I'm not a wee wifie but a beast needing to be milked, is that it?' Màiri roared, pretending to be outraged.

Their gusts of laughter lightened the air. 'I'll fetch some milk and make us tea'.

Màiri stayed sitting by the fire, watching the water heat up in the pot hanging over the flames. She thought about how she could usually find where her words were roosting. Maybe because she only learnt to write late in life she kept the old habit of storing everything in her memory. Pappa had told her about the people living on Saint Kilda, perched on islands on the edge of the world, pounded by winds and waves. It was hard to imagine how they could keep anything warm and dry but they had perfected a way of building small hollow cairns with turf roofs which preserved the carcasses of the seabirds they had caught. She too protected her words from the spoiling elements of time and forgetting.

Mairead returned with the milk from the cold press, 'I was remembering the gatherings we had in the old days. We had cèilidhs still in Australia but it wasn't the same without the glow of the peat fire. And what about waulking the cloth? All the women and lassies there – no man dared come for fear of being rolled up in the cloth and pounded.'

'I always thought it hard that we girls just got a sip of whisky, not a proper taste,' Màiri added, 'But what a feast afterwards! Everyone brought a contribution to the food and added their share to the bucket. You had to sing heartily to forget about the reek in your nostrils. Don't look so disapproving, Mairead. You squatted to give your portion, the same as the rest of us.'

'I prefer to remember the songs, how they got faster and faster. It's odd but I don't remember you being so much of a singer in those days.'

Màiri shrugged, 'Do you think this milk's a wee bit sour?'

CHAPTER 24

Bridge Street Station, Glasgow, 1876

Dr MacLaren was absorbed in his newspaper when the guard blew his whistle. As the train started to move he heard the carriage door flung open. From under his paper he could see a pair of heavy boots haul themselves aboard. They were black, scuffed and slack-laced as a loosened corset. Not the sort of footwear you would expect from a first class traveller. He lowered his newspaper to reveal a bulky woman wriggling and edging herself into the seat opposite. Rather like a cow backing carefully onto a tree to rub an itch, he thought.

She sighed softly, exhilarated yet tired. She had been performing at yet another cèilidh. She was brimming with new songs; they were pouring out of her. She was relishing John's praise too, 'It's so powerful when you sing about the speakers of English who mistreated you.' He had started to sing in a warm baritone,

> They gave me stone slabs
> To walk on, a board for a pillow.

'Then when you turn to the plight of our people,'

> Where the people lived
> Now sheep
> A shepherd on every hill
> And barking dogs on the moor.

'Now those are the words that rouse the spirit, much more than the poems where you praise people, even though I was flattered to be called "the hero who shifts the millstone about the necks of the stalwarts." '

He had smiled to remove the sting from his remarks. Still, Màiri frowned in vexation now, churning it over in her mind. Surely it was the bard's role to praise important people? She could only compose verses in the way she did and that was that.

Watching her covertly Dr MacLaren bit his lips to hold back a smile. He thought how this stolid woman looked for all the world like a cow in a summer pasture, tossing her head to get rid of irritating flies.

It was tiring though, rushing to catch the train home to Greenock. She had moved from Glasgow. It wasn't really suitable anymore staying with Flora now that she was married and had so little room. Effie was grown up too now and didn't need her there.

'I suppose you consider our poor wee close beneath you now you're so grand,' Flora had snapped, very unjustly Màiri thought.

Once she had qualified as a midwife she wanted the freedom to work outside the hospital and to have her own front door. It was the first time ever that she had lived on her own and she enjoyed suiting herself. It was other people who didn't like her bobbing free. They wanted to anchor her down to what they thought a widow should do. Did they imagine that she was gallivanting to cèilidhs for her own amusement? She was invited because her songs inspired people and put them at their ease after all the speechifying.

What would Isaac have made of it all? She closed her eyes, trying to summon up his face, his voice and his presence. It was difficult to gather them all together. She would remember one aspect of him but then it would shift and slide like uneven ground beneath her feet as she tried to assemble the whole man. She suspected that he would disapprove of her appearing in front of audiences. Maybe he would have changed his view of the world though, had he lived? After all, she had done so. Ten years ago she would never have imagined that she would be not only a qualified nurse with her own money but also a respected bard whom folk flocked to see. And all those important gentlemen listening to her songs and her opinions. She had done well for a simple girl from Skye. She sank back into her seat, letting her shoulders drop and looked out of the window. She wouldn't dwell on other people's disapproval.

Dr MacLaren noticed her relax. Now she's settled to chewing the cud, he thought. She turned her head and caught his eye.

'It's a hot evening to be travelling, Madam.'

Before replying she took in his tailored coat, neatly trimmed greying beard and smooth, well-tended hands. His scrutiny made her feel flustered. Then she chided herself, remembering that she was no longer a servant but a woman of substance, a lady even, who could hold her head up high.

'Indeed it is, Sir, and I was fortunate to catch the train.'

'Do I detect a Highland lilt in your voice?'

'Aye. I'm Skye born and bred. Màiri, nighean Iain Bhàin I was born, although I've passed more than half my life away from my home. I lived in Inverness for many years until my husband died.'

'May I introduce myself? I'm Dr Fergus MacLaren and originally my family hailed from Argyll. Like so many others my grandfather came to Glasgow in search of work.'

Màiri watched him intently and to his surprise he felt moved to continue.

'He was a canny man and married his employer's daughter. Thanks to his enterprise and good fortune I was able to train as a doctor.' He hesitated and then added, 'I too have lost my companion in life.'

He stared at her, his cool blue eyes scalpel sharp and she steeled herself not to look away.

'I hope that you won't consider me impolite if I ask you a question?'

Her deep set eyes were guarded but unflinching. She nodded.

'Have you ever been associated with the Royal?'

'Indeed I have. I trained there a few years ago as a nurse and midwife.'

He smiled in satisfaction, 'I thought so. You've remained famous. A colleague from the hospital told me about a nurse answering your description, a brave lady he said who had bearded the great Professor Lister in his den.'

She smiled, her treacle dark eyes gleaming.

He leaned forward, 'So you are the lady in question. Is it true that you attended one of his lectures and asked a question of the great man?'

'And why not? I've always believed that cleanliness was vital. I couldn't understand why some of the doctors wouldn't wash their hands and wore their dirty outdoor clothes when they tended patients. So I decided that I should seek his advice.'

'Did no-one warn you how much he abhors the female sex studying medicine? He won't allow lady medical students to attend his lectures, let alone ...'

'Common nurses,' she interrupted, laughing. 'I told no-one about my plan to speak to him. If I had, my resolve would have wavered. I needed to speak to him because I strive to be a good nurse.'

'Even if that means criticising doctors?'

'If needs be.'

'What did you think of the great man?'

'A very dignified gentleman who took great pains with his patient. He spoke to her gently but then after she was given chloroform he put on his operating coat.' She paused and shuddered. 'It was so stiff with dried blood and gore that he had to force his arms into the sleeves. How could he be so careful about keeping the wound clean and yet so heedless with his dress?'

He frowned, 'I think you are venturing into areas beyond a nurse's duties.' Seeing that she was about to retort he looked out of the window, 'I believe we're coming into Greenock now.'

Màiri watched him silently. Her spirits were buoyed up after her performance but there was something more stirring in her, a stronger swell making her rear and buck in the waves. The conversation with the doctor had stimulated her and she realised that she would like to know him better. After all, he was a widower and a well set up gentleman. Why shouldn't she harbour hopes for a second marriage? She was still lusty and healthy. The train was slowing down. How to find a way of prolonging their conversation? Should she speak or wait for him? How did the gentry act in this situation? She hesitated, unsure of herself.

CHAPTER 25

Greenock, 1876

'Well Madam, it's been a pleasure to speak with you. May I assist you onto the platform?'

The doctor swung the door open and stepped down, offering his arm to Màiri as she heaved herself onto the platform, still wondering how she could keep him talking. Neither of them noticed the stationmaster running up behind them, his round face crumpled into a frown and his watch chain beating against the mound of his waistcoated belly.

'Do forgive my intrusion, Sir, but another passenger has told me that you're a doctor and I'm in dire need of your services.' He edged closer and whispered, 'We have a young woman in the Ladies' waiting room. She collapsed at the station entrance. Well, she's not a lady as such but she appears to be in a delicate condition. I've closed the room to everyone else for the time being.'

The doctor looked bemused.

'An urgent, *delicate* condition, if you follow me.'

'Do say clearly what you mean, my good fellow,' Dr MacLaren snapped.

As the station master floundered Màiri stepped in, 'Do you mean that she's in labour?'

His shoulders slumped in relief as he nodded, 'Could you come and assist her, Sir?'

A shadow scudded across the doctor's face before disappearing behind his professional smile, 'Well, she is indeed fortunate. She has the skills of two people at her disposal. This lady here is a midwife, trained at the Royal. However, there is a minor difficulty. I'm returning from a social function so I don't have my medical bag with me. I shall go to collect it while the midwife examines the patient. In all likelihood she won't give birth within the next few moments.'

He strode off before the other two could reply. The stationmaster smiled and started chatting to Màiri as he showed her the way. He was relieved to be dealing with someone of his own class rather than the condescending doctor. As she puffed along beside him Màiri thought how Dr MacLaren was a typical medical man, issuing orders and leaving her to do the hard work. She would ruin her good clothes in the process, too. Then no doubt he would saunter in later to claim all the credit.

She sent the anxious stationmaster off to organise clean cloths and hot water before opening the door to the waiting room. She could hear stifled groans coming from what looked like a pile of discarded old clothes, strewn across two chairs, pushed together in a corner. As she moved closer she saw a pair of protruding feet, grubby toes clenched tightly, battered boots lying abandoned in the corner. Their laces had long gone and the escaped tongues lolled over. One sole was parted from the upper; it gaped open in a silent scream.

Màiri winced at her creaking knees as she knelt down. She reached out to ease back the matted shawl that the young woman was gnawing.

'I'm Màiri MacPherson, *isean*, a midwife. What are you called?'

The pale young woman opened greenish eyes clouded with pain. She let go of the blood flecked cloth. Her lips were bleached but her high cheekbones were flushed.

'Anna. I've had three babies already, all stillborn,' she whispered. 'This one's coming early. The pains gripped me as I walked past the station. I was going to find my man and see if he had been paid his wages. I must have passed out and someone brought me in here.'

Màiri carefully examined her patient. Her body was slight and bird-like except for the straining, distended mound of her belly. She moaned as another pain thrashed her, making her heave like a broken-backed boat trapped on rocks.

'I can't go on. I've no strength left.'

'Come on Anna – don't lose heart. It won't be long now. I can feel the baby's head.'

There was no time to wait for either Dr MacLaren or the promised clean cloths. She would just have to catch the baby in her newish, tweed cape. The tiny child flopped out, an exhausted fish spilt from a net. Màiri chaffed the limp little body to no avail.

'It's the same as the others, isn't it, born too soon?' muttered the young woman, her defeated eyes awash with unshed tears. 'Another wee lad was it, not that it matters now?'

Màiri busied herself cleaning up her patient. There was still no sign of the doctor. So she sat down in the drab waiting room, the sole witness at a silent wake while her patient sank into a sleep as heavy as a rock plummeting down a bottomless well.

Màiri could remember plunging into that sort of deathlike slumber when her own baby died and then again when Isaac breathed his last. Finally she had to haul herself back to life again to tend to the living. Women were supposed to be the weaker sex but they were the ones who had to endure. Where was this poor woman's husband? Probably drinking away his wages. Where was fine Dr MacLaren? He had likely never attended a confinement. He would, like many doctors, have considered it beneath him. But of course he would never have admitted his ignorance of childbirth. So he had slipped away, telling lies about his return. She wouldn't see him again and didn't want to, now that she had glimpsed his true colours. Màiri closed her eyes and let her head dip forward. Women, like boats, knew how to stay afloat in a storm, letting the waves drench and toss them until the winds died down. What did the men do? They pretended that they could defy the elements and steer the vessel through the gale.

'Where's my Anna?' Màiri was startled awake by a soft but insistent voice. She jolted her eyes open and hurried to the door.

'Hush, she's sleeping and she badly needs to. She's very weak, the baby came early. He was stillborn, I'm afraid. I wrapped him in my shawl.'

The father glanced briefly in the direction of the sad bundle and then turned his back abruptly, covering his face with his hands.

Màiri spoke to his narrow, bowed back, 'I'm Màiri MacPherson. The Station Master asked a doctor to come and help your wife but he disappeared. I'm a midwife, so I did what was needed.'

He made a noise, half sob and half snort, straightening his hunched shoulders and turned to face her. She saw a haggard man in early middle age but his scooped out cheeks and the crevices gouged beside his mouth made him look older than his years.

'Well, what else would you expect?' he sneered. 'I'm John Alec MacInnes. Poor Anna. She can't carry a child long enough for it to be born alive.' He scratched distractedly at the ginger stubble on his chin.

'How is her health usually? She seems very thin and flushed.'

'What are you saying? That I forced myself on a sick woman and made her pregnant when she was ill?' he snarled.

Màiri stared back steadily, 'No, John Alec, I'm saying no such thing.'

He shrugged, his anger deflated, 'We both work in a mill. I'm a weaver and she spins. It would make anyone weak, working in that hell hole – so much heat and dust. You're a Gael. You know that we're bred to an outdoor life.'

'Aye, that's true. And where are you from, John Alec?' She could hear the rise and fall of the Lewis accent in his voice.

He slumped down on a chair. 'I don't even think about where I came from any more,' he replied, knuckling his eyes, 'But since you ask, I'm from Carloway.'

'Where you come from matters. It makes you who you are. Were you driven from your home?'

'Aye. I was only a wee lad. All I can remember is the terrible hunger. I couldn't sleep with the empty hole in my belly. We dug up silverweed roots for my mother to grind into meal. And we had shellfish to stop us starving. One day I went down to the shore with my sisters to gather them. I made a fuss because I thought it was women's work. My mother smacked me for being so crabbit. It was so unlike her but she was expecting my wee brother and must have been demented with hunger herself.' He gulped and looked towards his sleeping wife.

'Anyway we collected two full pails and toiled up from the shore. There at the top stood the factor, hands on hips and a smirk on his face,

"What do you think you're doing?"

"Getting our tea," I said.

"Well, it's not yours to take," says he, kicking my pail over. I tried to pull it back but he knocked me down. Then he trampled the shellfish into the sand and swaggered away.'

'What happened next?'

'We waited until he'd gone, picked up the shellfish and washed the sand out of them.'

She shook her head, frowning, 'He'd no right to do that. We were always allowed a deer from the hill, a fish from the stream and wood from the forest.'

He jerked his head up and stared hard at her. 'So they say, but fine words don't mean anything. Anyway we left soon after that, carrying everything we could on our backs, like beggars. Ended up in Greenock. It's a pity my parents weren't wise enough to go to Canada.' He fell silent, his fingers rubbing the rough cloth of his trousers.

'I've heard so many tales like yours of people treated like vermin. We need men like you to join the fight against the landlords.'

He looked at her red indignant face and laughed bitterly, 'And who are these brave fighters? Not the likes of me, worn out mill slaves. You'll be meaning the gentlemen who parade themselves in kilts.'

Màiri gasped but rallied quickly, 'These gentlemen have told the world about the wrongs done to us Highlanders.'

'You can't turn the clock back. People have left their land for ever. The ones who emigrated have started a new life. And men like me have no time and no desire to listen to gentlemen and ladies,' he spat the words out, 'telling us to fight for justice.'

'But look at John Murdoch. He's not rich. He struggles to keep *The Highlander* going. He travels all over Scotland raising money for the paper.'

'Aye, I've heard of him. He's the one who strides over the hills in a kilt singing Gaelic songs at the top of his voice,' jeered John Alec.

'You mock our tongue even though you speak it yourself,' Màiri pointed out tartly.

'Well, it's my native tongue but what use is Gaelic here? If I had children ...' his voice shook, 'I would make certain that they spoke English so that they would get on in the world. Gaelic is like a fish caught on a hook, struggling to breathe in the English air.'

'All the more reason to fight for it.' She jabbed her forefinger at him, 'And don't imagine you're the only one who has suffered. I spent time in prison, found guilty of theft just because I couldn't understand what I was accused of.'

'Maybe you should have learnt English sooner then,' he mocked. 'If you want to do some good why don't you go back to Skye and help the poor folk there? I'm sure they've need of a midwife.'

Their raised voices woke Anna. She started to cough, gasping for breath. John Alec rushed over to her, 'How are you, *mo ghràidh*? I'm so sorry the wee one died.'

'I know. Surely you're not arguing with the kind midwife who took such good care of me.' She lowered her voice, 'You must pay her. Then go to find a box to put the baby in and take him to the churchyard.'

'To be thrown into a common grave,' he croaked.

'That doesn't matter. God will know where to find him.'

John Alec scrabbled in his pocket and awkwardly held out the coins to Màiri. She gravely accepted them and walked away out of the station. The Station Master caught sight of her and hurried to catch her but he was too late. She pushed forward through the crowd, a warship cutting through the smaller craft on every side.

CHAPTER 26

Glasgow, 1877

After the crowd had left, Màiri stepped outside the cramped hall
to escape the stifling atmosphere. The room was sour and damp
from the reek of sweat soaking through heavy clothes. That smell
reminded her of the stench of restless, penned-up animals at the
cattle sales in Portree where she'd gone with Pappa. Highland
houses smelt too – of peat-saturated walls – but at least in the
country she could escape to life-giving air outside. Here in
Glasgow the outside air was rank, choked and sooty.

Màiri had brooded for a long time about John Alec's words
once her anger had spent itself. His fierce comments had at first
snatched away her enjoyment of the cèilidhs. Being attacked in
court had been like a sword slash. Since then there had been
other, blunter, blows; the mocking lady nurses, Professor Lister's
chilly disapproval and Dr MacLaren's dishonesty. These had left
a dull throb of disappointment but being savaged by one of her
own was worse, like being hacked by a blunt saw.

As if she could just run off to live on Skye! Women there
needed her but they couldn't afford her services. She depended
on the money that she earned here. Mairead made her welcome
when she returned to the island for visits but it was a burden
being a guest. Her old friend refused any payment for her board
and Màiri hated being in debt to her hospitality.

Even if she could afford to live on Skye would she still be
able to create poetry there? Down here in the Lowlands her mind
could conjure up so clearly the details of her childhood. She
whispered quietly to herself one of the new verses she had added

to one of her songs. It was becoming a favourite with audiences and she had sung it again tonight,

> When Martinmas came
> And the livestock and crops put right
> The men making heather ropes
> And the rush-made bags in a heap;
> Beside the built heap of potatoes
> There would be a barrel full of meat;
> That was how we were reared
> In the high island of the mist.

Would her well run dry if she returned home for good? She knew how much Skye had changed since her youth. She saw the differences for herself each time she returned. For a number of years she had not ventured near her old home after the time she had gone there and had been chased away by the shepherd's barking dogs. Would the sadness of it all swamp her if she stayed on Skye? When she was away she could keep her anger sharp, like a wolf snarl; she could stoke her rage at the ruined homes sprouting nettles. If she lived there would the wolf's blood grow thin, his bones stiffen and his howl shrink to a weary whimper?

Still, John Alec had made her think about the younger, poorer Gaels in Glasgow, especially those who had been born in the city and only knew about the Highlands from the stories told them by their families. They didn't have the leisure or the smart clothes to go to the Highland Society meetings. Yet they were the ones who had suffered most from losing their birthright. How to reach them? She had spoken to John about her concerns.

'You're right, Màiri. I've spent so much time tramping the Highlands that I've forgotten about the streets of Glasgow. We need to follow the example of our Irish brethren. They've forged bonds with all their exiles, rich and poor. We've much to learn from them. As you know, my dream is that all the Celts will stand together, Gaels and Irish.'

'That'll be difficult. Haven't the Irish come over here and taken work from our folk?'

'But the real enemy to both the Gaels and the Irish are the landlords who've forced them to leave their homes. Anyway, I'll spend some time visiting the places where the poorer Gaels meet. Of course you can always find them under the *'Hielanman's Umbrella.'* Well, I had better be on my way.'

'And I shall speak with the women in the closes. I'm sure they won't mind a hand with the mangles on wash day.'

'If you wish,' he replied in a lukewarm way, 'But the men are the ones that matter. They're the ones who will get the vote and influence Government.'

'When it comes to fighting it's the wives and mothers who will be among the bravest, as it's been in the past. Didn't Flora MacDonald risk her own life for her prince's?' Màiri's dark eyes glinted steel.

John had the grace to look a little embarrassed, 'You're right. Never underestimate a Highland woman.'

So between them they had encouraged working men and their wives to come to the meeting that evening.

'I'll sing but as I'm a mere woman with no hope of a vote you won't be wanting any speeches from me,' Màiri had joked. They had both laughed. Màiri was a confident speaker now, talking with passion about the hardships she saw on Skye. And she had done plenty of both singing and speaking tonight. She sighed with satisfaction as she breathed in the damp Glasgow air. The door opened behind her and she turned.

'Ah, it's yourself Màiri,' he exclaimed as he joined her on the step, 'You gave a strong performance tonight.'

'In what way, John? Was my singing particularly fine?' she grinned.

'It was inspiring as always, but I meant how well you trounced those hecklers. Charles was worried about rough behaviour. The Glaswegian working men are especially fond of putting speakers on their mettle. He was right too. There wasn't much Highland courtesy there tonight. What was it that rude fellow called out when you were talking about the brave men of Skye?'

'"What use is that place to anyone?" he said, "There's nothing to see but rocks and nothing to eat but tatties."'

And I wondered if it was your voice I heard calling out, John Alec, she thought to herself. She had scanned the crowd for a gingerish head but there was a good scattering of redheads in the audience and she couldn't be sure. She wondered how his poor consumptive wife was faring.

'And then you drew yourself up to your considerable height, glared at him and slapped your … er …'

'"Rump", is the word you're after, I believe, John.'

'I prefer "haunch,"' he said, looking a little pink, '"That's how well they feed us on Skye", you declared. The crowd loved it.'

'Well, people like it if you laugh at yourself, and if you surprise them. I gave them all a shock when I turned my back on them and pretended that I was going to lift my skirts, "Look at the two bannocks I got on the Isle of Skye." That silenced him. Oh dear, I've embarrassed you now. Isaac always scolded me for not being ladylike. Many years ago I said something similar in Inverness at the time of the potato blight. At least my friend told me I had. I was a little the worse for wear with strong drink and don't remember. It was before we were married and he made me promise never to do anything like that again. What would he think of me now?'

Another figure appeared in the doorway, a tall upright man with a long, serious face and well-tended beard. John was relieved at the distraction.

'I never had the honour of meeting your husband but I can only hope he would applaud the way you strike such a spark with a Highland audience. I've advocated for a long time that the fairer sex should have a voice in local government. Maybe the day will come when there are ladies in Parliament itself.' Charles Fraser Mackintosh smiled as he spoke.

'You do me an honour but I fear that men like declaiming too much themselves to allow women to join in.'

Charles shrugged, 'Maybe so.' He turned to John, 'I've not had a chance to ask you about *The Highlander*.'

'Its fate is in the balance. Captain Fraser is taking me to court for libel,' Murdoch said softly.

'That scunner Fraser,' Màiri exclaimed, 'He's in the wrong for putting up the crofters' rents. Of course he was egged on by that sneak of a factor. Red Alick MacDonald may as well be a Lowlander for all he knows about crofting. How different from his grandfather, *An Dotair Bàn* – now he was loved by everyone on Skye.'

Charles raised an eyebrow, 'I don't understand, John, how you gave such a vengeful man a chance to attack you.'

John's shoulders slumped. 'I was away trying to raise money when those terrible floods hit Uig. I was remiss in not checking Finlayson's article before publishing it.'

'But he wrote the truth. Captain Fraser's house being flooded was a judgement on his wickedness.' Mairi said firmly.

Charles sighed and tugged at his beard with a sinewy hand, 'Even if it's true it can't be proved in a court of law. It will be seen as a matter of opinion and a slur on his character. You aren't schooled in the law, Màiri.'

She pursed her lips while he turned to John, 'Perhaps not all is lost. Have you offered Fraser an apology?'

'Aye, straightaway. But he wants his pound of flesh. He's threatened me through his lawyer. "You escaped when you attacked the landlord of the Skibo estate last year but we've got you now and we'll lock the door on you." That's what he said,' his expression was bleak.

'That's just bluster. We'll have to trust in the good sense of the judge and hope that he awards low damages,' Charles said firmly.

Màiri puffed up her feathers again, 'I would remind you that I had the misfortune to be forced to learn about the law. I had the shame of being named as a common thief in the Inverness newspapers, me who came from a clean nest. Should I have cried libel and gone to court? Even if I had the money to do so, the mocking laughter would have reached to Heaven. Although we are all equal in God's sight, on Earth the rich have all the laws on their side.'

'I know you have suffered, my friend,' John murmured.

'We shall have to wait and see,' Charles said. 'That flood was a terrible tragedy for Skye,' he said to her, feeling that he had been too dismissive.

'Aye, whole flocks of sheep were swept out to sea; and so were bodies from the graveyard. It's just a pity that it was the estate manager who drowned and not Fraser himself. After the bridge was carried away, two brave men from the village waded up to the house through shoulder high water to tell him to leave at once but he refused. They risked their lives for a man they had no reason to care about. I'll wish you goodnight gentlemen. This *cailleach*'s away to her bed.'

'May I escort you home? It's a rather insalubrious area here.' John asked.

She laughed and brandished her umbrella like a bayonet, 'Who do you imagine would dare to attack me? My daughter's expecting me tonight and it's not far. I'm among Gaels here, my own people.'

CHAPTER 27

Glasgow, 1877

The two men watched her disappear.

'She's a brave woman. You saw how she inspired the audience.'

'True, John, but she bites too. There's not much dulcet femininity there. Of course, like all women she lets her emotions overrun her reason.'

'She seemed a little weary tonight beneath all the bombast.'

'She still works, does she not, as a nurse?' Charles enquired, 'I wonder that she doesn't retire given her age.'

'I doubt if she can afford to. She's far too proud ever to admit it of course but she needs her income from nursing. Now she spends so much time campaigning for our cause she has less time available to work.' He let his words hang in the air.

'Hmm. I hadn't realised. She would be useful for electioneering too. She's certainly got the common touch. I need someone who speaks the Highlanders' language, literally and figuratively. It's rather irregular to have a woman as an agent but why not? She's a mother figure to the Gaels, after all, and a widow without family obligations. I could pay her expenses and some sort of retainer. What do you think?'

'That's very thoughtful of you, Charles.'

He laughed and tapped John on the shoulder, 'I admire her spirit but I do prefer ladies who are a little less like a bull mastiff in temperament. Keep me informed about the court case. I trust you'll escape your enemies, like Prince Charles after Culloden. May I offer you a nightcap John? Ah no, you're an abstainer. A cigar then?'

*

Màiri trudged along the empty street to Flora's home, feeling disgruntled. I'm useful for warming up audiences and silencing the loudmouths, she thought. On the other hand I'm still a bit common for their refined tastes and they certainly don't want my opinions. I'm still a sort of servant, really, and meant to know my place. All the same, I'm the lure that draws people in. The audiences respect the others but it's me they love.

She licked her lips, anticipating the wee dram she would enjoy before she went to bed. That was another thing that annoyed her; John's silly disapproval of all strong drink. While Charles was more tolerant you could see him flinching in disgust to see a woman drinking whisky.

Still, it was a pleasure these days to visit Flora and her husband Joseph when she came to Glasgow, now that they had their own home and a baby on the way, or as her friend Mairead used to say, "One in the loom." It had been so hard in the early days when she first came to Glasgow. As well as pining for Isaac she missed Inverness. She had been happy there but how could she have stayed when she had been so humiliated? She was grateful for the chance to train at the Royal but she had felt dispirited and friendless, having to sleep in that grim nurses' room off the ward. None of her children seemed to understand that although they had lost their Pappa she had suffered much more severely. After all, most animals push away their young when they are grown enough to fend for themselves, look at the deer or the swan. The young go on to build their own families and forget about their old home but she … she had lost her life companion, the one who shared both her yoke and her pasture. Like the swan that loses its mate she had hunched over with a drooping neck, staring at the water and willing the reflection to become the dead one returned to life. Was it so surprising that grief drove her a little mad for a time?

How strange that it was shinty that had helped her recover. It had been the turning point when she began to look forward more than back over her shoulder. Joseph loved shinty and was a fair player himself whereas Flora hated it.

'It's like a battle between the clans with split heads and spitting out teeth,' she said, glaring at her husband who had sacrificed a couple of teeth to the game himself. Màiri loved shinty too because she had grown up with the stories of the heroes playing the game, like the herdsman of Cruachan who beat the champion who had the gold ball and the silver caman. In the next few days she found herself remembering the shinty games of her youth down on the flat plain of the Snizort. They marked each corner of the pitch with a bottle. The game would go on for a long time, new players coming in to replace those who were exhausted. The high spirits of the young men spread to everyone watching. One and all brought mounds of bannocks and cheese which tasted as good as manna from Heaven to appetites sharpened by the open air.

'The Gaels of Greenock have challenged the Glasgow lads to a game at Hogmanay. Why don't you come and watch it?'

'I'll do more than just come, Joseph. I'll make a feast.'

So the day before the match found her in the Highlanders' Great Hall, sleeves turned up like a blacksmith and sweat dripping down her face as she rolled and baked and stacked. The President of the club sat beside her, surrounded by a thicket of sixty camans he was getting ready for the players.

On the day itself she organised a horse and cart to carry creels full of bannocks, cheeses as big and round as full moons, and whisky to spur on the lads. She followed behind the sixty players down to the park, their camans held like rifles on their shoulders, half in kilts and the rest in knickerbockers, with pipers fore and aft. The game started at 11 o'clock in the morning and continued until it was too dark to see the ball. She cheered the home players until she was hoarse, waving her scarf in the air and encouraging the children to leap up and down. 'I expect you to set an example to them, Mother. You're shrieking like a banshee,' said Flora, scowling in disapproval. But Màiri didn't even hear her. When had she last had so much fun? Not since she had rolled down the sloping meadow with Mairead or been in that crowd with Jeannie when the carts were thrown into the harbour. The game ebbed this way and that, with neither side gaining a clear advantage until, with the light fading fast, the visitors scored an audacious goal. Spurred on by this late set-back the Glasgow lads surged forward and scored the equalising goal with a thirty yard strike homing in on its target out of the gloom. Surely the game couldn't go on much longer? But then, from nowhere, Donald Ferguson outran his opponents to settle the score with a fine single-handed effort and the Glasgow lads had won a memorable match.

After the match Màiri handed out her refreshments, with a word and a joke for each man.

'Will you give us a song?' one asked.

'Not today. I've no voice left but I'll compose one later about your grand victory.'

'Come and join our team, you'd scare the other side witless!'

'Aye, especially if I stood in goal. No ball would get past me.'

It was then that she realised that this harsh, brash city had become a familiar, cheerful presence to her, even though her heart would always remain on Skye.

She kept her word about the song:

> These are the lads who give us a lift
> This is the New Year that brought us joy
> These are the lads so dear to my heart
> Far from home in Glasgow's streets.

Each strapping youth, caman in hand
The ball whistles through the air
Swift as deer on the run
And the cry: Up it goes, Donald.

Singing to herself she picked her feet up and swung her umbrella like a caman, startling a thin cat that was lurking in the shadows.

'Ah, *piseag*, I would give you some crowdie and milk if you came back with me,' she crooned, but the animal gave her a suspicious stare and slunk away.

'Another snooty Lowlander,' she called after it.

CHAPTER 28

Fleming's Hotel, Glasgow, 1881

John Murdoch stood against the weak wash of sunlight trickling through the tall windows and skimming over the table. Màiri smoothed her thick fingers along it, admiring its burnished surface. Her cornflower blue dress was vivid among the dark suited foliage. The secretary of the Skye Vigilance Committee, Henry Whyte, opened proceedings and invited John to speak. He nodded and began, his eyes sparkling and his voice breathy with excitement.

'Well, my friends and fellow Gaels, I don't wish to sound smug but it's a wonderful thing to have one's predictions proved right. I've long maintained that the spirit of the age is sympathetic to our ideals. Now Captain Fraser's unjust and inhumane actions have been roundly condemned in the Press. He ...'

Màiri interrupted, slapping her palms down onto the table, 'Yon dreadful man. He's the very devil for spite. First he tries to close down your paper, John, and when that doesn't work he's back to evicting tenants.'

The bearded, black garbed men sat around the long table like diners. They all turned to stare at Màiri, trussed and stuffed into her good dress, opening their eyes wide in amazement as if the celebratory turkey had suddenly come back to life and was squawking in protest.

Alexander Mackenzie winked across the table at Màiri, his fat schoolboy's face crinkling with amusement, 'You're right Màiri. He's as bad as Sellar was when he cleared the people from Sutherland.'

'No, he's far worse because this man is a hypocrite too,' Màiri thundered, 'I heard that two weeks before he sent out warnings about evictions he gave out wee gifts of tea and sugar to those he thought were deserving tenants; the ones who bow down to him.'

'He's cunning,' Alexander continued, 'He knows the newspapers are watching closely. He hopes to keep in good odour with them.'

'Good odour indeed! That man's doings reek to high heaven,' Màiri retorted, 'He's a very midden of ...'

Whyte cleared his throat and spoke in his soft voice, 'I think everyone is agreed about his wrongdoings. However, his misdeeds have achieved one useful purpose. They have strengthened opposition to him. Our good friend, Charles, and of course The Clach here,' he nodded at Alexander, 'have led the way in pressing for a Commission into the Land Laws. Now at last the Federation of Celtic Societies has come together to support Fraser's Valtos tenants in resisting him. Our committee's role is to keep track of his actions and be alert to other developments on Skye.'

Aye, thought Màiri, and how many Skye folk are there involved? John is from Islay, Alexander from Gairloch, Charles from Inverness and Angus Sutherland – well his name gives the answer to where he's from. And to think I wouldn't even know about the Committee if I hadn't done a wee bit of eavesdropping and heard Henry Whyte, the one they call Fionn and a Glaswegian to boot, talking about it. Then I had to stamp my feet to shame them into inviting me to join.

John's voice cut across her thoughts, 'For a long time I've advocated making common ground with our fellow Celts across the Irish Sea. Parnell and Davitt have made the Land League a powerful weapon and forced Gladstone's Government to pay attention to them. When the Irish Land Act becomes law it will give tenants fair rents, fixed tenure and the right of free sale. That measure seems to me to be one that we should emulate here, at least as a starting point.'

There were noises of agreement from the listeners. Whyte hurried onto the next item before any more squalls from Màiri or The Clach could blow them off course. He introduced Charles Fraser MacKintosh, 'He has done us the honour of attending our meeting despite the burden of his Parliamentary duties.'

The MP looked around with the slow deliberation of an experienced public speaker. 'In truth, we live in historic times and it is gratifying that the Government is more willing to bend an ear to the plight of our countrymen. John and The Clach have long campaigned for the beleaguered crofters. However, we Highlanders must take care not to lose our reputation as law-abiding people. A good name is hard to earn but perilously easy to lose. How different is our reputation for fortitude and restraint compared with that of the Irishmen whose intemperate and violent actions have horrified the English nation. The likes of Michael Davitt demand not only that land be given outright to the tenantry but want to sever completely Ireland's ties to the Empire. I can only condemn such disloyalty, nay treason.'

The raised volume of his final words made Màiri's head jolt backwards sharply. Surely she hadn't dozed off while Charles was speaking? Well he did have a low rumbling voice and now The Clach's lively tenor tones were in full spate.

'You speak of the Irish as being like rude boys who seize all the food set out on the table but their methods have succeeded. Their Members interrupt Parliamentary business until their voices are heard.'

'But at what cost? The greedy child is hated by his brothers and eventually the father will lose patience and punish him,' Charles replied.

John joined in, 'If I may continue in the spirit of your analogy, Charles, I see the head of the family as the English Government which keeps the other British nations on short rations so that they can't grow into independence. Isn't it right that brothers in blood, Gaels and Irish, combine together as we did in history against the overweening Saxons?'

The Clach sighed impatiently, 'We don't need the Irish. Our people can stand up for themselves. We must press for action to support the Valtos men.'

'I've no objection to doing so as long as there is no Fenian style lawlessness. It's vital that we keep a close watch on events,' Fraser MacKintosh observed.

'May I suggest we listen to a gentleman who is now waiting in the lobby?' John asked. 'As you know I spend many hours on my travels through the Highlands. I also have men who keep an ear to the ground for me. Here's one of them. His name's Peter Nicolson. I believe that the cauldron of discontent is coming to the boil and we need to be ready to use the head of steam it produces.'

While they were waiting for Nicolson to come in Màiri turned to Alexander, 'Where does your nickname "The Clach" come from? How are you like a stone? You're broad enough to be a standing stone. Or is it that you're as strong and solid as a rock, as Our Lord said to Peter?'

His round face split into a roar of laughter, 'Your first suggestion is true but not flattering. Your second one is flattering but not true. My name comes from the Clachnacuddin stone.'

Màiri laughed too, 'I stopped there often enough to put down my load of washing. But I don't see you as a washerwoman. I can imagine you stopping there for a gossip though.'

'There's a simple reason for the nickname. My first place of business when I came to Inverness was a drapery shop called the "Clachnacuddin House".'

'So we do have something in common through clothes, then,' Màiri smiled, digging him in his well-fleshed ribs.

CHAPTER 29

Charles straightened his back and summoned up a smile as Peter Nicolson was ushered in. He was a meaty man whose muscular shoulders strained the seams of his jacket. When John invited him to begin he spoke in English with a hesitant Gaelic lilt.

'I've come from Skye where I spoke with Captain Fraser's tenants. He seems to be universally despised.' Màiri nodded triumphantly. 'Also, I spent some time meeting crofters in the Braes townships near Portree. Three in particular: Gedintailear, Balmeanach and Peinchorran. They're all tenants of Lord MacDonald.'

'An absentee landlord,' John added.

'That's not true!' cried Màiri, 'He returns to Skye every summer.'

'He does indeed, by a special train all the way from his grand house in London up to Strome Ferry. Then he transfers to his private steam yacht, "The Lady of the Isles" isn't it called?' said John in a mocking tone.

'And he expects all his tenantry to cheer him as it sails to Armadale. I suggest we listen to what Peter has to say about the mood of the people after the terrible season Skye has suffered.' Henry Whyte motioned for him to continue.

'Aye, it's been a dreadful year. The potato blight struck again and most of the other crops have been lost, swept out of the fields in violent gales. The final blow was the loss of over two hundred fishing boats in the storms, but at least the rents of the Braes men have not been increased.'

Màiri grunted in approval.

'Surely the rents are already too high for their inferior land. So their yields will be poor even in good years. That's the trouble when landlords take away the best land for sporting estates and farms,' The Clach commented.

'It's more complicated than that,' replied Charles, 'After all, the sporting estates bring money and employment into the Highlands.'

'It's time the landlords listened to the grievances of their tenants. There's growing anger against them and if they don't take care they may indeed face the same violence that has happened in Ireland,' The Clach retorted.

'I suggest we hear Mr Nicolson's report before we enter into a debate,' Henry Whyte intervened. He nodded at their guest to carry on.

'The Braes crofters were talking about Ben Lee. Twenty years ago they lost their common pasture land there when a tacksman, called John MacKay, took it over and ran up to a thousand sheep on the hillside, but recently there've been rumours that he doesn't want to renew the lease. This has raised hopes that Lord MacDonald's factor, Alexander MacDonald, might return Ben Lee to them.'

'When I was a girl there used to be a big fair at Sligachan. The folk from Uist used to graze their cattle on Ben Lee while it was on.'

'As always, Màiri, you have a wealth of local knowledge,' observed Charles.

Again Peter Nicolson waited until the Secretary gestured for him to continue.

'I was invited to the cèilidh house and made welcome with a seat close to the fire and a dram pressed into my hand. I asked them why a stranger called MacKay held land in a place that since the beginning of time belonged to MacDonalds, MacLeods and MacKinnons. There was a silence and then a greybeard spoke up, Alasdair the Seer he was called.

"You're a Nicolson yourself?" he asked.

"Aye, indeed, from Mull," I replied, "It's a proud name too on Skye I believe."

The old man, a MacDonald himself, scrutinised me, "Maybe so but the Nicolsons are outsiders on Skye." Then he counted back the generations on his fingers and declared that the Nicolsons only arrived there three hundred years ago.'

The Clach seized the chance to scuttle off into the undergrowth and startle a wild goose into flight, 'How fascinating to see the oral tradition in action, going back through the Christian names and patronymics of their forefathers,' he enthused, leaning forward, 'I wonder how far back he could go – maybe even to the time of Somerled himself. As you know I've a great interest in genealogical research. I've even discovered that William Gladstone and I are related to each other.'

'Would that be on the right side of the blanket?' cackled Màiri.

'Fascinating indeed. Perhaps you could deliver a lecture on the topic later at a Gaelic Society meeting,' suggested Charles, moving his words around slowly as if shifting heavy pieces of furniture. 'Proceed, Mr Nicolson.'

'So the *bodach* went on, saying how generous the Lord MacDonald of the time was in giving land at Scorrybreac, near Portree, to the exiled Nicolsons and upsetting his old enemy MacLeod of Dunvegan in the process. Anyway, it looked as if a quarrel might break out then and there between the different clan members. Fortunately a younger man spoke up, asking them all to give me a chance to be heard.

'So I painted a vision of the future, of how life could be for them if they had their rightful land returned. How they would have better crops and more money from selling their beasts. How they wouldn't be living hand to mouth any longer. How their sons could learn trades; masons, carpenters and tailors would be needed. They started to nod as I spoke but that old man interrupted, "It's not the future you're talking about but the old days before the tacksmen took all the best land. What we've been left with will never be any good to raise more crops. All we have in abundance is our children. They go off to the Lowlands and send us money to keep us going. Aye, we're good at breeding children here." He cackled with laughter and they all joined in.

'"But surely," I said, "Once those children go away they never return? They raise their own children in other places and the link to the land is lost." But I knew that they'd stopped listening to me. When I left I could hear them mocking me behind my back.'

'In what way?' enquired John.

'They were muttering under their breath the words of that old song about the man from Islay, the man from Mull and the Devil himself.'

'And the worst of the three was the man from Mull,' added Màiri, smiling in amusement, 'That's a very ancient joke.'

A mottled flush spread up Peter Nicolson's neck, 'And a bad one,' he said through clenched teeth.

'There's always been rivalry between the different islands,' said John gently, 'I know I'm laughed at behind my back as the strange Islay man in the kilt who tramps through the countryside.'

'Did you meet with any other crofters while you were in the Braes?' Henry Whyte asked.

'Well,' Nicolson continued, 'Later I spoke with the Free Church elders and the schoolmaster. They listened politely enough. I was cautious, pointing out that Lord MacDonald was nothing like Captain Fraser. Nevertheless I suggested that his taking Ben Lee sixteen years earlier had caused hardship and that he now had the chance to return the pasture to its rightful owners.'

'Did they agree?' The Clach asked.

'Did they, indeed,' Nicolson sighed, 'They all leapt to his defence. "But Lord MacDonald was only a boy of twelve years old at that time. He can't be held responsible," said one. "He's such a busy man. How can we expect him to deal with such matters directly when he is only here for a short time each year?" said another of them. Then the schoolmaster joined in. I hoped he might be bolder in his opinions, "We must remember all the generosity of the MacDonalds over the years," was what he said. And so it went on. Every time I cut down one argument they raised up another. "We've heard about the fighting in Ireland. We don't want anything like that here. We must trust in our faith in the Lord to show us the way,"' Nicolson quoted with a sigh.

'They're not used to new ideas,' John suggested. 'The old loyalties to the chief run deep. MacDonald is not a tyrant like Fraser. His sins are those of omission rather than commission. He deludes himself that he can enjoy the life of an English milord while forgetting about his tenants. We mustn't be too downcast. I'll visit them myself and encourage them to demand the return of Ben Lee.'

Màiri had been tapping her fingers on the table's shiny surface while the discussion went on around her. Now she placed her hands down firmly on it and half rose to her feet. Sweat glistened on her brow and basted her face.

'I can't listen in silence any more. Why is your message not being heard? It's because you're talking to the wrong people.' She gulped a breath, '*Bodachs* steeped in old battles and elders too preoccupied with the state of their immortal souls – and other people's – to notice what's happening around them. Who is it who has to endure the worst hardships? Who has to do the hard work, the beast's work, carrying creels full of peats or pulling a harrow through stones because no-one can afford a horse to do the work? Who is it who stands up to the sheriff's creature when he comes to deliver the eviction notice?' She glowered fiercely at each of the men in turn, 'It's the women of the townships, of course. They're the ones who thirst for change and justice.'

They were all temporarily silenced, except for The Clach, 'But surely it's the men who do the heavy labour on the land?' he asked.

She hooted in derision, 'You've written plenty about the Highlands but have you ever visited them? The men work hard when they're there but they have to go away to the fishing so that the family doesn't starve in the lean months before the harvest.' Her voice rose like a wind scouring the shore and bending the trees beyond. 'And the women do the milking, the spinning, cooking meals from what little they have,' she paused for breath, 'And what about the hardest labour of all – bearing and rearing large families? Those big families they joked about come at a high cost for the mothers who bear them. I attend poor women in Greenock who are worn out by long hours working in the mills. But they at least can afford a midwife. The women on Skye have no such help and if their labour is long and difficult they die in childbirth or are left broken in health. They suffer the most. So they are the ones who most desire change.'

Her listeners were shifting uneasily in their seats.

'Màiri, we know that you understand the plight of the women folk,' Charles said smoothly, 'We should listen to their concerns. However, except in the case of widows, it's the men who are the named tenants. Soon these men will be given the vote. They're the ones we must win over to our cause.'

As Màiri sank back into her chair John spoke, 'There's truth in what Màiri says. The womenfolk have influence with their families.' Seeing that she was about to speak again, he hurried on, 'We need to win them over. But I come back to what I said earlier. We must follow the example of the Irish and work closely with the Scottish supporters of the Irish Land League here in Glasgow.'

Charles looked grim while The Clach openly groaned at his words.

The sullen silence that followed was broken by Angus Sutherland, a small man with neat, alert features who had been listening to the earlier discussion with a glint of amusement in his eyes, 'You met Charles Parnell himself while you were in America, I believe. What opinion did you form of him?'

John smiled, 'Aye, I did meet him, in Philadelphia. He's not a typical Irish orator, no poetical language or striking poses. He spoke quietly and earnestly about a suffering people. I didn't have a chance to speak privately with him as he had to leave straight away after his speech.'

'Hmm. I've heard that he doesn't like sharing the stage. Maybe he was envious of your oratorical skills,' Angus said.

John shrugged, embarrassed.

'What's your opinion, Angus, of that Land League fellow Davitt? What sort of man is he?' asked The Clach, wanting to turn attention away from John.

'A powerful speaker with a soldier's bearing. The ladies see him as a tragic hero with his missing arm and solemn demeanour. A freelance by nature, but sensible enough to throw in his lot with Parnell after he was released from prison.'

'A man after my own heart. He must be a grand fellow if he went to prison,' laughed Màiri, The Clach joining in while John shook his head.

'Now, Màiri, you cannot maintain that all those sent to prison are necessarily of good character.'

She turned to face John. Her eyes flashed, 'I cannot speak for others but I know that for me prison was my university and a hard one. It's many a rock I've rubbed against in my life but that one was the worst. When I stood in that courtroom it was as if I was trapped in a madhouse. I could understand nothing. I lost sight of who I was, like when the Old Man of Storr is covered in mist and the whole rock disappears as if it had never existed. You can't ever understand what it was like and no words of mine can ever convey it.'

For a moment time hung suspended. Then Charles coughed and spoke, 'I am opposed to any sort of alliance with the Irish, either in their own land or here in Scotland. Davitt has been associated with violence in the past although he's taken up a more moderate stance recently. As I've said already we cannot risk losing the good reputation of Highlanders.'

Peter Nicolson had been listening intently, forgotten by the others, 'You may not be able to stop it. The links have already been made with the Irish. The young men from the Braes go fishing in the summer and they have been talking with Irish sailors in Kinsale. The language there's not so different that they can't understand each other.'

The Clach was listening hard, his small predatory eyes gleaming, 'We need to find a way to get all these groups in the Lowlands and Highlands working together. We need someone who can be at the centre of the web. Charles has his parliamentary duties in London and the rest of you stay in Glasgow. However, I'm based in Inverness which is a good position for gaining intelligence from all sides.'

'You see yourself as the big spider, do you, Clach?' broke in Màiri, 'Who are the flies that you'll trap, I wonder?'

While The Clach struggled to hide his annoyance behind a pinched smile, Charles glided in, 'It's an excellent idea to develop intelligence throughout Scotland. For the time being though I think we should make further use of John's network, men like

Mr Nicholson here who has worked so diligently while Angus has an ear to the ground in Sutherland and Màiri of course on Skye. Despite the tepid response Mr Nicolson received in The Braes I believe that we'll soon have veritable thunder and lightning. If we have advance warning we can moderate its effects.'

As if anyone could control either the Highland weather or the Highland people once roused, thought Màiri, but this time she kept her opinions to herself.

CHAPTER 30

Skeabost, Isle of Skye, 1881

Lachlan MacDonald was in a good humour as he breathed deeply in the summer afternoon's sunshine. He still felt somewhat shaky and shivery but overarching everything was his enormous gratitude at being free from pain. Three months of throbbing agony in his right big toe seemed torment enough but then the gout had ravaged his left elbow as well. He considered himself to be, in general contented with his lot, but the illness had driven him to the very limit of despair. Still, in the last two weeks he had hauled himself out of the deepest part of the pit. Now he could drink moderately again and, even better, not be restricted to the miserly two cheroots a day that the doctor permitted. The vile tasting medicine that had given him a few hours of nightmare-drenched oblivion each night was again banished to the back of the cupboard. He felt strong enough to turn his mind to business and had just finished casting his eye over the letters from India, noting with pleasure that the indigo planting had been successful.

What a miracle it was to feel the warmth on his face and to anticipate the short ride in the dog cart without the fear of agonising jolts. He patted his jacket pocket to check that his notes were there, not that he really needed them. It would be amusing too to see the antics of the Land Leaguers; John, affable as ever, would be trying to keep his unruly colleagues in line. The Clach would be throwing his voice and his weight around as usual while Blackie would be preening his feathers. At least I'm quick enough on my feet now to sidestep his theatrical embraces, he thought. There, at the heart of events, would be Màiri herself, roistering one moment, imperious the next but she deserved her moment of glory.

The circus of Land Leaguers had been in Portree the day before when he had made a brief visit to the bank. He had heard them outside the Royal Hotel before he had seen them.

'Look at me now, I'm as brown as the heather after spending so much time in the Highlands,' Blackie had cackled.

Lachlan had kept his distance and hurried away to go shooting with Captain Jackson. It had been a fair bag too; a hare and a brace of snipe, a much more rewarding occupation than listening to reformers spouting hot air.

Damnation! Who were those figures walking from their carriage towards him? Was it some of the mob he'd missed yesterday? Yes, he could see John's leonine head bobbing among them. Well, now that he had been cornered there was nothing for it but to be civil.

Lachlan fixed a smile on his face and welcomed them to his home. John explained that most of the party had gone on ahead but just as he was about to set out himself three more friends had arrived. It seemed a good opportunity to introduce them to Lachlan before the ceremony. Two of them he knew already. The neat, slightly built Glaswegian schoolmaster Angus Sutherland was the candidate for the Sutherlandshire seat. He seemed a cold fish, ambitious rather than passionate. The bluff Reverend MacCallum from Waternish had too much swagger for Lachlan's taste. He had a fanatic's gleam in his eye and a disputatious manner. Clergymen should stick to their proper sphere. They shouldn't confuse their flock by meddling in political matters. Their companion was a stranger but his thin soled shoes and sharply tailored coat marked him as a city dweller. John introduced him as Mr William Saunders from London, a gentleman with a keen interest in land matters. Lachlan hid his scepticism behind a mask of attentive politeness.

The party settled themselves back into their carriage and followed behind Lachlan for the short journey. As they arrived they could see a gathering of a considerable crowd; local people, Land Leaguers from the Island, John MacPherson of Glendale, among others, and Norman Stewart, nicknamed Parnell, from Staffin. There was a scattering too of tradespeople from Portree but the gentry were conspicuous by their absence.

Lachlan leant into the gathering breeze as he walked up the gentle slope. A louring sky threatened and he felt the splash of the first raindrops on his face. He looked down towards the loops of the Skeabost River as it coiled through the plain of the *Bugha Mòr*. Over to his right the hummocks of tough grass were swallowing up the parings of previous lives. The gashes of lazy-beds, the broken stumps of walls and the scratches of paths were all that remained. Were there ghosts in that abandoned landscape, watching and listening? He brushed away the fanciful thought as he wiped away the speckles of rain on his face. He looked at the living ahead of him. There among them was the poetess herself, a dignified statue standing beside a sack-covered stone. Her face radiated anticipation and pride as he greeted her.

'Where's the well then? Oh, is it that small thing?' Saunders' cawing voice slashed across the hum of Gaelic. He strolled over and dipped his fingers in the water, letting it spatter over the mud of his shoes. He failed to notice the sudden intake of breath from those near him. How could the ignorant dolt commit such a desecration? Didn't he know that wells were sacred and carried deep wisdom from within the earth up to the surface? Màiri looked thunderous. So Lachlan hurried to start his speech before the foolish fellow was set upon.

'Màiri, nighean Iain Bhàin is a bard who needs no introduction. Like so many sons and daughters of Skye she was forced to leave her home to make a living for herself. Unlike most of them she has been able to return, cloaked in fame and honour.'

Then he asked her to remove the sacking. She did so with a magician's flourish, revealing the inscription, '*Tobar Iain Bhàin*'.

Màiri enjoyed listening to Lachlan's speech. Like a fluent minister he had the gift of speaking naturally, without relying on a book of words. As he spoke of the Gael's love of the mountains and the sea and the exile's pain in losing them she looked about her. She saw the mingled colours of a bale of tweed tumbling out; the greyish cushioned clumps of heather splashed with the sharp green of mosses, the rocks studded white with lichen and the spiky whin whose gaudy flowers could burst out at any time of year, like kissing it was never out of fashion. It was odd though to hear herself described as a poet of nature. She just sang about what she could see and remember. It would be grand today to sing in the open air with a background chorus of birdsong, rather than in a stuffy Glasgow hall.

She decided to sing a new song first, a sad one that might seem surprising at a celebration. They were the words that had given their birth cry inside her head all those years ago when she returned for her father's wake,

> I left my well-beloved Skye
> Over forty years ago
> They have destroyed the life of it –
> It breaks my heart to sing of it.
>
> When I came to my old home
> Where my people lived
> I was welcomed bitterly
> By barking dogs.
>
> I went to the well made by Fair John
> My beloved father
> I found the stones he'd laid
> Left for me, treasured memory.

Tears ran from my eyes
As I stood there
Remembering my people
Now sleeping in the grave.

My senses grew feeble and
Death touched my cheek
The water from the well
Restored my spirits.

She paused and for a moment there was silence except for the soughing wind and the rasp of a seagull's call. Then she smiled and opened her arms wide, 'But now that sadness is changing. I have a song of blessing and prophecy for you, one that I was saving for the New Year. But it seems to me that a new dawn is beginning for us Gaels, so I shall sing it now,

Take this prophecy and blessing
To every place where the Gaels are –
To Glenelg of the heroes
To Kintail and its great people

To Glenelg of the heroes
To Kintail and its great people
To the Island of the Mist
I was not the only one to have to leave it

To the island of the Mist
I was not the only one to have to leave it
And when I'm between the boards
My words will be seen as a Prophecy

And when I'm between the boards
My words will be seen as a Prophecy
For the children of our people
Driven over the seas will come back again

For the children of our people
Driven over the seas will come back again
And the thieving lairds and landlords
Will be driven out, as they were
The sheep and deer will be cleared
And the glens will be fertile again

The sheep and the deer will be cleared
And the glens will be fertile again
Time to sow, time to reap
And time for the thieves to get their reward.

Time to sow, time to reap
And time for the thieves to get their reward
Time for us and our friends to put back in place
The cold stones of our broken down homes
And when New Year's Day comes round
We'll see happiness for all of us.

The applause swooped and wheeled around her. Before it was over Professor Blackie's voice fluted above it, 'Màiri sang about the new landlords who, like the Vikings before them, invaded to seize what didn't belong to them. No Turkish sultan is more absolute than an absentee laird in the Highlands with a factor to do his dirty business. However, we are fortunate to have among us Mr MacDonald of Skeabost who is very different, a true father to his people. He is also a champion of our ancient, poetic tongue. He's made a generous contribution towards the fund to create a chair in the Gaelic language.'

There was a pause as the audience tried to make sense of Blackie's mangled Gaelic and the strange idea that you could somehow sit on what you spoke.

'I think he speaks through what he sits on,' an old woman declared, causing ripples of laughter to spread through the crowd. Lachlan's name though brought a hearty cheer.

Afterwards they went back to Skeabost House for luncheon. Màiri was gratified to be seated next to the Laird. Lachlan was determined to keep the conversation light among the motley crowd of Land Leaguers and assorted worthies.

'Mr Saunders, did you know that Mrs MacPherson is renowned for her poetry?' he said, drawing her into the conversation. But she just stared back vacantly, letting her mouth hang open.

'You'll have to translate for the poor woman,' Saunders cackled.

Lachlan frowned but obliged.

Màiri simpered. 'Indeed, I have written a great deal,' was all that she offered in reply.

'Ask her what she thinks about the land question. Does she agree that the land should be taken from the landlords and given to the crofters?' He spluttered a fusillade of crumbs.

'I don't agree,' she boomed. 'I want the wheel to turn back to the old ways. The true Highland lords, like the laird here, have always taken care of their people. It's the grasping *Sasannachs* and Lowlanders who have treated us badly.'

Lachlan smiled ironically, 'The good lady believes that the Highland landlords can be trusted, unlike the outsiders.'

Saunders gazed at both of them in contempt before turning to listen to The Clach on his other side.

'I believe that proprietors' rents should be spent on educating crofters' children', he said.

Saunders took a hearty bite of venison and said, 'That doesn't go far enough. Crofters should follow the Irish example and refuse to pay any rent at all.'

Lachlan looked at the shrapnel sprayed around the Englishman's plate.

'If you've finished eating perhaps you would like a brief tour of the estate before you return to Portree?'

'Indeed, I would. However I shall be staying in Portree a little longer and I should welcome the opportunity to find out about the life of the peasan ... crofters. Some of them are fishermen too, I believe. I should like to have a trip on a fishing boat.'

Màiri had been sitting still, her heavy features totem like, but now she turned to Lachlan, her eyebrows raised. He sighed and then translated. She became animated and grinned broadly, promising to arrange the trip for the next day, as long as Lachlan would come as interpreter. What was she scheming, he wondered. He opened his mouth to decline but to his astonishment it was the voice of his younger rapscallion self that hurtled out, 'What a first rate idea.'

So the next day saw the three of them waiting at Bayfield, on Portree Bay. They stood on the shore of the tidal inlet where the fishermen's houses clustered together with their toes in the sea.

Kenneth MacRae welcomed Màiri aboard 'The Brothers' Pride'.

'We fishermen are superstitious about a woman coming aboard but as it's yourself Mistress MacPherson, you can only bring us good luck.'

'Are you saying I don't count as a real woman?' she said, punching his arm playfully.

As a brisk wind made the boat skip through the water Saunders plagued the fishermen with questions. Màiri he ignored completely.

'Well, my good man, what drove you to take to the sea? No doubt you suffered at the hands of a landlord?'

'No', replied Kenneth, 'My parents had a croft, a good one, in Camustianavaig. My father was offered the tacksman's house when he came over from Raasay. We're a big family though, so we couldn't all stay there. He helped me get started with the boat. There's plenty herring and salmon, enough for my three sons to make a living when they're grown.'

'But it would have been better if your father had owned the land rather than just renting it.'

'How is that? If we had all stayed it would still have had to be divided up between us.' He looked hard at Saunders through clear blue eyes, deep set in a weather-beaten face.

'How are these matters arranged in England? Does the land go to one son or does the government hand out more land so that all the children can have a decent share?'

'Er ... the eldest son usually inherits but the tenant has more rights of course and ...'

'Well Sir, may I suggest that you sort out the problems in your own land where you are more familiar with how things are done.'

Màiri meanwhile was deep in a whispered conversation with one of the crew. The man went to lie down on his stomach at the prow of the boat, his head over the side, inhaling deeply with his eyes closed.

'What on earth is that fellow doing?' asked Saunders.

'Oh, Sir, didn't you know?' asked Kenneth. 'That's how we tell where the fish are hiding. We smell them out. Some fishermen, like my cousin Donald here, have a special gift for it. But we have to stay absolutely still and quiet for it to work.'

For the next ten minutes Donald made his way trance-like around the boat, frequently stopping to lie down and sniff noisily. Finally he rose, tossed his head from side to side and pointed to starboard. The nets were lowered. Saunders hopped from foot to foot in great excitement.

'This could be the basis for an interesting scientific study. I wonder if other primitive peoples have retained this skill?'

Later, the bulging net was raised on deck and its glittering load spewed out.

'It makes me think of our Lord on the Sea of Galilee with the fishermen, James and John,' Màiri observed.

Saunders curled his lip. She bent down to pick up two mackerel, their brindled scales still shining with life and held them out.

'Perhaps the English gentleman would enjoy these for his supper,' she boomed in English. He jumped in surprise, knocking against her so that the fish flew out of her hands and landed on him, leaving a silvery saliva trail trickling down his fine dark coat. He stumbled ashore to a chorus of jubilant laughter.

CHAPTER 31

Strome Ferry, Highlands, April 1882

The steamer at Strome Ferry gave a final blast from its hooter. The last passengers hurried to board her, some from the Inverness train and others who had come on the earlier steamer from Skye, celebrating while they waited for the return trip. The last to hurry up the gangplank on his spidery legs was Colin the piper who had accompanied Màiri from Portree. He bundled his pipes under his arm as if he was quietening a squirming piglet. As he did so his instrument let out protesting digestive noises, making his companions laugh. Once aboard they joined a swirling crowd. At first sight the waves of movement appeared to be random but the tide was splashing towards a small group of older men dressed in rough tweeds. In their midst, rooted to the deck and towering over them like a protective oak was Màiri, with a wide smile on her face and a wicker basket by her side. The shuddering of the ship's engines made the bottles inside it clink. Alexander Finlayson, at nearly seventy, was the oldest of those around her. He smiled warmly beneath his wiry grey beard and shook her hand with shy deliberation. She pulled out a bottle of whisky, 'Talisker from home – take a good slurp and pass it round. There's plenty more,' she urged.

Although she joined in the high spirits around her, another hidden part of her sizzled and seethed like a glowing horse shoe thrust into cold water. Why couldn't she have been there, among those brave women? Would her presence have made a difference? Whether it would or not, how much she would have enjoyed sending stones winging through the air. It would be a just reward for all those times when her hand had been stayed – by Captain Bolland's soldiers, by the Reverend Carmichael at Tuasdale, by Isaac at the riots in Inverness.

'Now I want to hear the whole story,' she declared, 'but first of all, this Sheriff Ivory. Is he truly as mad as they say?'

Finlayson chuckled, 'He's been jumping around like a man plagued by midges ever since we burnt the eviction notices. When Ivory was told what had happened he shouted for a hundred soldiers to subdue the island. The wee man's imagination was running away with him. He claimed there were hordes of us, like the plagues of Egypt, watching on all the hills, day and night. '

'Highland regiments would never agree to march against their own people,' Màiri said stoutly.

'No. That's why they got Glasgow police instead … and tried to bring them over secretly.'

'As if Glaswegians could ever keep a secret,' she chuckled.

'Aye, there was a newspaper reporter aboard the *Clansman* with them,' added Peter MacDonald, a stocky man with a shrewd, wind-battered face.

'Then best of all,' continued Finlayson, 'the steamer ran aground as she came into Portree on a low tide during the night, so the whole village could see the fleet of boats bringing them all ashore.'

'And what a cèilidh there'll be when we get to Portree, but watch out for the Raasay folk when we stop there. They'll try to get you all off the steamer to celebrate with them. Anyway, carry on with the story about Sheriff Ivory,' she said, nudging him in the ribs.

'Well, the wee bantam led the troop from Portree to the Braes – he was in a waggonette with the Portree Sheriff, the Procurator Fiscal and the Glasgow police commander, all of them too important to tread on God's earth. But it was a terrible day with water enough to drown in. Rain poured down from the heavens and the wheels stuck fast in the mud. So they had to walk for the last two miles with the policemen. All Ivory's fine plumage drooped.' They all laughed.

'They weren't much of an army but they still caught us napping,' Peter MacDonald continued in a more serious tone. 'We didn't expect them to come so early. They got to Gedintailear at the crack of dawn when everyone was still abed. We were just rising when they reached us in Balmeanach. So they caught the five of us.'

'But everyone put up a brave fight', Màiri said.

'Aye, the village folk harried them and tried to rescue us. They rushed to trap them as they took us through *An Cumhang* where the hill rears up on one side and there's the sheer drop down to the Sound of Raasay on the other. That's where the police laid about them with their truncheons. We kept shouting for the Peinchorran men who should have helped us but they were still in their beds more than a mile away.'

'I believe the women gave a good account of themselves,' Màiri interjected.

'They fought like lionesses. One of them got Ivory with a clod right on the jaw. I've never seen a man look so amazed as he measured his length in the mire,' Alexander Finlayson roared with laughter. 'When they arrived to arrest us my daughter-in-law had a big pot of water heating up and she threw it over one of the policemen. Sadly he was so wet already that it didn't do much damage.'

'But it grieves me that the women and lassies took the brunt of it. Seven of them badly hurt, including poor old Widow Nicolson,' said Peter MacDonald sadly, 'I hope the police felt ashamed.'

'Maybe they were. They looked more like mourners than a victorious army when they took us to Portree jail,' Alexander

Finlayson said, 'The hissing and cursing from the crowd would chill your blood, especially when they came from the lips of white haired old grandmothers, "Cursed be you and yours for all eternity",' he shuddered.

Màiri shook her head, 'And they should feel ashamed of themselves. It wasn't manly work they were doing. I'm sorry the women suffered but there's no disgrace on the men of the Braes. The shame is on the sheriffs, the factors and the rest of them for invading the homes of peaceable folk to arrest them.'

The Clach came over to join the group, 'But this time the authorities miscalculated. They didn't think that the papers would expose their misdeeds. Now they stand condemned in the eyes of the world. Let me introduce you to some of the gentlemen of the Press,' he suggested, taking her arm. His florid face was grim. 'I have to tell you how horrified I've been by what I've seen on the island. Those tiny houses, bare of any comforts. Their boats were in better condition than their homes.'

'Aye, but you have to remember it's the boats that bring them a livelihood.'

He carried on, seeming not to hear her, 'And the people as worn out as the barren land itself. But they're not objects of pity; they're dignified. Look at what Alexander Finlayson said after his arrest, "I didn't intend to break the law. I didn't think I was doing anything wrong but defending our rights. I refused to pay full rent when land had been taken away from us, land our fathers, grandfathers and great grandfathers – I cannot remember further back than that – had held before us." To think that such an enormous force of policemen were sent all the way from Glasgow and Inverness to arrest five such decent men.'

She patted his arm, 'It's not just a game to you any more, is it?'

He nodded, for once bereft of words. Then he swallowed, 'I spoke to one of the policemen.'

'Why?' she spluttered, 'They're brutes and Papists, most of them.'

'But the young policeman I spoke to was no thug, he was limping and bloodied. No, don't sneer – hear me out. He told me that he'd no idea about the sort of people he had been sent to arrest. He was told that they were fierce outlaws, wild as rabid dogs. But when he saw their homes he could have wept, "I remembered my mother's tales about the famine in Ireland. Folk were fainting with starvation on the roads or dying of pestilence in their houses. Yet the landlords were blaming them for their plight. I saw the same thing happening in Scotland and I'd no stomach for such a cowardly fight."'

She sniffed, 'I hope that he tells other people. Then maybe next time the police will refuse to march against us. There'll be no more blue-backed hordes in the glens.'

'You calling them blue-backs reminds me of a strange story I was told about Alasdair, the old soothsayer. He saw a vision of a tide of blue helmets coming up the brae to Balmeanach. When they actually did come though they looked as if they would march past the place where he had seen them stop. He stood there open mouthed, horrified that his vision had been wrong. But at the last minute that silly wee Napoleon of a sheriff ordered them to halt. The old man fell to his knees in relief that he'd not been mistaken ... Ah, here's Patrick Kelly, one of the reporters who's been writing about the Braes.'

The reporter's jovial face was red and glistening, 'You're talking about Second Sight? Well, of course we have that too, over in the old country. Now what I find so odd about that story was that the fellow was so relieved to have been proved right about the place where the police stopped. I would have thought he would be tearing his hair out for not predicting the right time of their arrival. Had he known the raid was going to be early ... well, who knows ...'

Màiri looked scornfully down her nose at him, 'Second sight is God-given. The seer is only the recipient. He can't control what he sees.'

Patrick Kelly shrugged, 'Answer me another conundrum then, if you will. After the five were hauled away to jail there was a plan hatched for men from the Braes to march on the square in Portree, carrying a mast as a battering ram so they could break down the doors of the jail. The men from Balmeanach marched off on their own when the promised reinforcement from the other villages didn't arrive. As they neared Portree they passed Viewfield, where they heard that the wife of the factor's brother had just given birth. So what did they do but stop to raise a cheer for the infant. Now why, by all the saints, would they do that? Why would they pour blessings on the head of the child born to one of Lord MacDonald's creatures when MacDonald was the enemy they had been fighting against?'

Màiri stared hard at him and spoke in a dangerously quiet voice, 'Tell me, when you look down at the sea from a hillside, what colour is the water?'

He looked quizzical but decided to humour her, 'Blue, of course, but the sea mirrors the sky and the exact shade will depend on the weather.'

'True. And even on the same day the colours will vary across a stretch of water, from dark greenish blue where it's deep to grey-green or colourless in the shallows. We Gaels hold different shades of colour in our minds. You Irish hate your landlords. That's understandable, they aren't of your race and they spend their time in England with no care for their tenants. We too hate the outsiders who have bought estates in the Highlands and use their factors to clear people off the lands they've held for generations. But we have room in our hearts for the lairds whose forefathers looked after their people.'

'And that's why you won't win the battle to keep your land. The lords as a class of men are your enemies. You can't make exceptions and feel a tenderness for some. The old lords are as heartless as the new ones. There's no room for softness in war time. That's why the Braes men lost their courage and carried their mast back home,' Kelly retorted.

'And if they'd attacked the jail and broken heads would they still have the support of so many people across the length and breadth of our nation? Why do you think so many distrust your Irish Land League? It's because you use violence,' Màiri insisted.

'Think of the *Fianna* who won all those battles in Ireland and Scotland. Did they win them by being polite and drinking tea with their enemies?' he replied. But he found himself addressing the broad buttress of Màiri's rear as she bent down to fetch more provisions from her basket.

'Come on Màiri, Nighean Iain Bhàin, are you going to give us a song about the fight at the Cumhang?' a voice called out.

'Not yet. I shall compose it after the court case is over and you've been cleared. Or even better, I shall sing it when you have Ben Lee back again.'

'You'll give us a good thirty verses then?' someone else shouted.

'At the very least,' Màiri laughed. 'You'll have to make do with my older songs for now. How about *"Nuair a bha mi òg?"'*

'That's a few years ago for some of us,' observed Alexander Finlayson.

'But the mature whisky is the best of the lot,' she countered.

'Do you know that the papers are calling it "The Battle of the Braes?"' The Clach asked.

'And so they should, for it was a battle between good and evil, a battle that we shall win.' Then she planted her feet down firmly, lifted her head and sang,

> As I strolled round each glen and stack
> Where I was happy tending the cattle
> With the lively youngsters, stock of country people
> Without vanity or guile and who are now in exile
> The mossy bank and pastures are under heather and rushes
> Where I once gathered the sheaves of corn
> And if I could see people dwelling there
> I would become joyous as when I was young.

CHAPTER 32

Inverness, May 1882

Inverness, May 1882

My Dear Friend,

I trust this letter finds you in good health. You have certainly chosen an auspicious time to return to your native island now that it's become so important in the campaign. I heard that other Skye stalwart in our cause, John MacPherson, declare that the imprisonment of the Glendale crofters had done more to remove tyranny and oppression from Skye than anything that has happened during the present century. He declared that if Joseph had never been sent into Egyptian bondage, the children of Israel might never have escaped from slavery. I fancy that he sees himself in the role of Joseph although as a staunch adherent of the Free Church he could not allow himself to clothe that thought in words. However, I would dispute his claim. It was the Battle of the Braes and the trial of the five men from there which lit the fire of protest. And whose voice was it that rallied the warriors? It was the voice of Màiri nighean Iain Bhàin herself.

I'm writing to give you an account of the trial. I've been sitting there in the courtroom, scribbling away in my notebook so that I can publish a verbatim account of the proceedings. The events of the trial are as absorbing as any stage play. Even if you've already heard the outcome I'm sure that you will enjoy reading the details of what happened.

Our supporters sought my advice about which lawyer we should appoint as defence counsel. My recommendation was Mr Kenneth

MacDonald, the Town Clerk of Inverness. From the beginning he has shown a sure hand at the helm. He secured bail for the Braes men which resulted in their triumphant return to Skye.

Also, Mr MacDonald has made the world aware of the injustice of the Crown Agent in insisting on a summary trial before the Sheriff, far from their homes rather than trial by a jury. Even when Charles raised the issue in the House of Commons the Lord Advocate remained firm in his resolve to have a summary trial. What a heavy weight of legal process has been brought to bear against a few older men of peaceful habits and general good character whose worst weapon was a lump of wet turf!

When I was a boy I had a great fondness for the novels of Sir Walter Scott. I was stirred by all those sturdy heroes like Ivanhoe and Rob Roy. I have learnt now from the Battle of the Braes that it's not the flamboyant leaders who change the world but the slow-burning determination of ordinary men, and indeed women, who risk losing everything they own when they fight for justice.

Mr Macdonald convinced the Sheriff to withdraw the first charge of impeding the sheriff-officer from delivering his summonses. Only the second offence of assault remained.

By the time that the witnesses were summoned and questioned our lawyer was at full tilt, trampling reputations underfoot. Allow me to give you a flavour of his sparring when he examined Alexander MacDonald:

Mr K MacDonald: You are a solicitor at Portree and act as factor for Lord MacDonald. Martin is your clerk and a sheriff-officer. Does he hold other offices?

Witness: He is clerk to the Road Trustees and Collector of Rates for the parish of Snizort, about five miles from Portree, and Collector of Poor Rates for Bracadale, nine miles away. I do not recollect if he is Collector for any other parish.

Mr K MacD: How many proprietors are you factor for besides Lord MacDonald?

Witness: MacLeod of MacLeod, Mr MacAllister of Strathaird, Mr MacDonald of Skeabost and Major Fraser of Kilmuir.

Mr K MacD: I suppose that is the greater part of Skye?

Witness: Yes, decidedly.

Mr K MacD: And in addition to this you are also a landed proprietor yourself?

Witness: Well, I believe I am. (Laughter)

Mr K MacD: You are also a solicitor and bank agent?

Witness: Yes.

Mr K MacD: And I believe you are Agent for Captain MacDonald of Waternish?

Witness: Oh, I have a number of appointments besides these, and lots of clients.

Mr K MacD: And your influence extends all over the Isle of Skye?

Witness: I do not know about my influence but I hold the positions mentioned.

Mr K MacD: You are distributor of stamps?

Witness: Yes.

Mr K MacD: And Clerk of the Peace for the Skye district?

Witness: Yes, depute under Mr Andrew MacDonald. (Laughter)

Mr K MacD: Any other offices?

Witness: I may have some but I do not remember any more. I do not see what right you have to ask these questions. Do you mean to assess *my income? I will tell the Assessor of Taxes when he asks me but you have no right to enquire.*

Mr K MacD: You are also a coal merchant?

Witness: I am not aware, Mr MacDonald. (Laughter)

Mr K MacD: And how many School Boards and Parochial Boards are you a member of?

Witness: Several.

The Sheriff: I don't want to interrupt you but what has this to do with the case?

Mr K MacD: To show that this gentleman is the King of Skye, the uncrowned king of the island, (laughter) an absolute monarch who punishes a murmur by transportation to the mainland. There are some other offices which you hold on Skye?

Witness: Yes.

Mr K MacD: In point of fact, you and Martin hold between you pretty much all the valuable offices in Skye except that of parish minister? (Great laughter)

Witness: (warmly) Not at all, Sir; not at all. (Laughter)

Mr MacDonald's cleverness in making the chief witness look ridiculous gave us all great hope. The Sheriff's summing up however raised alarm. He spoke of Alexander Finlayson having a stick in his hand and acting in a threatening manner.

At that point I could sense everyone in the courtroom collectively holding their breath – our party in dread and our enemies in hopeful anticipation. Then there was enormous relief when moderate fines were announced, rather than the long sentences we had feared; a mere £2 10s for Alexander Finlayson and Donald Nicolson and 20s only demanded of the other three. As you can imagine it gave me *much pleasure to brandish a cheque in payment of the fines in front of the court official's face.*

My dear friend, Màiri, nighean Iain Bhàin, even if my letter is old news to you by the time it arrives I hope that you will relish hearing about how foolish our enemies were made to look.

Kind regards from a joyful friend,

The Clach

CHAPTER 33

Portree, Isle of Skye, May 1882

Dear Mairead,

My dearest old friend, what must you be thinking of me? It's so long since I came to visit you. You'll be saying I deserve a good skelping for my neglect. What can I say to excuse myself? I've been so busy in Portree and the Braes that I've not had time to draw breath, let alone come up to the North End. Much as I would rather have a good cèilidh with yourself I've had to accept bed and board with good folk down here.

I've been keeping you in mind though. I was remembering how fondly you spoke of your mother singing the old Skye songs when you were a wee lassie in Australia. Once I'm more settled I shall write you a song to atone for abandoning you.

As I cannot provide you with any diversion in my own person, I shall tell you what has been going on here since the fight at An Cumhang or 'The Battle of the Braes', as people are calling it now. The Clach is putting the trial of the Braes men into a book. All those English Lords in Parliament will have to sit up and pay attention to us now.

I've been busy travelling with that old warrior John. He's brought a new young hero to tramp around the island and put fire into bellies. He's an Ulsterman called Edward McHugh. He has a fine broad brow, a full dark beard and a piercing gaze. When he addresses a meeting he speaks with such power and conviction that you feel yourself being swept along on the tide of his words. He speaks in English and in the Irish tongue which is not so hard to follow once you tune yourself to it. At first though it was like listening through a seashell held to your ear – lots of swishing, muffled sounds. It's close to our Gaelic but not quite the same, like when you hail a friend across the street and when she turns round you see it's not her but her sister or someone who walks in the same way. Anyway he spoke with such passion about us Gaels and our Irish brethren who have both suffered so much at the hands of the Sasannachs. We should stand shoulder to shoulder with them in our struggles for fair rents and more land. He said that even in England many farmers had been cheated out of their land in days gone by. He gave us an old English verse:

> *Why prosecute the man or woman*
> *Who steals a goose from off the common?*
> *And let the greater felon loose,*
> *Who steals the common from the goose.*

Then when he had us all hanging on his words he held out a single stick, quite a thick one and broke it across his knee with a loud crack that made me gasp. Next he picked up a bundle of thin sticks tied together with rope and struggled to break them, to no avail. He let the silence grow while he stood and smiled.

'I don't need to spell the message out,' he said softly, 'I believe, as all of you do, that God created the Earth as a dwelling place for us, his children. He intends us to share in his bounty and to labour together to provide for the needs of us all. Everyone has a right to the natural elements essential for life; air, water and land. When the right to land is denied, as it is here, the result is terrible misery and poverty. However, if we stand together we can't be broken.'

By then the whole audience was breathing in every word as if their lives depended on it. He carried on speaking for an hour in the open air and kept us under his spell. Maybe you judge me impious for praising him to the heavens, especially as he is a Papist. How I wish that there were more leaders in our Church who could be so inspiring.

He was wise as well as brave. The tide of his words never swept out of control. He warned us not to break the laws of the land but to be as cunning as our enemies. When he left Ireland as a young man and moved to Greenock he learnt the printing trade.

'And how did we printers deal with bosses who worked us too long and too hard? We didn't strike only to find ourselves having to crawl back to work later, half-starved. No, we practised 'ca' canny' – we didn't work too fast at our tasks. We took our time over them. So in the end they had to take on more workers. Now you might say that factory owners in the cities are not the same beast as landlords in the countryside but they're not so different. When the crofters refuse to pay for rent increases it makes the landowners pay attention. Will they dare to send soldiers against poor, peaceable folk? Never! Public opinion would crucify them.'

What applause he got! I'm surprised that it didn't carry over the miles to you. The poor young man looked hollow-cheeked and ravenous afterwards but he refused the offer of a dram.

'I'll not help the liquor trade that takes advantage of the poor man, stealing his wages and sapping his strength. Neither will I eat meat for it inflames anger. Don't you think that our enemies would be delighted if they had an excuse to accuse me of drunkenness and arrest me?'

'But surely you need some sort of recreation?' I asked him, 'I'd wager that Irishmen, like Gaels enjoy music and dancing.'

He shook his head solemnly, 'I think life is so short and the struggle for justice so hard that I've no time or inclination for frivolity.'

'I hope though you would make time for courting – a fine young man like yourself.' That made him blush a little.

Well, my dear friend, I must rest my weary hand now. I remember how hard I found it to write when I first started to train at the hospital.

I trust that this letter finds you in good health and spirits,

Màiri, the penitent.

*

Os, June

My Dear Màiri,

I hope you're not exhausting yourself gadding around with handsome young strangers. Neither of us are spring lambs any longer. Of course I'm disappointed not to see you but I realise that an eminence like yourself has many calls on her time. I shall have to wait my turn.

I was interested to hear about Edward McHugh. His name has been carried on the wind all over Skye but as you know I dislike attending big meetings, so I've not had the chance to hear him speak. Your account of his character reminded me of what you've told me about Isaac. He was a powerful speaker too. No wonder you've fallen in love with this Ulsterman. I can hear your protests but as one of your oldest friends I'm allowed to tease you a little.

Anyway, there has been much talk about him here. He's made an amazing impression for a man who never appeared. That sounds like a riddle but I'll explain. A stranger has been travelling around the North End this last week, inquiring about the Irishman. He's a tall, well-built fellow in a good dark suit of clothes, with big hands and feet. The big feet are shod in well-polished shoes. He stayed at the Staffin Inn and kept poor Mr Nicolson up to the wee small hours with idle conversation until he was desperate for his bed.

Eventually the stranger says, 'You must know about everyone who lives round about.'

'Aye.'

'And off course all the goings on among the crofters.'

'Aye'.

'There's been lots of newspaper men about, Scots and English. Have you seen an Irishman at all?'

'No.'

'This Irishman was travelling around the Stenscholl area, I believe. Did you hear anything about him being there?'

'No.'

'I heard he was travelling around telling men in the townships to seize land for themselves. Do you know anything about that?'

'No.' Then he loosens his tongue a wee bit. 'There wasn't hide nor hair of any Irishman round here. Maybe you should go up to Uig and ask there about him.'

'Thank you for your advice,' says the stranger, plodding off to Uig. But he learns nothing about your fine fellow there. Eventually he arrives footsore at Donald Ross's shop in Idrigill while Donald is serving Angus MacLeod. This time the stranger steers the conversation round to the land troubles. Angus drops in McHugh's name.

'Who's this McHugh?' pants the stranger, as excited as a dog smelling dinner.

'I've heard tell that he's one of those Land Leaguers,' says Angus, wide eyed.

'Has he visited the crofters in Idrigill?' the large stranger demands.

'No, indeed not,' shouts Donald, slapping his hands down on the counter, 'Why would we want him here? Didn't we get our rents reduced by a quarter this year?'

'He's a trusair I hear,' Angus joins in, ' Do we need a Catholic Irishman to tell us what to do?' says he spitting on the floor, near the well-polished shoes, although I imagine they were a little worn after all that trudging around.

'Well, that's very interesting,' says our stranger, reaching inside his jacket to lift out a wee book before thinking better of it and groping for his handkerchief instead.

Donald and Angus don't dare open their mouths for fear of laughing.

But our sturdy hero continues on the trail of the invisible Irishman. He huffs and puffs off to Earlish and ends up outside the door of Archibald Gillies's house.

'Aye, McHugh was here on Saturday.' Now our man is foaming at the bit while Archie takes his time lighting his pipe, 'But we didn't want to see the man at all. So we stayed quietly at the other end of the house when he called out and left my youngest daughter to speak to him. He waited in the kitchen for a while and when no-one else appeared he left some pamphlets with her.'

'Do you still have them?' he asks, hopping from one big foot to the other in excitement.

Archie scratches his head and frowns, 'Ah, I remember now. We left them beside the door of the byre. We didn't want to read any Papist rubbish. Oh, did you want to read them yourself?'

So our fine fellow plods back to Portree, carrying the pamphlets as carefully as if he had an orphan lamb in his arms and sends his report to Sheriff Ivory, that champion of justice. For our mysterious stranger was none other than Sergeant Malcolm MacDonald, travelling disguised in plain clothes. I'm sure your Mr McHugh will be pleased to know that he's worrying the authorities so much. You'd better warn him that they're hot on his trail.

With affectionate regards,

Mairead

CHAPTER 34

Skeabost, Isle of Skye, May 1883

The two men emerged from the plain whitewashed church and walked towards the waiting pony and trap. Suddenly the shorter, broader figure yelped in surprise as he felt a heavy hand on his shoulder.

'I'd know that sailor's roll of a walk anywhere. Will the pair of you come and have a *strupag* with me?'

Without waiting for a reply Màiri started to stride ahead. The two men glanced at each other behind her back. The Clach twisted his mouth downwards while John smiled and replied, 'That's kind of you, Màiri. Watching history being made gives you a dry mouth. I should like a rest before chasing after the Commissioners to Uig.'

Màiri's words bubbled out in excitement, 'Did you see their ship sail into Portree Bay? What a beautiful vessel! And our own Charles himself is one of the Commissioners.'

'Well, it's right that he should be here. After all, he stood up in Parliament and insisted on a Royal Commission. Mind you ...' The Clach paused with a smug smile, '... it was me who first put the idea in his head back in '77 when I spoke at a meeting of the Gaelic Society in Inverness. As for the other ones – Napier appears to be an honest man, albeit a Lowlander, but all the rest are landowners.'

'Sheriff Nicolson is a Skye man and not so high born,' she retorted.

The Clach frowned, 'I dare say but I'm concerned that there's no-one to speak up for the crofters. It's fortunate that John and I have been travelling around to help the witnesses prepare their statements. You know how it is with the crofters, especially the *bodachs*, rambling on for ever about the old days and who owned what before the Famine. We need to drive home the message about getting fair rents and more land.'

Màiri laughed, 'So that's why one of the Commissioner gentlemen was a bit sharp with old MacLure today, "We need to hear what it is that you want, my good man, not catch phrases about fixity of tenure." He could tell he was a blackbird mimicking another bird's call.'

Seeing The Clach's face stiffen, John changed the subject, 'The Commission's timing couldn't be better. They're arriving for the hearings in Glendale just after John MacPherson and the others return from prison. The reporters will be there in force. John has such a gift with words. The first time I heard him speak he told the audience how they would raise a spark in the heather that would set it all ablaze. How true that was.'

Màiri sniffed, 'Aye, they did well enough in Glendale but they weren't heroes like the Braes folk who faced the police and ended up bloodied and broken for their pains.'

John spoke with deliberation, 'The Braes men – and women – were indeed the stuff of legend but times have changed. The whole of Britain heard about the violence meted out to innocent people and were horrified. But if we have more fighting now we could be accused of being as wild as the Irish Land League. That's why John MacPherson was wise in agreeing to be arrested. "If we refuse to surrender and run to the hills we will be seen as being like chaff blown to the wind. But if we stand against the wind though we bend to the blast – yet we have shown that our principles are strong and just." He's right, we must keep our reputation for restraint.'

'Well I prefer a good, honest fight, like when the Fianna set out for battle,' she grumbled. 'Here's my house now,' she said proudly, pointing to a substantial single storey cottage.

She ushered them into a comfortable room with a wooden settle in front of the fire. After prodding the peats back to life she swept into the kitchen, returning with bannocks, cheese and cold herring which she set before them. Watching her, John was struck by how neat and fastidious she was, darting around as she organised the meal. He could imagine how efficient and calm she would be as a nurse. Once they had started eating she spoke again, 'I thought that Mr Lachlan himself might have been at the meeting today but maybe he thought that the witnesses would feel easier about speaking if he wasn't there.'

'That's to his credit,' observed John, 'It was a very different matter yesterday at the Braes meeting. Lord MacDonald didn't deign to attend in person but he sent that scunner of a factor, Alexander MacDonald, to represent him.'

'Ah, the uncrowned king of Skye himself,' laughed The Clach.

'Well he didn't seem so royal, squirming like an otter in a trap when the Commissioners asked him to give an assurance that none of the witnesses would be evicted for giving their evidence.'

'I wish I'd been there to see it,' said Màiri, 'but I haven't got the walking legs of my youth to march all that way from Skeabost. I'd have been glad for a place in a carriage,' she added pointedly.

John looked uncomfortable but The Clach ignored her and continued, 'He had no choice but to agree there would be no retribution for the witnesses. Then what did the fool do in the interval? He cursed Angus Stewart to his face for daring to ask for a guarantee of safety before giving his evidence. The Secretary heard what had happened and forced the factor to make an official statement promising immunity.'

Màiri nodded empatically, 'Mr Lachlan is so different from that. He's a fair and generous landlord; the evidence today showed that. It was made very clear that he has never evicted tenants.

Mind you, I was annoyed to hear William McClure complaining that Mr Lachlan had taken away the trap on the loch they had used for catching fish. But the sheriff cooked his goose on that one, "Are you aware that such devices for catching salmon are now prohibited by Act of Parliament?" What an ungrateful wretch! In the end McCLure had to agree that all those things were done by landlords who were there before Mr Lachlan.'

'I think the people speak about old wrongs because no-one has listened to them before,' said John mildly, 'Lachlan MacDonald is much better than the usual appalling specimens of landowners but he's not a saint is he? There were justified complaints about him not letting the crofters take shellfish from the shore or collect seaweed.'

'I don't know about all of that but there's no denying that he paid for houses to be built and gave out free milk to the children,' Màiri retorted.

Meanwhile The Clach had been tapping his fingers on his teeth and now he spoke, 'This isn't a black house that you're living in, is it?'

'Of course not,' she bristled, 'It's whitewashed and full of light, by far the best house I've ever lived in.'

He smiled sardonically, 'That's exactly what I mean. And who gave it to you? The very same Lachlan MacDonald. No wonder you can see no wrong in the man.'

Màiri was red in the face now, 'I praise him because he deserves it. He's a good man who treats his tenants well.'

'I don't deny that he charges reasonable rents but as we heard today his tenants don't have enough land. They're poorer than their fathers and grandfathers were. They need bigger crofts to provide for their families, yet MacDonald rents out some of his better land to farmers and keeps some back for himself. He enjoys his shooting doesn't he, with his friend Sheriff Nicolson?

Would he be willing to hand over any of that land to the crofters? I think not.' The Clach shook his head vigorously.

Seeing the furious expression on Màiri's face John intervened, 'You know how vehement The Clach can be. I think he's saying that no matter how fair a landlord might be – and there are a few honourable ones like Lachlan who don't grind their tenants' faces into the dust – he is like the sound apple in a barrel of rotten ones. He can't help but be tainted by the others. He's still one of a class of men who oppose true land reform. He can't or won't see that the solution to land hunger is in his own hands; give more land to the crofters. And I'm sorry to say it but your acceptance of this house rent free means that people will think that you're in his pocket.'

'What could I do? I could never have afforded to return to Skye without his help. I had to live in the Lowlands to earn my living.' Her eyes flashed, 'Both of you have fine houses, much grander than mine. You could afford to buy them for yourselves. I've had to make my own way as a widow … and one who was unjustly treated.'

John reached out to touch her trembling hand, 'We've no wish to upset you or abuse your kind hospitality. I know what sterling work you have done for our cause. Your songs have touched so many hearts. But battle lines are hardening now. Landlords as a class are our enemy and we can't make exceptions for the one or two who are more humane.'

Màiri sighed, shaking her head, 'For the first time in my life I feel old. I can't understand these new ideas.' Her solid form sagged and shrank back in her chair. A heavy silence fell. Murdoch stared hard at The Clach, willing him to be quiet.

'You're a bard Màiri and bards are expected to be a law unto themselves. Now I'm afraid that we must continue our journey before nightfall. Your *strupag* has revived us for the next meeting.'

After they left she sat for a long time, staring into the fire. When she was a child she used to gaze at the flames, willing them to show her a vision of her future, but now all she could see was glowing peats. She felt as if she was being left behind. Down in Glasgow she had a position. People looked up to her. Maybe it had been a mistake to come home.

CHAPTER 35

London, October 1884

They sat buttressed by their deep leather armchairs in the shabby opulence of the Oxford and Cambridge Club. Both were tall, striking figures although Sir William Harcourt at six feet four inches was taller and broader than Lachlan MacDonald. Glasses of malt whisky waited at their elbows and a fug of smoke coiled from Harcourt's cigar, braced between his fleshy lips.

'I'm grateful, Home Secretary, for the opportunity to talk to you about the situation in the Isle of Skye. I hope I can give you an accurate report of what's happening there. There are so many highly coloured newspaper accounts about lawlessness and rebellion,' Lachlan spoke in a quiet but emphatic voice.

'Yes, indeed, lurid tales of landowners being kidnapped and forced to appear before a jury of crofters and other similar nonsense. You're a landowner yourself, of course, albeit an unusual one. I've been told that you're known as the richest man on Skye.'

Lachlan grimaced.

Harcourt continued, 'Whether true or not your fortune was honestly earned in the colonies, rather than inherited wealth. I also heard the interesting observation that you are the only landlord on the island who can safely venture out in a pony and trap. I take that to mean that your tenants have enough regard for you not to hurl missiles at you when you appear. If we were talking about Ireland those missiles would be bullets but in the Highlands only clods of earth or stones. An affront to the dignity but not deadly.' He removed his cigar to expel smoke and to grin broadly.

Lachlan smiled politely, 'It's taken injustice on an unimaginable scale to rouse the slumbering rage of the Highlanders. It would be a black day indeed if warships were sent against such loyal and long suffering people. The last time such a force was sent was against the Jacobite rebellion, one hundred and fifty years ago.'

'I know the history,' Harcourt replied curtly, 'You've no need to convince me of their loyalty. I've spent many summers sailing in the Hebrides. I've a deep regard – nay sympathy – for the people there. The Highlanders, and the Irish for that matter, have legitimate grievances. Some of the landlords in both countries have brought discredit to their class by conduct which no circumstances could justify. However, Her Majesty's Government will not countenance violence. I have no compunction at striking down the Irish Dynamitards with their wicked bomb plots but, *entre nous*,' here he leant forward and spoke in a stage whisper, 'I have been begged by the landowners to send troops to Skye but on no account should they be from Highland regiments. What a damnable admission!'

The glassy blue of his eyes was bleak as winter seas. He sank back, his ageing gladiator's face drooping with weariness, 'Would to God that I could be like Pontius Pilate and wipe my hands of ruthless landowners and vicious officials.' He stared hard at Lachlan who kept his dark, deep set eyes expressionless.

'I'm concerned that violence could erupt in Skye at this difficult time when the Government has so many other urgent matters to deal with. I sense you're an honourable man. We're both pragmatists, younger sons who've had to make our own way in the world.' He sighed heavily, 'Everyone bombards me with their opinion. Her Majesty says that she can't understand why her dear Highlanders have become so difficult. Her solution is mass emigration.'

Lachlan gritted his teeth, 'That idea was tried before and has caused the groundswell of opposition we see now,' he retorted sharply. Then he added hastily, 'Although of course Her Majesty is entitled to her views on the subject.'

'Even when they're wrong,' Harcourt grinned wolfishly, clamping his teeth around his cigar. 'I merely quoted the Queen, Sir. I didn't say I agreed with her sentiments. On the contrary, I believe the crofters should have security of tenure and the landlords manage their estates properly, with humanity and restraint. However, as Home Secretary I can't turn a blind eye if crofters break the law of the land and attack sheriff officers who are only carrying out their duty in delivering summonses.' He took a sip of his malt, swishing it appreciatively around his teeth before placing the glass down firmly. Lachlan waited, alert and watchful as a heron.

Harcourt took a deep breath and cleared his throat, 'Now, Lord Napier. I can't criticise him publicly of course, but he has fanned the flames of discontent by raising false hopes. Advocating fair rents is acceptable but his fantastical scheme for recreating townships is another matter. He's allowed the crofters to believe they will be given more land by Act of Parliament. As if the Government could confiscate landlords' property and hand it over to the crofters!'

Both men shook their heads at the preposterousness of such an idea. Then Harcourt leaned forward with a boyish chuckle to tap the arm of Lachlan's chair, 'Come on, tell me more about the two characters who are screaming for gunboats. What are Ivory and MacDonald really like?'

Lachlan took a slow sip from his glass to give himself time to compose his answer. He was the cautious stalker while Harcourt was the sportsman who would squeeze his trigger too early, spooking the stag, 'Well, if I start with Alexander MacDonald. He's been the factor for Lord MacDonald – and many other landowners – for a considerable time. Alasdair Ruaidh, Red Alick is his nickname. He's a decent man and his family has a long history on Skye.'

'He also has the nickname of "The uncrowned king of Skye" I believe.'

Lachlan gave a sharp barking laugh, 'His grandfather, Dr Alexander MacDonald, was known as An Dotair Bàn – the fair-haired Doctor – and was well regarded. He too was a factor. The tenants liked him even though he used to go into their homes, opening all the windows to clear the peat smoke out and force fresh air on them. "But the smoke keeps the midges at bay," they complained. His grandson wants to be fair but he's become the scapegoat for the people's anger against the landowners. His pride was hurt by the mockery he received at the trial of the Braes men. He's like a sort of Gulliver, tied down fast by the laws he's trying to enforce. The worry of it all has aged him prematurely.'

'That sounds like a fair assessment. What about William Ivory?' prompted Harcourt with a gleam of malice in his eye, 'Not a man renowned for his diplomacy. If only the wretched homunculus would resign,' he spluttered.

Lachlan's lips curled into a smile despite himself.

'I know I'm being indiscreet but the man has driven me to distraction,' continued Harcourt, 'Surely he can see that the dangers we have in Ireland; the murders in Phoenix Park, the risk of an armed uprising, might well need a military response while the agitation in Skye is only a skirmish in comparison. He seems to be determined to whip up hysteria so that he can force me into sending a gunboat. Have you any influence over the demented midget?'

'I wish I had. Alasdair Ruaidh and Sheriff Spiers, both sensible men, can't control him. I believe Ivory is determined to exact revenge for what he sees as the humiliations he suffered at the hands of the crofters. Fool he may be but he's a fool who can cause a great deal of harm.'

He looked hard at the Home Secretary, 'I think you're warning me that the gunboat is likely to come. If our pocket Napoleon gets his marines, what will their orders be?'

Harcourt grunted, 'From what I've heard Ivory's tactics are to lead from the rear.'

Lachlan's gaze didn't falter, 'He's a ridiculous man but a dangerous one too. I must press you, Home Secretary, on this matter. Would the troops open fire if crofters resisted the police when they were trying to make an arrest? Would they enter the houses of tenants who had arrears of rent? Would they break up public meetings? I fear another Peterloo Massacre and the disorder that would follow.'

Harcourt crushed his cigar and stared back, his stony face reddening, 'It's not your place, Sir, to question my possible orders in a hypothetical situation. I have told you I have no inclination to send an expedition at all.'

Lachlan continued, unflinching, 'I believe you have also intimated that your hand could be forced in this matter. The crofters would see it as a terrible betrayal if armed soldiers were used against them. After all, generations of Highlanders have fought and died valiantly for Queen and country, at Waterloo and in the Crimea. The Isle of Skye sent ten thousand fighting men, six hundred officers and twenty one generals to fight for our nation between 1780 and 1810 alone.'

He watched mesmerised as the veins in Harcourt's forehead bulged and his eyes blazed. Lachlan remembered the time years ago when he was in India and a tiger had suddenly burst out of the forest ahead of him. He had held the animal's ferocious glare while quietening his terrified horse. Then, as now, fear hung suspended for a breathless moment in time. Finally the tiger had turned around and loped away. Now Harcourt exhaled loudly and unclenched his fists.

'Very well. If the gunboat were to be sent I would make it clear to the Lord Advocate that the troops would not under any circumstances be used to carry out police duties. They could march harmlessly around the island looking suitably martial, making young women's hearts flutter and satisfying Ivory's desire for glory. They would show the flag in the disturbed areas.'

'As if Skye were some outpost of Empire?'

Harcourt grimaced but then adjusted his mouth into a half smile, 'Come on now, that's the best I can offer. Remember I'm a friend of the Highland people.' He rubbed a large hand over his face, making it crumple like a creased handkerchief, 'Politics is a hard trade. My family were all Tories. Tories don't need policies but I believed that inactivity was not enough. So I horrified my family by becoming a Liberal. Now a Liberal government has to have policies or it would be like a doctor without patients. So we set up the Napier Commission to recommend changes to the land laws. Now we're blamed because the Commission doesn't meet every demand made. You're known as an exemplary landowner but I would wager that you've been criticised by discontented tenants.'

'Yes. I have. I've been publicly blamed for actions taken by my predecessor and lectured to by Radical gentlemen who told me that all property is theft. However, they are a small minority and the Skye crofters are almost to a man decent and God fearing. So it grieves me if they are treated harshly because the authorities imagine that they are Fenians.'

'You've my word that any troops would only be used to show the government's authority, not as armed police.'

'I thank you for that assurance. We should offer a toast to the brave men of Skye.'

Harcourt stretched out his legs and raised his glass, 'And we must drink to the downfall of Emperor Ivory, too. I've said how much I love the Highlands. Let me tell you about the first occasion I travelled there. I was staying in Argyllshire and we were out for a gentle stroll one night when I spotted a magnificent horned head grazing on the hill. In the gloaming it looked like a truly mighty stag. So I rushed back to the house to seize my gun. I advanced cautiously on the beast and once I was close enough I put my finger to the trigger and …' he paused for dramatic effect, '… then a voice boomed in my ear, "You're not gaen to shoot the meenister's goat are ye?" There, I thought that would make you laugh. My friend Millais was with me and he's always telling that story at my expense. He claims it's the artist's duty to mock the politician's pretensions.'

They sat a little longer, talking warily about lighter matters. When he walked out into the street later Lachlan mused about how his duty seemed so often to be coaxing people into reasonable behaviour, whether it was a minister of the Crown touchy about his authority or vengeful crofters set on burning down a man's house because they suspected, with no proof, that he had committed incest with his sister. Perhaps tigers were simpler to deal with.

CHAPTER 36

Os, North Skye, December 1884

The door was flung open so that it shuddered on its hinges.

'Ah, it's yourself, Màiri,' her friend observed as she hurried to see who had stormed into her kitchen, 'Do come through,' she muttered ironically to the broad, rigid back blustering into her front room, 'Will you be wanting a wee *strupag*?'

'I've no time for that, Mairead,' Màiri wheezed as she thumped her basket down on the table. 'I need to get a place on a cart to Uig in a moment.'

'And why would you be going all the way there? And when it's getting dark too?'

'I have to be at the Land League meeting at the school of course. John MacPherson is speaking and yon Reverend MacCallum.'

'Did no-one arrange more suitable transport for you?' Then seeing the furtive look in Màiri's eyes she tutted gently, 'You've not been invited to be on the platform?'

'Do you know those two are paid £1 a week, just fancy it, to speak at Land League meetings,' she blustered, 'as well as the Reverend being paid by his church. And there was me being invited to all those meetings in Glasgow and up here, just for a wee bit of money to pay for my travel. It's not right.'

'Well, you know I don't understand these political matters but I know John has a family to keep. Anyway, I thought you were a supporter of the Reverend MacCallum.'

'Well, he's a Reverend but not a Free Church minister. So he can't have the same depth of learning,' she declared, waving a triumphant finger, 'and with all that gallivanting round the island he can't be ministering properly to his flock.'

'You've changed your tune, Màiri. Back in May you were praising him to the heavens after hearing him speak at the Fairy Bridge. "The Prophet of Waternish" you called him.'

'Well, I've had cause to revise my opinion since then. His head's been turned and he's too full of his own importance now.'

'And of course he can't compare with a handsome young prophet from over the water,' Mairead laughed.

Màiri fell silent and Mairead glimpsed a flicker of pain in the peaty depths of her friend's eyes.

'Come on, take the weight off your legs. The water's nearly boiling and you can spare a moment for a cup of tea. If you want to go to the meeting you should go. I'm sure folk will be pleased to see you. I just hope the young men don't get too excited. We don't want any trouble while there are still marines on the island.'

'From what I hear the soldiers are more interested in chasing the lassies than in chasing crofters,' Màiri sighed as she plumped down onto a chair and her louring expression lifted. 'Some of them will soon need my services as a midwife. It'll be an important meeting. The reporter from the *Oban Times* will be there.'

Mairead handed her a cup, 'Yon Duncan Cameron? He's a funny one. Did you hear about what happened to him? Last month when the gunboats arrived all those reporters were desperate to get their telegrams sent from Portree. That fellow Cameron usually borrowed a horse from the minister at Stenscholl but he was a hopeless horseman, sitting on the beast like a sack of tatties. So he was relieved when another reporter offered him a place on the waggonette that the rest of them travelled in. He was thankfully lowering his aching backside onto the seat when he glanced up and saw the other reporter riding off like the Devil on the minister's horse to get to the Post Office first.'

Màiri slurped her tea and laughed, 'Men can be such fools. They're taken in so easily. Even more so when there's a woman involved. Remember that Mrs Gordon Baillie? She fooled that popinjay Ivory. He invited her to dinner with Alasdair Ruaidh and the pair of them drooled over her fair hair and tinkling laugh. Then later she went with Ivory over to Glendale. When they arrived they heard a crowd cheering ahead of them. And who was it holding forth to the crowd, there in his city suit with a waxed moustache and tam o' shanter but Mrs Baillie's so-called secretary? "The landowners have stolen your land. Are you going to wait for the government to act or are you going to be men and seize the day?" And Mrs Baillie meanwhile was gathering the folk together in the centre of the village to sing "God save the Queen."'

'It would've helped if they'd known the English words and even then they wouldn't have approved of singing something that wasn't a psalm', Mairead smiled, 'Still, as I recall, it was you who described to me the wonderful reception in Portree where she presented her grandfather's sword to John MacPherson. You praised her for her speech comparing the Braes folk to some warriors from long ago who held back the Persians from getting through some pass or other in Greece. She was as gracious as a Queen you said, wishing Lord MacDonald a long life in the affection of his people. You all lapped it up like fresh crowdie.'

'Well she was a very convincing actress,' Màiri conceded, pouting, 'Who would have guessed that she would have left the island without paying her bills? I wonder if she still has her *'bide-a-wee'* secretary to keep her warm at night,' she added wistfully. 'Anyway, time I was away.' She hoisted herself to her feet and picked up her basket.

'Is that a bottle I can hear clanking, Màiri? You're a caution!'

'I never go visiting empty-handed.'

'Nor without something to say either.'

Màiri swept through the door in full sail.

CHAPTER 37

Uig, Isle of Skye, December 1884

The schoolhouse in Uig was already crammed to bursting but Màiri squeezed herself through the press of bodies. The audience was mostly men. There were only a few shawls and bonnets bobbing among the caps. She wriggled through, elbowing a space for herself and inhaling the smells of peat fire, rough tobacco and the sweat of man and beast rising like a mist from the audience. She nudged the young man standing next to her and introduced herself. At first he looked blank but then his face split in a broad grin.

'I'm Donnie MacLeod and I've heard about you right enough. You helped bring my wee brother Archie into the world. My mother said that he was slow about making an appearance. He's still like that now, late for everything. She heard you were up in Skye and sent my father off hot-foot to fetch you. Everyone breathed a sigh of relief when you came in the door and you soon chivvied my wee brother up. When it was all over you poured out a dram. Pappa had his hand out ready but you said, "It's the mother who needs it," and he was packed off to get water straight from the stream to bathe the baby in. He went out muttering about what a mad idea it was.'

'And has your brother grown up strong?'

'Aye and he never takes a cold at all,' Donnie laughed.

'As it happens I've brought a bottle with me tonight. Take a swig and pass it along.'

'Well that's grand, thank you. We'll have to be careful as there's plenty of Temperance folk here tonight.'

John MacPherson came forward to open the meeting, a solid man with a bushy beard. He stood calmly, watching until all the shuffling and murmuring ceased. He spoke in a quiet but penetrating voice, 'In the last few months I've been travelling the length and breadth of the Highlands; on foot, on horseback and by boat, through weather sometimes fair but more often foul, to talk with people like yourselves, loyal members of the Land League. There are so many of us now that it would be easier to stop the waves of the ocean than to slow our advance. We'll continue the struggle against the landlords and the agents of the government until we have justice, both for the crofters with too little land and for the cottars who have none at all. When I was released from prison I vowed that the spark of protest in the heather would become a blaze. The heat of that fire is now singeing the ears of our nation's leaders down in London.'

He waited for the foot stamping and cheering to stop, a smile curving his lips, 'The landlords and their factors often have the advantage over us because they're cunning, while we honest men say what we mean. Think of that wily old fox, MacLeod of MacLeod.'

He was greeted with groans and shouts. 'What does a cunning fox do when he's troubled by fleas? He picks up some dry wool in his mouth and goes backwards into a burn against the current. Then he puts his whole body under the water until only his long snout is showing. When all the fleas are gathered on the wool he suddenly thrusts his muzzle below the surface and lets the wool float away with the fleas aboard. Then they become someone else's problem. That's what old MacLeod did. First he evicted the folk from Bracadale and sent them to Glendale where of course they were given less land than they held before. Later he sold the land in Glendale so that the crofters, like the fleas, became someone else's responsibility. That's how ...'

'And I'm sure that the new owner would be blamed for the old laird's wrongdoing,' interrupted Màiri in a booming voice, 'That's what happened to poor Mr Lachlan MacDonald. He was wrongly accused before the Commissioner gentlemen of evicting tenants when the deed had been done before he ever bought the land. Of course it's the rich men who come up from the South to buy up estates who are the real devils, not so much the lairds from the old families who ...'

'Just what I was leading up to Madam,' MacPherson intervened smoothly, aware of the craning necks and frowns of disapproval in Màiri's direction, 'When I spoke to the Commissioners I told them we wanted to own our land, not just the poor scraps we have now but the land that was wrongfully taken from our forefathers. All men are equal in the sight of God and all are entitled to use the land that He has given us. I said the landlords in Glendale could not give us a satisfactory reply but kept telling us to have patience. Our ancestors died after waiting patiently all their lives and we can wait no longer. Yet here we are now waiting for the Commissioners to write their report. We've been treated as badly as if we were Irish Fenians who use the club and the gun. Warships have brought soldiers to our shores. Still we've been forbearing and welcomed the marines as guests but our forbearance can't last much longer. It's said that the mills of God grind slowly but exceedingly small. I trust that the mills of the Commissioners will grind a little faster and render the landowners just as small.'

His voice dropped to a fierce whisper towards the end. His head drooped and he reached out his arms in front of him. It seemed to Màiri as if he was drawing his listeners in to hold them against his heart. She cheered with everyone else, thinking what an inspiring speaker he was, glowing with life like a hot peat. Every word pealed out, summoning each of his listeners personally. Then he smiled modestly and turned to introduce MacCallum.

The minister stepped forward, a slighter and younger figure than the middle aged MacPherson. His features were less careworn. Well, thought Màiri, he had enjoyed a softer life. His burning eyes darted over the audience and when he spoke he used dramatic gestures, sweeping his arms wide and repeating phrases for emphasis. He must have been practising those tricks when he was in the pulpit, she thought. His strange Argyllshire Gaelic wasn't easy to follow either. Still he was a vigorous speaker, well versed in the Bible. He spoke in a vivid way so that she could picture Moses, carrying his staff aloft and leading the Israelites out of slavery in Egypt and forward to the Promised Land. 'Do not be slaves to men but children of God. Be of good courage. There are many that will stand against you. It is better to fall in righteousness than to stand in injustice.'

His words have a fine ring, she thought. I was right to describe it as a new dawn breaking when he stood with us at Fairy Bridge. Maybe Mairead was right about me being contrary in turning against him.

'As Lazarus, the brother of Mary and Martha of Bethany, was held in the sleep of death for so many years, so too were we Highlanders held in the sleep of slavery. In the fearful darkness of the house of death, he that was dead heard the quickening voice of the Son of God saying to him, "Lazarus come forth," and he came forth, still bound in his grave clothes. It's the quickening voice that our brethren heard in the house of bondage and they too are coming out.'

His voice crackled and sputtered with emotion. As he ended he wiped his glistening forehead. As the gusts of applause began to wear themselves out, MacPherson stepped forward to thank him. Donnie whispered in Màiri's ear, 'Come on, get up and sing while everyone's on fire.'

'I fully intend to, young man,' she replied with dignity as she squeezed herself to the end of the row before advancing to the front. 'After all that fine speechifying we should open our mouths and hearts for a song or two,' she shouted.

MacCallum's mouth gaped open in surprise before snapping shut again. He squared his shoulders and intoned, 'Well, Mistress MacPherson, it's indeed a surprise to see you here tonight. I didn't know you were expected.' His eyes bored into her, daring her to challenge his authority.

'Surely, Sir, it matters not whether I was expected. I'm ready and willing to sing some of my verses and I believe the folk here would be pleased to hear me.' Her voice was firm although she could feel her legs quivering at the minister's fierce stare. Everyone waited, spectators at a trial of strength.

'On the contrary, it certainly does matter. Look around you. This is a meeting for men, for crofters to discuss serious matters, not a cèilidh.'

'We want to hear Màiri sing,' called out Donnie in a slurred voice, 'better a song than a speech any day.'

MacCallum fingered his clerical collar and glowered, 'It seems I need to remind both you and the good lady of what St Paul said, "Let your women keep silence."'

Donnie spoke in a soft, boyish voice, 'Tell me please, Sir, does St Paul mean that women should not speak in front of men at a meeting?'

'Indeed he does. He was speaking about women in church but I think we can take him to mean all public places. That's why I would request Mrs MacPherson to resume her seat and behave with modesty.'

Donnie grinned, 'Well I do believe that we have a solution to this wee problem. Mrs MacPherson isn't going to speak, is she? She's going to sing. Does St Paul have anything to tell us about women *singing* in public?'

MacCallum's voice sliced through the laughter which followed, 'Young man, do not bandy the word of God with me. I have a closer knowledge of the Scriptures than you. 1 Timothy reads, "I do not permit a woman to teach or have authority over a man." That statement can brook no argument.'

'She's only going to sing a song or too, not lead us into battle or become a Member of Parliament,' another voice called out.

'And she's one of our own. We want to hear her,' shouted a man from the back.

MacCallum drew himself up to his full height and proclaimed in his strongest pulpit voice, 'The time is over for women to sing. We need manly resolve to go forward now. Mrs MacPherson, you've played your part in voicing the pains that the Gaels have endured. However, you are of the weaker sex and heavy with years. I suggest you should stay quietly at home and leave the task of land reform to the men.'

'Do I look weak and delicate to you?' Màiri boomed, turning on the spot and flexing her arms, 'Am I some poor *cailleach*?'

Cheers and clapping rebounded from the walls and ceiling.

'You could pick up the wee minister and tuck him under your arm, like a pet lamb,' someone else in the audience shouted.

Màiri waited for the noise to abate and spoke again, 'Were the brave women who fought the police at the Braes weak and delicate? They had the blood of brave clansmen coursing through their veins.'

'We don't need sermons from a minister of the Established Church, the Church that's hand in glove with the landlords,' shouted Donnie, 'Our Free Church ministers support their flocks. How many parishioners do you have in Waternish? I've heard it's only your family and housekeeper that take Communion. That won't keep you very busy.'

A different voice from the back could be heard chanting the mocking rhyme, composed at the time when the Free Church had broken away, leaving many of the Church of Scotland kirks nearly empty:

'The Free Kirk, the Wee Kirk, the Kirk without the Steeple,'

and other voices joined in –

'The Auld Kirk, the Cauld Kirk, the Kirk without the People.'

MacPherson decided it was time to intervene. He walked forward to stand beside MacCallum who was glowing with rage. MacPherson raised one hand and spoke, not too loudly so that people had to quieten down to hear him, 'All of us here are standing shoulder to shoulder for the cause of justice. We're all marching behind the same banner. Our enemies – the landlords, Sheriff Ivory, the politicians in London – would be rubbing their hands in glee if they could hear us now, attacking each other.' He mimicked a clipped Edinburgh accent, '"Just look at those ignorant savages, still fighting their clan battles. If we leave them alone they'll destroy each other and save us the trouble of doing it."'

He waited a minute for his words to sink in and turned to Màiri, 'Màiri, nighean Iain Bhàin, you have been a mother of song to us and a light of inspiration. You'll always be welcome in our midst. Please sing for us.'

While all the arguing had been going on Màiri had been running through in her head which songs she would sing. She glanced at MacCallum, who was silent although his eyes glittered angrily. She was determined that her performance would last longer than his. She would sing "Farewell to Skye," one of her best known and liked songs. She ran through her favourite verses:

> The rock of the ravens
> Its waterfall rushing down
> To the pool you could sail a boat on

Even with a telescope
You couldn't see the bottom
Since Finn the giant bathed his feet there
And turned the water brown

Let all music makers sing with joy
Of their own homeland,
Boast of its fame,
Its honour and dignity
We don't mind, we know
That over all of you
No place the dew falls on
Can be more beautiful.

And there were a good twenty more verses too. "Island of Mists" she would save to the end, with its message of hope,

Remember your hardships,
Keep up the fight
The wheel will turn for you.

But before then I'll surprise them by singing, "The Crofters' Meeting," she decided.

They came from all corners,
Like streams running down the hillside,

And when she came to the lines;

The clouds of slavery lifting,
The day MacCallum stood with us at Fairy Bridge.

she would sing lustily and nod to him in acknowledgement. She would be gracious in victory. Well, Mairead, you had no need to be so fearful on my behalf. You'll be amazed at my feat, she thought as she stood, head held high, legs planted firmly – a captain sure of her vessel and riding the waves of fame.

CHAPTER 38

Sailing from the Isle of Skye, September 1885

Màiri only stopped waving when she could no longer see the fluttering handkerchiefs on the Braes shore. She pulled her shawl more tightly around her shoulders. Departures by sea always made her shiver, ever since that first time when she left home on the ship with no sail so many years ago. She leant on the rail of the steam yacht, stroking the supple wood and shaking her head to dislodge the cuckoo sadness that had nested there, uninvited. After all, she had much to feel joyful about. Here she was aboard the *Carlotta,* a beautiful vessel belonging to Mr Charles Fraser Mackintosh, soon to be Member of Parliament for Inverness-shire. And she wasn't merely a passenger but a keystone of his election campaign. How she loved to say his full name to herself, sinking her teeth into each word, even though he insisted that she call him Charles. Ah, there was the mighty named man himself, coming over with Hector MacKenzie, less stout than his father The Clach, but with the same gleam in his eye.

'Will you come below now, Màiri? It's chilly on deck,' Charles enquired.

'I'll come later. I like to feel the sea spray on my face.'

The boat was breasting the waves a little heavily as they sailed down the Sound of Raasay, between the spread palm of Skye and the long thin finger of the smaller island. Màiri looked out on the gulleys gouged out of Raasay's flanks; valleys left by dried out tears. No wonder, she mused, when you remembered what had happened there, only a generation ago, during the famine years. Rainy, the landlord had been decent towards those who had decided to emigrate to Australia. He had bought their cattle, given them shoes and clothes for the journey and paid for their passage out from Liverpool. Those who stayed behind believed their lives would improve now they were not so overcrowded.

But then the blow fell. All the people living in the thirteen townships he owned had been forced out, their houses pulled down around them and their fires doused. Everyone had to leave, although some of them could barely crawl through hunger and illness. When she closed her eyes and felt the spray splatter her face she could sense the salt tears of the families who were driven out.

Charles was a true warrior and friend to the Gaels but she knew he would frown at such a fanciful idea. His life was too far removed from the tragedy of eviction and exile. John would have an inkling of what she meant and maybe The Clach would too. What would Isaac have made of it? Strain as she might she couldn't summon up his voice in her head any more. His slow rumble of a voice was silenced. She could still see him; his sturdy body and his padding walk, his full head of reddish hair and his hands, broad as a bear's but light of touch. His smell, sharp and smoky had vanished too. His scent was the reason she had decided to train as a midwife – so that she could escape from nursing men and breathing in the raw maleness that made her want to howl in despair at her loneliness.

He would shake his head in wonder at how times had changed. Not just her appearing on platforms all over Scotland but what about the Braes women who had fought as hard as, if not harder than, their men? Even Charles believed that women should have the vote if they owned their own house, but that would only be ladies of course. He was a strange mixture, Charles, so smooth and confident in many ways but shy in others. It came out in his speeches. He had a good taste of Gaelic on his tongue and knew when to use proverbs that his listeners would enjoy but when it came to answering questions he would often reply in English, claiming that his Gaelic was rusty. Was it spending so much time down in London that made him water down his Gaelic malt? Well, the two of them together were able to deal with awkward characters in both languages. What was that rhyme that rude fellow had shouted out at the Inverness meeting? She was practised at herding verses together but the English rhythms were harder to keep penned in her mind:

> A Tory first and then a Whig,
> He always was a wretched prig,
> He'll preach all day about the land
> His words are like a rope of sand

Then dum de dum – until the stinging insult at the end –

> O crofters, you softers
> To listen to such tosh
> Or vote for that daoter, Fraser Mackintosh.

She had felled the heckler – 'I've better words that those' – and sung the poem she wrote to commemorate his first victory, when he won the seat for the Inverness Burghs over ten years before. What a hero's welcome they had given him, clapping their hands loud as thunder.

Lost in her thoughts, she hadn't noticed a wiry, fair man in a sailor's jacket come towards her, 'Mrs MacPherson? Welcome aboard. I'm Sandy MacKellar, the mate on this yacht.'

'How are you Mr MacKellar? It's a fine boat. I shall enjoy my trip.'

'Do call me Sandy. She looks well but she wallows in stormy weather. When we were in South Uist she was stuck off Ushinish lighthouse. She couldn't make any headway, even at full steam. The Captain wanted to return to Lochmaddy but Mr Fraser

Mackintosh wouldn't hear of it. Why can't they have election campaigns when there's better weather?'

'Charles wouldn't let tides or storms stop him,' she laughed, 'How has the trip been otherwise?'

'Not bad. The gentlemen like to have wee visits ashore, so that gives us some peace. Mr Mackenzie was off visiting Eilean Donan Castle and very disappointed to find it a ruin with great lumps of the stones lying in Loch Duich. Still I cheered him up with the story of the pet lamb of Kintail. The crew have had a grand cèilidh or two ashore as well. Great sport it was too without the toffs there. Perhaps we'll have the chance of another one while you're ...' He stumbled to an embarrassed halt.

Màiri laughed, 'I might spend time with toffs but I'm not one of them. I'll be happy to sing for you. But what about this pet lamb of the MacRaes?'

He smiled and tamped down the liquorice black tobacco in his pipe while he chose his words.

'You know the MacRaes?'

She nodded, memories of her sister's husband at their wedding brushing her cheek in a cold draught.

'The lamb belonged to *Murchadh Ruadh MacRath* from Carn Gorm. He's a crofter and shoemaker, descended from Finlay, the first MacRae ever in Kintail. Three of his uncles fought against the Redcoats. His family had been removed from a township in Morvich and then been given a scrap of land and no grazing. Meanwhile the land at Morvich was let out as a deer forest by the landlord, Mr James Thompson Mackenzie, to a tenant called Winans, an American. There wouldn't be sight nor sound of him for years and then suddenly he would appear, demanding a deer drive.' Sandy curled his lip.

'He was too idle to stalk the stags and just waited for the animals to be chased towards the guns. Then he told the crofters that they weren't allowed to graze any animals in the forest and he claimed that the forest reached to the high water mark of Loch Duich. So when any of them stepped over their doorsteps they were trespassing on the deer forest.'

Màiri snorted in disgust.

'Not long after this Murdo was out cutting peats when he found a lamb that had lost its mother. So he carried the poor creature home as a pet for his children. At first it was so frail that his wife had to give it milk or eggs with a little sugar from her own mouth but it recovered.'

'I can remember having a lamb like that. It never got used to being outside when it was grown. It used to come in to lie in front of the fire or sit on a chair with its four wee feet waving in the air.'

'Aye,' he continued, 'hand reared lambs imagine they're some sort of woolly dog, don't they? Anyway, Winans got to hear about the lamb getting out to eat a few blades of grass, so he sent his stalker, Willie Ross, to chastise Murdo. He's got a redhead's temper and he shouted at Ross, "Devil a hair of the lamb will I put away for Winans. I'm thinking of getting more sheep and a cow too. Let Winans go his length and I will too. He's a rich man and I'm a poor one but let him remember that God is stronger than man."'

'He sounds like a man after my own heart. What happened next?'

Sandy took his time relighting his stuttering pipe, 'Winans couldn't bear to be flouted. He sent for a sheriff officer from Dingwall. Murdo was out when he arrived but the man saw the sheep and started to follow it. When the township folk spotted him they started to follow the man. He was scared, poor thing, and hid until Murdo came back home. Then he found his courage again and told him he would be sent to prison if he didn't get rid of the lamb. By now Murdo was heartily sick of the whole business and the next day he sent the animal to Dingwall to be sold.'

'Amid lamentations from his children, I'll be bound. Was that the end of it?'

'For the lamb. It ended up on someone's plate but Winans was set on revenge. He tried to force Murdo to agree never to keep any stock again, but being a proud man he refused. So the case came to court. Murdo had to travel down to Dingwall, but Winans and MacKenzie, the landlord, were allowed to give their evidence down in London. MacKenzie thought Winans was mad to claim that one sheep would damage the forest and offered to cancel his lease. But he wouldn't hear of it. He claimed that the low ground was needed for the deer in the winter and what if all nineteen of the cottars got a pet lamb? They would eat the whole forest. The lawyer who cross-examined Winans asked, "Are pet lambs really more of a disturbance to the deer than are the cottars?"

"What I desire is to get rid of the cottages and their inhabitants. I shan't leave a stone unturned until I get rid of them," Winans replied.

The sheriff found in Murdo's favour and told Winans that he would have to pay the expenses of the trial.'

'I should hope so.'

'But Winans was like a dog snarling over his bone and he got another sheriff to turn the judgement upside down so that Murdo would have to pay the costs. Finally there was another court case and the decision went against Winans. The judges said that the whole question was about whether the lamb was trespassing and it couldn't be trespassing when it had been killed and eaten before the case came to court.'

'So there was justice in the end. One thing puzzles me though. Who paid for Murdo to appeal to the court? He could never have afforded to himself.'

'Now, that's a mystery. Some folk suspect it could have been Thompson MacKenzie himself as he was so shamed by that lunatic Winans.'

'It's good to hear the Highland gentleman had a conscience, unlike yon dreadful foreigner.'

'You should compose a song about Winans', Sandy said, 'and show the world what dangerous madmen we have to deal with.'

'Aye, I might but I'm kept busy with our own Skye devil, Sheriff Ivory.'

Captain MacClachlan was right yet again in his gloomy predictions about the weather. There were tempestuous winds and rain. The people coming from Knoydart to hear Charles speak were already drenched from their journey before they reached the open air meeting. Màiri was gratified to see Mr Eneas MacDonell of Camusdarroch there, standing tall and majestic in his plaids, ignoring the rain. Intent faces looked up in the eerie light of the moon. They strained to hear Charles' voice against the howling of the raging elements and the jangling of the harness as the miserable horses tossed their heads.

Màiri was on her best behaviour in the presence of the gentry, applauding the speeches in a dignified manner and singing her more respectable songs. Then back home to Skeabost again while the *Carlotta* toured the Outer Isles before returning for the final big meeting in Portree.

Charles was given a true Highland welcome when the boat arrived. As he boarded the carriage waiting at the pier men leapt forward from the crowd to unyoke the horses and haul the carriage up the steep brae to the Portree Hotel. Later he spoke to the crush of people in the schoolhouse. Màiri was pleased to see his glow of confidence as he rose to speak, 'Mr Chairman, Ladies and Gentlemen, I'm leaving Skye tomorrow morning and this is the last meeting that I'm to address in the

Hebrides, with the exception of one tomorrow at the Braes. There are about three weeks elapsed since I arrived on the West Coast from Inverness and I have been very much engaged during that time. There has not been a day when I have not addressed one, two, three and sometimes four meetings and I must say that I've obtained a reception in the islands which, I don't believe, has ever been given to any private individual before. If I might be allowed to put myself for one moment in comparison with a man who was once the greatest chief in the islands, Somerled of the Isles. I don't believe he himself was received in his journeyings with the cordiality that I was. He no doubt got good receptions because he was a man of great territorial position but I have no such claims upon the people. I come merely professing to be their friend and they apparently know and believe that I am.'

The applause exploded around him and she could see that Charles' eyes were gleaming with unshed tears. She clapped her hands until her palms smarted, delighted that he had been able to lose his usual reserve and speak from the heart. He learnt that from me, she thought proudly.

He continued his speech in the same warm tone, encouraging the new voters to elect him and praising the Skye people for their bravery in supporting the land agitation that had led to the setting up of the Royal Commission. He was among friends, so there were few hecklers. However, he was asked again the question that had dogged his campaign, 'Were you ever a member of the Junior Carlton Club?'

Màiri opened her mouth to boom out a response but he caught her eye and put his finger to his lips.

'I think that question is very personal,' he declared to the accompaniment of cheers, 'I resigned my position in the Club before I became a Member of Parliament. Also, wasn't our venerable

Liberal leader, William Gladstone himself, once a member? That puts me in very august company.'

The audience laughed and the meeting ended with him being accepted as the fit and proper person to represent Inverness-shire in Parliament. Màiri was flushed with motherly pride. At long last the wheel was starting to turn.

CHAPTER 39

Skeabost, Isle of Skye, July 1886

'Come in John and warm yourself by the fire.' Màiri was shocked to see how haggard her old friend had become. When he loosened his plaid she could see his gaunt frame, like a family cow after a hungry winter in the byre. She hid her concern by bustling around, bringing him crowdie and oatcakes. She watched over him while he ate as if he were a patient.

'I wish you'd take a dram, John. It would revive you.'

'Now, Màiri, you know my opinion on strong drink,' he muttered impatiently, his usual good humour vanished.

'As you wish, John,' she soothed him. 'Tell me about your travels on Tiree. It still has a Highland landlord, doesn't it?'

'Aye, the Duke of Argyll, and very pleased he is with himself,' he snorted. 'During the famine he encouraged, no doubt with a good push, nearly half of his tenants to emigrate. He took what he called their wretched scraps of land and joined them together to create larger crofts, nearly twice the size of the ones on Skye.'

'Wasn't that a good thing for those who were left?'

'Aye, as far as it goes. But at the same time there are three hundred cottars on the island with barely any land at all. There's an active branch of the Land League there and the Commission raised their hopes. But the crofters are under the iron fist of Hugh MacDiarmid. The "Black Factor" he's called, and not for his hair colour. He keeps them working on the Duke's land three or four times a week, as if they were Russian serfs. Then more trouble started to brew last year after the *Cairnsmuir* ran aground off the island.'

'Aye, I remember hearing about that. It was carrying drink, wasn't it? So at least the islanders could toast the ship.'

He smiled thinly, 'I wouldn't begrudge them a few gleanings from the sea to warm their blood but the Duke was very heavy handed. The customs officers complained that threatening groups of islanders kept them away from the wreck. All the officials could find were empty cases on the beach.'

'What did they expect? The tides would have swept the bottles away,' she chuckled.

'The Duke wasn't amused at all. He had notices put up in the churches forbidding his tenants from drinking spirits at weddings or any other gathering. I think it was that action that hardened the people's resolve.'

'And no wonder!' Màiri declared.

'Anyway, resistance came to a head with the lease on Griannal Farm ending. Everyone expected the land would be divided up among the crofters but, no, the lease was given to one man, Lachlan MacNeill, a crofter who had done well for himself. He was also a leading member of the Land League branch while his brother Neil was the President. You may well look shocked, so were the other crofters. They expelled the brothers and elected a new President.'

'Quite right, those two acted like Judas, betraying their fellows,' she shook her head, making her jowls wobble like the wattles of an agitated hen, 'How can Gaels betray each other for a mess of pottage? And what about you, John? You were betrayed too in losing the election in Glasgow? I thought the Irish there were supposed to be shoulder to shoulder with us, so why didn't they vote for you? I heard that when that fine young Mr McHugh urged them to support you he was booed.'

John rubbed his aching eyes, 'Aye, he was brave to do that but you must understand that the Irish voting for the Tories wasn't a personal attack against me.' He snapped his eyes open and looked at her intently, 'It was about political strategy. Parnell had made a deal with the Tories. He was promised their support in Parliament if he helped them win the election. So all the Irishmen in Britain were told to vote Tory.'

Seeing her disapproving expression, he continued, 'Let me put it another way. Parnell was like a maiden being courted by two men, a Liberal and a Tory. He had to decide who would be the better marriage prospect and accept that offer. So he chose the Tory. Davitt wasn't happy at the idea of allying with the Tories but his hands were tied. He didn't want to publicly disagree with Parnell and split the Home Rule party, especially when it's on the cusp of winning. So, in a way Davitt and McHugh are like the bride's relatives, not impressed by the successful suitor but making the best fist of it so that they can avoid fighting in the family. You don't look convinced, Màiri.'

'No, I'm not. I don't like all that scheming and plotting, but I'm not such an innocent that I don't know it happens.' She folded her sturdy arms like a resting prize fighter, 'But what I can't stomach is knowing who did win the seat; that Alexander Craig Sellar. I can hardly bring myself to spit out his surname, the son of that devil who drove the folk out of Sutherland for that witch of a duchess. May Patrick Sellar's name be damned for all eternity.'

John's shoulders slumped, 'Aye, that name turns my blood to ice too but we mustn't condemn the son for his father's sins.'

'You're too long suffering John. You should have heard what The Clach said about it. He was as white as snow with the shock. The son is cut from the same cloth as his father. It was the son who threatened to take The Clach to court for writing about his scunner of a father. And now he's been elected to Parliament.'

'Aye, The Clach took a risk in publishing his book. I was surprised, I didn't think he had so much steel in his soul.'

Màiri raised her eyebrows at the sharp edge in his voice. He reached out to touch her arm, 'Take no notice of me. I'm a battle weary sour old man. I've never seen eye to eye with The Clach. I've always suspected he was more interested in fame than in the plight of the crofters. And I can't help feeling envious that he survived libel threats while I didn't.'

Màiri squeezed his hand, 'Aye, John you've laboured hard in the vineyard and seen The Clach treated like the Prodigal Son while your efforts are forgotten. He likes fame right enough but he changed after the Battle of the Braes. His eyes were opened to all the injustice.'

John swallowed hard and cleared his throat, 'I fear there's more trouble to come. I urged the Land League on Tiree to be careful if, more likely *when*, the police are sent there. I told them not to help the police but not to attack them either. I worry about the more irresponsible reporters too; the ones who exaggerate the dangers. It means the authorities start jumping at shadows.'

'Everyone's weary of waiting for the Commissioners to decide on fair rents. They're bound to reduce them in the end, so you can't blame folk for not paying them until they know what's happening,' Màiri replied.

'Aye, but they should own their land outright and not be paying rent at all.'

'But if we have fair rents won't that be like the old days before the Clearances?'

He gazed at her before replying softly, 'The old days are gone for ever and I doubt they were ever that golden. You're a dear old friend and I have no desire to offend you but even the decent landlords like Lachlan MacDonald still keep the best land for their own use. And they drive a wedge between their tenants by treating some of them more generously than others.'

Màiri's jaw was set firm, 'I know full well what you're hinting at, John. I've nothing to be ashamed of in living in this house rent free. Lairds have always kept bards and pipers. It's part of an old tradition and I'll have no more said about it. But I'm fearful we'll have marines and police here on Skye again. One of the teachers in Skeabost told me that they aren't going to be paid any more because the rates haven't been coming in. He said it's the fault of the crofters for not paying anything. I don't see how that could be.'

'Ah, Alexander MacDonald, the man with a finger in every pie, is the one causing trouble. He's pressing Ivory – how ironic that such a black soul should have such a white name – and the Secretary for Scotland, begging for another military expedition because the crofters have refused to pay, not only their rents, but also the school and poor rates. So MacDonald claims that because the crofters refuse to pay their share of the rates there's no money to pay the teachers. Well, our friend Charles with his sharp lawyer's brain smelt a rat. He asked the Government for the full details of the arrears of rates on Skye. I'm sure you can guess who owed the lion's share, nearly three quarters of the total – the landlords. And which of the landlords owed the most? None other than Alexander's own employer, Lord MacDonald himself. It would be a wonderful sight to see Ivory himself marching down to Sleat to serve a summons on Lord MacDonald.'

He stretched and stifled a yawn, 'Your good food and fire have revived me Màiri, but I'm ready for my bed now.'

'Off you go, John. Everything's ready for you. That factor MacDonald will surely be shown up as a fool, as he was at the trial of the Braes men.'

CHAPTER 40

Inverness and Portree, Isle of Skye, November 1886

Inverness, November 1886

My Dear Màiri,

I trust this letter finds you in good health. I know how much you thirst for news. So I'll do my best to refresh you. Things have gone from bad to worse since John's visit to Tiree. I've been rendered speechless. A rare occurrence, I can hear you say.

As I feared the new Tory government is as prone to panic as the old Liberal one was, like an old lady screaming and lifting her skirts when she sees a mouse. The landlords squawked and the gunboats were sent in again as if the government were dealing with Indian or Chinese natives. Three ships with four hundred marines and police! Soon there'll be enough of them for every family in Tiree to take one home as a household pet. As always the crofters treated the soldiers with kindness. They offered them milk to drink when they were overheated with carrying guns and ammunition round the island. So much for them being savages as the Duke of Argyll claims.

What a travesty of justice that the Tiree men were found guilty of trespass and obstructing the Messenger at Arms. Lord Balfour claimed that sentences of four to six months would have a 'wholesome effect on the people of Skye.' I would like to ask him how these sentences compare with the scant eight months meted out to the directors of the City of Glasgow Bank when it collapsed not long ago after losing six million pounds. Argyll's new tenant is ensconced at Griannal farm now. We can only hope that the Duke won't try to bully the Commissioners when they finally arrive on Tiree to set the rents.

And what about the trouble on the Misty Isle? I can't believe that marines and police are back again. Ivory's back to his old trick of making enemies. Did you hear about him picking a fight with Chief Constable MacHardy because he wouldn't allow his men to wear the 'Ivory medals' the sheriff gave them for their 'valour' in attacking women and boys? While the two of them were quarrelling aboard ship the marines and policemen were left waiting in open boats in the pouring rain. I feel some sympathy for the poor fellows having to follow Ivory's orders when their hearts are probably not in it. It's almost impossible to see Ivory himself as a human being rather than a bogey man but I wonder if he's scared witless underneath all that bravado. I'm enough of a cynic to believe that the government, whether Liberal or Tory, is making use of him. Like a magnet he draws everyone's hatred to himself and he'll be the scapegoat if the unrest gets worse.

Enough of gloom! We both like to find the lighter side in any story. I heard a tale from Tiree that will amuse you. It concerns the reporter from The Scotsman. The newspaper men descended like vultures on the island but they couldn't transmit their stories because the march took place on a Sunday. What an affront to God-fearing folk. So this particular correspondent suggested a sort of cease fire to the other reporters. Why didn't they all delay sending out their articles until Monday? Then they wouldn't offend anyone by asking for the reports to be sent by telegraph on the Sabbath. The others agreed.

What did the cunning fellow do then? He sent off a carrier pigeon with his report. I suppose it was acceptable for a bird to break the sanctity of the Sabbath but it was attacked by seagulls. So it flew back to the hotel at Scarinish, scattering the pages of the report through the island as it tried to escape its tormentors. The Tiree branch of the Land League called for the reporter to be expelled from the island. Would that we could do that with Ivory!

I was thinking back to some of the merriment we had in the earlier days. What about that time we were on the wee ferry boat

at Strome with Charles and Hector? Calum had said he would risk
taking us across all together but I noticed his lips moving in prayer as
we sailed over. Didn't you make a song about that trip?

Have you composed anything new recently? Why don't you pen some
verses about Ivory for me to publish? Don't hold back, after all I prevailed
against Sellar's son when he threatened libel action against me.

Your dear friend,

The Clach

*

Portree, November 1886

Màiri banged the door of Donald Stewart's shop as she left. She
had been looking at two gowns he had brought out for her. One
was navy blue, but it was the other one that had caught her eye;
an unusual shade of deep red. He must have seen how much she
coveted it because when she asked the price he narrowed his eyes
and said, 'Seven shillings and sixpence'.

She dropped it as if it was on fire and shook her head. 'I've
changed my mind.'

'Why don't you want it?'

'Because it's terribly dear.'

He smirked, showing sharp little teeth. 'Well, if you compose
a song for me I could reduce the price.'

The impudence of the man! The words flooded through her
mind and out of her mouth,

> My double-edged blessings on Donald Stewart,
> Offering me a dress for composing a song.
> I won't give a song to a man unless he deserves it
> Even if a hundred dresses land on my doorstep.

That had wiped the silly smile off his face. The day wasn't going well at all. The Clach's letters usually made her laugh but this morning's one had left her troubled. He had forced her to see Ivory in a different light, as a puppet whose strings were being pulled by unseen hands down in London. She would much prefer to see him as an imp of the Devil. Then she could flay him in verse. She had put the letter to one side and decided to go and buy herself a new gown, only to have Stewart try to swindle her. Now she stood outside the shop, uncertain what to do next.

A woman was walking towards her, her head bent over her shawl. She looked up at Màiri and smiled in recognition.

'It's Mistress MacRae from Peiness, isn't it and this wee *isean* is one of mine,' she said, stroking the top of the baby's head that was poking out of the shawl, 'I've just had words with Donald Stewart. Fancy him thinking he could cheat me! But what's the matter? You're crying. Is there something wrong with the baby or is it one of your other children?'

The mother wiped her face with the end of her shawl. 'Please tell me Mistress MacPherson, How much is a baby worth?'

'What an odd question. A baby's a gift from God. You can't put a value on a baby. A baby is priceless.'

'He's worth more than six pence, then?'

Màiri put her hands on the other woman's shoulders and squeezed them.

'Something has happened to distress you but I don't understand what you're talking about.'

The mother gulped, 'Well, you know the sheriff has been sending men around Skye to seize people's belongings for not paying their rates.'

'I know. He had to bring in carters from Inverness because no-one here would do his dirty work,' Màiri glowered.

'It was our turn yesterday. He sent his man MacDonald. In he came to our house with his notebook, looking at everything and shouting out prices, "Dresser and crockery, 1s.6d; wooden seats, 2s; chair, 1s; bed, 2s; puppy dog, 1s." Then he saw the cradle …' Tears sprang into her eyes again, 'and without drawing breath, he shouted out, "cradle and child, 6d." I thought it was some sort of strange joke. But he said with a straight face, "I'll take the baby too."'

Màiri's face gaped open in disbelief as she put her arms around her.

'My man came in and ordered him out. Six or so soldiers and police came in and took everything away, except the wee one.'

Later when she returned home Màiri sat down and unfolded The Clach's letter to read it again. Then she started her reply, slashing her pen across the paper:

Woodside Cottage
Skeabost Bridge.

My Dear Clach,

I'm in excellent health except for a touch of rheumatics but Mairead tells me I've nothing to complain about for an old boiling fowl. I smiled when you reminded me about the overloaded boat. I've been singing the song to myself since you reminded me of it:

> *Clach said to you Màiri, stay ashore*
> *Calum will come back for you*
> *You take up three places by yourself*
>
> *Don't you worry about Màiri –*
> *The captain's game to take a chance*
> *We'll get safe across the dark waves*
> *And into harbour.*

I know I was never one of Pharoah's lean cattle. Mind you, high living has turned you into a fatted calf yourself. So the two of us together would certainly sink the vessel if we boarded it now. We're not like poor John who has become so scraggy.

My heart is overflowing with rage when I think about Ivory. I've just heard about his latest crime and I'm so angry that I can't even write about it. If wishes were deeds he would have fallen dead to the ground from the weight of curses heaped on his head.

Then I thought about the bards of old who wrote elegies when the chief or a noble warrior died. I've written an elegy of a different sort for Ivory. I imagined that his body had been found in a black pool in the Mointeach Mhòr, near St Columba's Loch.

Ivory can't scare me with the threat of prison. I've faced Hell on Earth already. If you don't want to risk him hauling you through the courts you could write that the song was composed by "Mary of the Poems" to throw him off the scent.

> *Elegy song on Ivory*
>
> *I heard a story*
> *On a very happy note*
> *And were it not true,*
> *It would be a hard blow*
> *That the mean Coward*
> *Had been stuffed in a hole*
> *Without a board or a rag fixed about him*
>
> *Blessed be the hand*
> *That tightened the knot,*
> *Pressing down the hard, surly head;*
> *It put the bald-pated Coward*
> *In a scanty, narrow cage,*
> *And no official or officer will free him.*

Every floor under roof-trees
Will be swept smoothly;
Musicians will make a joyful noise;
Dancing will be seen on every field,
And music will be heard on every height
Where the Coward acted as a worthless pursuer.

A soldier, supposedly;
He was to be seen in action
Only on a dung-hill or on grey muck-heaps;
He was a spectre haunting children
And women at night,
Until he disgusted Europe.

A grey stone will certainly be placed above you
Which will record every one of your iniquitous bribes,
And how you sold your entire reputation
For a little booty,
For the sake of your corrupt ground,
Exactly like Judas.

There, I feel better for spitting that out.

With kindest regards,

Màiri

CHAPTER 41

Portree, Isle of Skye, May 1887

Màiri smiled as the crowds in Wentworth Street parted respectfully to allow her a place in the front row. Banners with hand written slogans swayed above their heads; 'The Earth He created for the Children of Men', 'Land for the People' and 'The Crofters are mightier than the Landlords'. The old were cheering as heartily as the young and women were waving their handkerchiefs. There was a cry of, 'Up with the bonnets!' and arms shot up like masts, their bonnets whirling on the top of walking sticks. How rousing it was, so different from the curses and hisses that had greeted Ivory not so long ago.

He was coming now, striding up towards the Portree Hotel. The cheers redoubled. Voices called out for a speech.

'We won't move until you talk to us,' a man shouted. He stood in the hotel doorway and turned to face them, his lips curving slightly. He was a tall slender figure, standing very upright and not at all self-conscious about the droop of his empty right sleeve. Suddenly the mouth beneath his bushy dark moustache burst into a boyish grin, 'It looks as if I've been taken prisoner. Never mind, I'm used to that. Wait a moment. I'll be back.'

Michael Davitt leapt through the door and a moment or so later appeared at the window on the floor above, nimbly pushing the sash up one handed. The window was set in the wedge shaped front of the hotel, jutting out at the corner of the street, facing the Square. As he leant forward holding on to the balcony he looked like a spectator in a box at the theatre gazing down at the stage. He waved to acknowledge the cheering and then he spoke in a clear voice with only a hint of an Irish accent.

'I'll speak first in Gaelic and then in our Irish tongue. That way the important people can understand.' He smiled and paused, 'Those unlucky souls who only have the English will have to wait for a translation.' The crowd laughed and then fell silent to drink in his words.

'I know that the sympathy you've shown in this enthusiastic welcome is extended more to the people I represent than to myself on account of anything I have done personally. I'm glad to know that recent distinguished visitors to your island haven't succeeded in convincing you that the people of Ireland are wrong in their struggle for Home Rule. I never believed for a moment that the people of this island, or of any part of the Highlands of Scotland, could be convinced by any amount of sophistry that the Irish cause was not a cause deserving of the sympathy of the Scottish people.

'In many respects we are not only identical in race, but in political and social aspirations as well. The land system that has impoverished Ireland and made it the home of agrarian misery and crime has also been felt in this island and in other parts of Scotland. I am sure that the people of Skye are convinced that if the Irish succeed in abolishing landlordism, an effective blow will be struck at the root of a similar evil system in your islands.

'Reading the mottoes you have on your banners, I see you are a people who study the Bible. Well, many of our modern philanthropists would rather you gave your spare time to the study of political economy. They think it was a mistake for the Creator to lay down a doctrine that the earth was created for the children of men. They would rather call your attention to the study of Adam Smith and Malthus, writers who, they say, show that Providence made a mistake when he said the land was created for the people to live on. They would rather you put the Bible on one side and took up the doctrines of those distinguished writers, and they would be better pleased if you agreed that your duty is to put up with misery and small patches of land in order that sheep and deer may enjoy the soil which God Almighty created for you.

'I believe that the land of Scotland, like the land of Ireland, was made by Providence to be enjoyed by the people. I've come here to advise the people to follow our example in Ireland; to go in for the complete abolition of landlordism. That system of legalised robbery is a social evil that must be got at in order to be torn up root and branch.

'This must be done before the misery, suffering and degradation existing in Ireland can be cured; and my advice to the people of Portree and the people of this island is, not to be satisfied with half measures of change, but to go in for what is your just and your natural right, the ownership of the land of Skye for its people.

'For Ireland I know well that in the coming struggle we'll have the moral support of public opinion in Scotland, and with that strength behind us I hope that the next time I come to Skye it will be my privilege to say that Home Rule has been won in Ireland, and that landlordism is ready to give up the ghost.'

After the peals of applause had fallen silent he introduced his colleagues, John Murdoch and Angus Sutherland MP, 'I'll bid you farewell for I think this window is becoming too crowded.' Then he smiled and withdrew into the upstairs room. Màiri, wedged tight in the shoulder to shoulder crowd, noted how everyone listened attentively enough to them but the first froth of excitement had blown away.

Later, while Davitt was being shown to his room, Angus, slender like the Irishman but shorter, turned to John, 'A good speech, I thought,' he said in his slightly abrasive, high pitched voice, 'His Biblical references went down well of course. Then he flattered them by talking about political economists as if the audience had the likes of Malthus on the tips of their tongues. Of course he kept the message vague; all Celts together fighting for their rights. Then he neatly slipped in the idea of abolishing landlordism.'

John shook his head, 'Aye, but I fear the Skye folk will let the idea of land nationalisation go over their heads. They just want the Land Commission to set them fair rents. They don't want to get rid of the landlords altogether, I'm afraid. It's Davitt the man they're drawn to, not to his ideas, more's the pity. I've spent years trying to drum up some radicalism here but it's a thankless task. If you'll excuse me I must go and find my old friend Màiri and invite her to join us. She was standing out there right at the front, like an old warhorse smelling the battle and pawing the ground. Although I fear that she doesn't always know which side she's fighting for – crofters or landlords.' He sighed and half smiled.

Angus grimaced, 'From what I've heard she's less like a warhorse and more like an old cow feeling frisky in the spring. I hear she half suffocated poor Edward McHugh with her unwelcome attentions. Has she developed a taste for gobbling up young Irish patriots, do you think?'

John frowned before replying sharply, 'I'm sure Michael will be pleased to meet her. He knows how highly people here regard her and he's always a gentleman.'

'Oh, don't be so prim, John. Michael can look after himself but I'll keep out of her way. I can't endure listening to her assuring me how wonderful the Duke of Sutherland is now that he's changed his spots and become the complete model landlord. I've been lectured enough already on that subject by Professor Blackie. The Good Lord preserve me from sentimental Gaels who fawn over landowners just because they're from old Highland stock.'

'Well Angus, we must keep a broad church if we're all to work together. We should follow Michael's example. He heartily disapproves of Parnell trying to be all things to all nationalists but never a word of criticism passes his lips in public.'

*

After bringing Màiri in, John introduced her to Davitt, 'I'm sure you two will have much to discuss. Did you know, Màiri, that Michael here has written poetry?' John clasped his hands behind his back and declaimed,

> In England's felon garb we're clad,
> And by her vengeance bound;
> Her concentrated hate we've had –
> Her justice never found.

'Please stop there,' Michael said, raising his hand and flushing, 'In the name of all the poets who have ever sung in Erin, I will not have my past poetic transgressions disinterred from a kindly oblivion.'

'As you wish,' John shrugged, 'but you can't deny that your prose is very stirring, even if you disclaim your poetry. The audience today certainly thought so. I shall leave you two to become better acquainted.'

'What despair your poor mother must have felt when you had that terrible accident,' said Màiri pointing at Michael's dangling right sleeve.

He was nonplussed. Usually people pretended not to notice his missing limb although he would often catch them looking furtively at it when they thought he wasn't aware. Unbidden, the memory came to him of his nine year old self, lying in a feverish half-conscious state. He could hear the urgency in the doctor's upper class tones and the softer gusts of his mother's voice. The whispering in his ear though was more distinct. It was their neighbour Molly Maden, murmuring, insistent as a creeping tide, "Don't let the doctors butcher your arm. What will you be with only one arm? A cripple for life. Every *Sasannach* boy will insult and beat you." The coils of her voice slithered into his mind, hissing about a life in Heaven free of pain and suffering, squeezing his will to live.

But his determined mother had prevailed. He was pinned down and gagged by a chloroform-soaked cloth. He awoke mourning the loss of his right arm, taken off almost to the shoulder. He knew though that he was relieved to be alive.

With an effort he wrenched his mind back to the present, 'It was a terrible shock to her when she saw me brought back from the mill in a cart, dripping blood along the cobbles. She feared I'd never be able to earn a living. Providence works in strange ways though, doesn't it? I lost a limb and my job but I went back to school and gained an education. The parish priest sent me to the best local school and it happened to be a Wesleyan one. That's where I learnt that religious differences don't have to be a barrier to working together. It's not religion but the ownership of land that's the sword that divides. After my schooling I was even able to find work as a one handed printer before I got caught up in the cause of Irish freedom. If I'd kept my arm I would have stayed as a factory slave.'

'And if I hadn't been sent to prison I wouldn't have become the bard of the Land League.' She jabbed him in the ribs with her elbow, 'We're both jailbirds. Of course *I* was innocent and wrongly accused. What about you?'

Again he was startled by this elderly woman's bluntness. Well, she was a simple soul, a sturdy peasant woman, like so many of those Irish exiles he remembered from his youth. 'I was wrongly accused of planning to murder an associate. The police found a letter written in my hand sent to another member of the Brotherhood. They claimed it was proof that I intended to bring about the death of a third party, to punish him for being a police informer. The truth of it was that I had written telling the other man not to assassinate the traitor.'

'So like me, you were innocent of the accusation made against you. Were you able to understand what was said in the courtroom? I had the double tribulation of being innocent of any crime and of not being able to follow what they were saying about me.'

'Fortunately I was fluent in English as well as Gaelic but I know that many of my countrymen have suffered in the same way as yourself,' he replied gently.

'One thing surprises me in your story. What I've seen of the police here shows me that they aren't wise enough to outwit a Gael using only half his brain. So how did they manage to catch such a smart young man as yourself?'

'Bad luck and treachery too. They arrested me at Paddington Station on my way to pick up a consignment of guns being brought down by a passenger from Birmingham.'

Màiri laughed aloud, 'Wasn't this a giveaway when they were looking out for you. She flicked his limp sleeve. His eyes sparked but he held his peace.

'Would those guns have been used against policemen or soldiers?'

'They were never used in anger,' he said with quiet emphasis.

'So maybe we are different, after all. I was completely innocent but in your case you were not proved to be guilty.'

'I do believe that you would have made a lawyer of great distinction,' he retorted, with an abrupt laugh.

She touched his hand, 'Forgive my forthright words. I'm a *cailleach* who speaks her mind. I know your cause is a true one and you've paid a high price for your beliefs. I was only in prison for a month but you had to endure a long sentence. It must have been terrible to hear the judge's words when he sent you down.'

How hard it was to keep up with this woman's twists and turns, one moment sympathetic, the next probing. Softening, he replied, 'I can remember waiting in the cell under the courtroom in Newgate Prison and reading the words scratched on the walls by prisoners who had waited there before me. "M.D. expects ten years for the crime of being an Irish Nationalist and the victim of an informer's perjury" is what I wrote.' He laughed bitterly, 'I was wrong. I was sentenced to fifteen years.'

'How were you able to work in prison with only one arm?'

He screwed his eyes up, 'A good question. They couldn't find suitable work for me in Dartmoor; one-armed men are rare birds in prison. I was put to stone breaking until the blisters on my hand made it impossible for me to continue. Then I had to haul a cart around the prison until the harness rubbed my stump raw. The next job was by far the worst of them all – bone breaking.'

'What's that?'

'You may well ask. The bone shed, next to the cesspool, was where all the bones from the meat supplied to the prison were collected. They stank to the very heavens after being left outside in the sun. My job was to pound this decaying mess into dust to be used as manure.'

Màiri wrinkled her nose and laughed, 'Well, I was foolish enough to ask.'

'Later I was moved to the washhouse. After being frozen for so long I was now too hot, drenched in sweat from working the wringing machine. Of course, as a political prisoner I was treated worse than the common criminals.'

'You were like me. Your pride wouldn't submit to prison.'

'Only men who have no honour can bow to injustice.'

'How your poor mother must have suffered again. Still, I suppose even the English would not be harsh enough to stop her visiting you.'

'No, she never came to see me but that was my choice.'

Màiri looked perplexed.

'I wanted to spare her further pain. So I persuaded my parents to join my sister in America. So my mother uprooted herself for a second time.'

'Not as hard I hope as when she had to leave Ireland.'

'No indeed,' he replied with a harsh laugh, 'In the old country she had to stand outside her house with three young children, and me a babe in arms, all her possessions at their feet, watching the roof of the house falling in as the thatch was set alight.'

Màiri nodded, her face bleak, 'And the men who did it not caring if you lived or died.'

'My mother used to tell me the story of how they teamed up with another emigrating family who let them travel on their cart.' He chuckled, 'All I can remember is the horse. He was a rascal or a true Irish patriot. He kept breaking his traces and bolting back the way we came. He didn't want to go to England either.'

'How did you keep your spirits up in prison through those long years?'

'I told myself that although my poor body was imprisoned my mind was a bird flying through the high windows. I paced up and down in my cell planning my future. The other thing that helped me was finding a way to send letters out secretly. My mother was greatly amused to hear I had become a washerwoman. '

'I was a washerwoman when first I arrived in Inverness. I was good at it too but I can't imagine you were much use.'

'I did manage to tangle the clothes and trample on them with my big boots.'

They both threw their heads back and laughed. The sound carried across the room to where John and Angus were talking to a much more serious group. 'Well, Angus, do you still think Michael needs to be prised from her clutches?' John muttered under his breath.

'And are your parents still alive?' Màiri was asking him.

'Sadly my father died while I was in prison but both of them took pride in me.'

'How grand it must be when your family applaud your actions. My children could never understand why I've worked so hard for the Land League. They wanted me to be a quiet, respectable widow, sitting in my doorway, knitting,' Màiri's voice dropped.

He reached out to touch her arm, 'I'm sorry to hear that. It's lonely in the world of politics, especially for a woman. Would you be my Scottish Godmother and slap my leg when I get too big for my boots?' He smiled and took her arm, 'Perhaps we'd better go and rescue John and Angus. They look as if they've been trapped by the brigade of bores over there.'

Màiri looked over at the two men with a stern face, as solemn as Queen Victoria herself.

CHAPTER 42

Oban, 1892

It was evening on a calm September day as Màiri plodded alongside the town's broad bay. Admittedly, it was a fine sight with the island of Kerrara standing guard at its entrance but was not to be compared to the view spilling out from Portree harbour. After all, the name 'Oban' only meant 'small bay'. She felt tired and sank down on a wrought iron bench to brood over the events of the day. She had been looking forward to the first meeting of the Mòd, a chance for Gaels to compete for prizes in singing. The Clach had told her all about it,

'Of course the Inverness folk were snooty. They said the name was not Gaelic enough because it sounded like the English word, "moot". Their noses were put out of joint because the upstarts of Oban thought of the idea first.'

She had been determined to come as it was so long since she had sung in a big hall but the journey had exhausted her. Ten years ago she would have taken the travelling in her stride. The event itself had all started off in the familiar way with a full hall and scores of greetings as she made her way to sit at the front and listen to the men's competition. Not an inspiring collection either, except for the young fellow who won; a Skyeman with some fire in him.

Then it was the turn of the women. She went up first, to murmurings of recognition. She knew most of the men on the platform of course and there was *Fionn* Whyte himself from the old Skye committee, sitting at the centre, his fair hair turned to dandelion down. So naturally she had shaken hands with them all and walked over to speak with the judges sitting behind a desk to one side. They had looked startled for some reason and hustled her over to the singers' stance. That was when she had suddenly realised that she was alone.

In the early days when she had stood up to sing in the rough, smoky Glasgow halls she had steadied herself by imagining that Bran, Finn MacCoul's fierce and loyal dog was standing beside her, his warm flank leaning against her leg so that she could reach down to ruffle through the black tufts of his hair. He was afraid of nothing and the heat of his courage pulsed from her hand and coursed through her body. As time went on and cheering replaced heckling in the halls she allowed the hound to leave her side. As she stood up to begin singing she would imagine herself at the top of Fingal's Seat, overlooking Portree, and repeat her own words silently,

> Sit on a green hillock
> On Fingal's Seat,
> Look all round about you
> Between both land and sea.

In her mind's eye she would send Bran loping down the hill to hunt deer on the *Mointeach Mòr* below. This morning though she had need of him again by her side but despite her desperate whistling he wouldn't come back. She felt her throat tightening as she began to sing, releasing a squeaky, bleating voice,

> The beautiful, fashionable tartan.
> That you can't get in the shops
> Is white, blue and scarlet,
> In Mary Hutchinson's tartan.

A mist of swirling doubt engulfed her and there was no sign of Bran. She had thought that a light-hearted song would be right for the competition. Everyone would expect her to sing one of her own compositions. As most of them were well-known already she had gone back to a poem from her early days as a bard, a ditty joking about the Union Jack tartan. Now she wondered if she should have chosen something more serious. Well, there was nothing for it, she would have to keep going,

> Although my voice is failing me
> It's so long since I left my homeland,
> And sang you Gaelic verses
> About Mary Hutchinson's tartan.

If only I had the second sight I would have known that this verse contained a prophecy, she thought, ruefully. She pressed on regardless,

> When I was busy herding cattle
> By the streams and pastures of my homeland
> I would be kept warm by my plaid
> Of Mary Hutchinson's tartan.

> When I came to Glasgow
> Expecting to see it in the shops
> I couldn't get hold of a length
> Of Mary Hutchinson's tartan.

Her voice had rallied as she soldiered on through all the twenty-two verses, gaining strength as she described the heroes who had worn the tartan, starting with William Wallace and Rob Roy MacGregor and leading up to the Highland Brigade in the Crimea. As she ended, she felt, too late, Bran's trembling flank rub against her side. The applause was loud enough but it wasn't like in the past when she had waited, a still moon in a clear sky, feeling the waves of sound drawn towards her. So it was no surprise to hear that she had not won first or even second prize but a blow to the pride none the less. How she wished that she could talk to Mairead. She could say what no-one else would dare to, giving her a good dousing of cold water from the well. Why did she have to go away to Australia, so far away that the two of them would never meet again in this life?

'I'm old and a widow, Màiri, there's nothing to hold me here. I want to return while I still have the strength for the journey. Surely you, of all people can understand that?'

So what would Mairead say about the competition?

'You've overcome much worse in your life. It's only your vanity that's been dented. How much applause does one *cailleach* need in a lifetime? Isn't it time to stand aside for the younger folk?'

All true enough my old friend, Màiri thought, but not what I want to hear. She shifted her weight on the hard bench as she brought her thoughts back to the present. Looking about her she noticed a thickset man of her own age strolling by. He had sun bleached sandy hair and neat features that looked marooned in his fleshy face. She caught his eye and greeted him in Gaelic.

He looked startled and stuttered a reply. 'I'm very rusty, I'm afraid. I've lived in Australia most of my life. So Gaelic sounds like the calling of gulls to my ears now.' He looked hot and flustered in his good tweed suit.

'Why don't you rest your legs for a moment?'

'Thank you, Madam. The name's MacLeod. I'm over from Australia. I took a fancy to see my homeland one more time.'

'Màiri MacPherson. My good friend has gone back there, she's near Sydney. Maybe you know her?'

He rumbled with laughter, 'I stay hundreds of miles from there. People in Scotland have no idea of how enormous Australia is. The horizon goes on for ever. It's dry too of course. You need plenty of land to keep the stock going in droughts.'

'If only Highlanders had plenty of land, and less rain.'

'That's why so many left, wasn't it? For the empty space. Mind you we had to clear the natives out first. They thought they could wander where they liked. Naked savages with no idea about farming. In the early days I always carried a rifle in case of trouble.'

'So what happened to them?'

'A few work for the settlers but most of them are idle fellows who want to lie in the sun with a bottle for company.'

'Outsiders used to call us Highlanders ignorant savages too,' she said frowning.

'That's quite different, you're Christian souls. Have you come for the Mòd?'

'Aye. I'm a bard. I've sung plenty about the Gaels being driven from the land and exiled abroad. I believe the wheel will turn again and their children will return.'

'Never! Emigrating was hard but if you put your back into it in Australia you can get rich. It's shocked me coming back and seeing how poor people are. Wee hovels and raggedy clothes – no better than when I left.'

'Where did your family live?'

'On Skye'.

'Well, that's where I'm from, from Skeabost. Maybe we met in our youth.'

'No, impossible. We lived down in the south, in Sleat, before we were evicted.' He clamped his lips together, his bluster deflated.

'That's no shame on you but on the landlord who forced you out. Do you farm now?

'I started out on a sheep station and worked my way up to overseer. But I longed to work with horses although I'd never owned one myself. So I put my savings into a teamstering business, carrying goods between the sheep stations and the town.'

Màiri saw how his eyes shone. She looked at his thick fingers, flexed together in his lap and remembered supple hands plaited through a horse's springy mane. 'What did you say your Christian name was?'

'Maybe I didn't. It's Andrew … well, Anndra really but I stopped calling myself that years ago.'

'Why on Earth would you deny your birth name?'

He grunted, 'Because I got tired of defending it with my fists. "Sounds like a girl's name" was what I heard all the time.'

She watched him while she sang softly,

> Young ones dancing, making music,
> All gone, the glen is empty,
> Anndra's ruined home full of nettles
> Reminding me of when I was young.

He looked wary, 'I'm sure my old home's ruined but you never saw it'.

'True, but I meant it to stand for all the exiled people and their ruined houses. Do you remember being at the Fairy Bridge with the other lads who untethered the horses and raced them?'

'I don't think so. I don't remember. That was years ago.' His expression was as empty and forlorn as an abandoned house, 'I must be on my way.' He tipped his hat and scuttled off quickly for such a large man.

Màiri sat motionless, thinking of that laughing young man, beautiful as a water horse. She had expected to see grains of sand and tiny glistening shells in his hair, signs of the creature's treacherous disguise. She would have led another life if she had come to know him and followed him to Australia. Her songs would never have been born. How relieved she felt that her desire to know him had not come true. It would have been like the granting of a Fairy wish, one that turned into a poisoned chalice.

Anyway, he had become so ugly and bloated now that she had barely recognised him. "And do you imagine the years have been any kinder to you?" It was Mairead's mocking tones again. Màiri shook her head to dislodge them.

'There she is!' The shrill voice of Professor Blackie pierced the air. He trotted away from his companions and stood in front of her, waving his gnarled stick, 'Where've you been hiding, Màiri? We've been hunting high and low for you. You must come and partake of a little refreshment with us before the cèilidh tonight.'

Like a tired but willing old hound summoned for a walk she struggled awkwardly to her feet, taking his arm as he pranced around her.

CHAPTER 43

Inverness, July 1893

The Clach sat nursing his malt, swirling it around the glass with a sigh. He always felt a prickle of envy when he sat in the restrained and expensive décor of Charles' house. He looked up and spoke to his host, 'It's a great pity John didn't attend tonight. It left a gap in the ranks of us old stalwarts. I'm surprised he didn't take the train up. Is he in good health? I always think of him as the immortal *Murchadh na Fèilidh*, forever striding through the heather.'

'I believe he's well although he's older than he seems – well into his seventies now – still active, of course and campaigning for working men in Glasgow. One of them described him as a man "as sturdy in frame as in opinions." I think that sums him up exactly,' Charles replied with a smile.

'He did say that he would come to the meeting, didn't he? Then he declined at the last minute. It's not like him to be so changeable. Anyway, I miss the old fellow, even though he can never quite lose his earnestness, like a minister on holiday.'

Charles cocked his head as he heard the thud of the heavy knocker on the front door. There were quick footsteps, a mumble of voices and a minute later the maid was introducing John himself.

'Well, talk of the Devil! We were just saying how we missed your company tonight,' exclaimed The Clach, while Charles offered him refreshment.

'No, I'm not hungry, thank you, just a little tired.' John sat down, smoothing his kilt and stretching his legs before continuing,

'I'm sorry to be so discourteous in arriving late. I had said that I wouldn't attend but today a restlessness overcame me and I found myself hastening to the railway station. Of course once I boarded the train I realised that it would not be right to arrive unannounced at the Assembly. So I whiled away some time eating dinner in the town.'

The Clach's eyes were sparkling pebbles in the doughy folds of his face, 'Now John, if you weren't a total abstainer I would say that your story has a suspicious whiff about it.'

'Well now,' John replied with a weary smile, 'That's an old joke of yours but I do believe that my abstention from strong drink will outlive your jesting about it.'

'You'll want to hear about Charles' speech tonight. It was superb. His theme of course was about the Society reaching its majority. It's hard to believe back then, here in Inverness, how little interest there was in the Highlands. At that time the Lowland cities seemed much more fertile ground for a Gaelic renaissance.'

John nodded but didn't speak.

'Of course it's a real boon for the Society now that Charles has more time to devote to it. Parliament's loss is our gain. Still it's a great pity that Charles lost his seat. It was down to the disloyalty of the Portree clique. I find it impossible to comprehend how they treated him so shabbily after his magnificent record of service to the Highlands. Why did ...'

Charles raised a hand to cut him off, 'All that's done with now and maybe it's for the best. I had thought earlier on about retiring from politics and there was some discussion about you taking over the seat if ...'

The Clach's torrent of words swept on, 'Some Skyeman had even approached Michael Davitt to stand as their Member. I mean no disrespect to the man, he's a talented orator and politician, but an Irishman to represent Scots? And what about our new sitting member, the fine Dr MacGregor who has spent his whole career in London?'

Charles sighed, 'Times change. The Crofter Members are no longer free agents as we used to be, we're expected to follow the beat of the Liberal drum. So my refusal to support Irish Home Rule put me beyond the pale, if you'll pardon an Irish idiom. The Skye men interpreted this as hostility towards their Celtic friends.'

'But not all of them were so misguided, I'm pleased to say. A Mr MacDonald, from Garafad, resigned in protest as the President of his local Land League branch when Charles wasn't re-selected.'

Charles chuckled, 'Ah, yes, the good Mr MacDonald wrote that he disagreed with my opinions on matters not directly impinging on the Highlands but he considered my past and present services to be considerable. He took strong exception to having an unknown candidate foisted on him and said that this highhandedness was what would have been expected of an Eastern potentate. Now that's a fine example of an independent minded Highlander – a Gaelic Voltaire. Didn't Voltaire declare that even if he detested another man's opinions he would defend to the death his opponent's right to hold them?' He shrugged, 'If you enter politics you can't expect universal admiration. Anyway, I shan't be idle in my retirement. I'll continue my research on the Clan Mackintosh and write antiquarian articles for The Clach's newspaper.'

Both men turned to look at John, disconcerted by his unusual silence. He sat forward in his chair and shook off enough of his lethargy to reply, 'You've worked tirelessly for the crofters, Charles, but now it's time to leave the stricken ship before it finally sinks. I fear that the best days of the Land League are over. I heard from

Màiri that a mass meeting organised on Skye by the League had – can you guess how many people attending? Several thousand you say? Too high. Can you hazard an estimate, Charles? Five hundred? A tenth of that would be nearer the mark.'

'Talking of Màiri, how is the old termagent?' asked The Clach, grinning, 'I've heard she spends her time gallivanting around the island, inviting herself into people's homes and hectoring them about how they should do their own spinning and weaving in the old way as if folk didn't have shops now.'

'She's still in robust health,' John replied with an expression of reproof, 'I dare say that she's feeling a little at a loss now that all the excitement over the publication of her book has died down. She's been put out to grass like the rest of us.'

'She always enjoyed the limelight. I can't imagine her sinking back graciously into retirement,' chuckled The Clach.

John suddenly banged his fist on the arm of his chair and spoke loudly, 'She's right to be disappointed. So am I. She always believed that the wheel would turn back to the better days before the Clearances but the turning back has only been a notch or two. Little's been achieved. True, the crofters have secure tenure and fair rents but they haven't gained any more land and the cottars still have nothing. Meanwhile the Gaelic societies, like the one here, have stayed as complacent as ever, filled with well-meaning exiles, cramming their thickening figures into Highland dress. They talk fervently about Gaelic rather than speaking it and listen to Gaelic songs they can barely follow. That's why I couldn't face the celebration tonight.'

Seeing the stiff expressions of the other two he lowered his voice, 'Of course the historical research is valuable, but Gaelic is being treated like a mummified language. Forgive me for speaking bluntly. I don't want to sound like an embittered old man.'

John stayed silent, looking down at his hands, clenched on his lap. Charles finally broke the silence, 'Well, old friends, we've been fortunate to live through momentous times and played our part in making history. We've stayed together despite our different opinions. I'm heartily glad, John, that you boarded the train and joined us. By the way, I think you would have agreed with a suggestion I made in my speech tonight about promoting Gaelic among the propertied classes. We hear much nowadays about competitive examinations, for entering the Civil Service for instance. Now, I suggested that when a Scottish mother was seeking to employ a nursemaid she should look for good health and character but also require her to pass creditably in the singing of Gaelic airs. Think of the effect on the rising generation. What we learn in the cradle is fixed in our hearts for life. At the very least such a measure would improve greatly the repertoire of songs heard at Gaelic Society concerts.'

He smiled and The Clach nodded. John stretched his reluctant mouth into a smile but his downcast eyes reflected a mute desperation.

CHAPTER 44

Temperance Hotel, Portree, Isle of Skye, 1898

How strange that it had come to this, her world shrunk to one small, bare room where she lay stranded on the bed. The floor had become a treacherous sea; she could barely cross to the door, a harbour out of reach. There was a great beast astride her chest, pinning her down, as heavy and pitiless as the Black Dog in the old tales. But where was brave Bran? He had killed the black beast and she could push off this panting, breathless weight if she used all her strength.

It had been only a few weeks past that she had been able to walk, slowly but steadily, a basket of bannocks on her arm for when she went visiting. Well, if she couldn't walk she could still sing. Those miseries downstairs with their curdled faces couldn't shut her up; always muttering about praying for her immortal soul. Had they forgotten the old saying that when the world ends only love and music will endure? She would use her last breath to sing. It was for her music that people had flocked to see her. So she would sing a rousing song, the one about Ben Lee. She had been so overjoyed when the Land Court had, at last, ruled that the grazings there should go back to the crofters. It was a sign that the wheel would turn,

> Give thanks to the people
> under the rule of the Queen,
> Who made the law so secure
> That we won't lose Ben Lee.

Bear greetings with gladness
To the farmers of Valtos,
Who were first in the battle
And did not flinch in the fray.

Those heroes most noble
Who were never in trouble
Had their fists put in handcuffs
Wrapped hard round their wrists

And the kindliest women
Of the most mannerly bearing
Their skulls were split open
On the sides of Ben Lee.

Many an eye will moisten,
Travelling over by steamship,
As people look with affection
On the braes of Ben Lee.

And although the Cuillin and Glamaig
Are among the loveliest mountains,
Their history will rank no higher
Than the foot slopes of Ben Lee.

That was all she could manage for the time being. She
would have a wee rest and then sing the rest of the verses. She
had taken care to praise everyone who fought on their side; the
newspapers who supported them, all the leaders of the League in
Skye, Norman 'Parnell' Stewart who had won £25 from Ivory for
libel. That was a sweet victory. They would all be remembered
in history and so would she, as the bard who wrote about them.
No one would silence her. It took a mortal shock for her to find
her voice in the first place and she had never fallen silent since.
It had been hard to always stand tall and steady when so many

thought her too strong a brew for a mere woman. She knew that envious people mocked her behind her back. She had suffered too in moving away from her children and losing the solace of their company. It was a lonely life being a female bard. If only Mairead had not returned to Australia. She was the only person she could truly allow to tease or cajole her, to wrangle and wrestle her with words – the sister she would have wanted. The only soul still alive who had known her back in the days when they had the dew of spring on them and their lives stretched out like shadows at dawn. Why did she have to go? She had never been the same since her husband's death. Màiri knew herself, too well, how hearing your footsteps echo through an empty house made you long to flee it. But to go *so* far away.

'You can't understand, Màiri because you see only the sadness of exile. But I've seen the scattered seed take root and flourish in Australia. I want to see that hope for the future once more before I die.'

Now if she could have a wee dram, not for nothing was it called the water of life, she could haul up her unresponsive body into a sitting position and look out of the window at the shreds and scraps of sunlight she was sure would be in the sky above Portree Bay even on this murky November day. If you were here, Mairead, we could laugh together about how my world has changed. There were times when having taken refreshment after singing at a cèilidh I found it hard to reach my bed, but never before have I found it so difficult to rise from it. Do you remember that time at the inn at Isle Oronsay when it took two or three brawny fellows to help me up the stairs? Now I'm so weak I need a dram to get me to my feet. No chance of a pain quenching draught in this benighted place. What was it Michael said about how he survived the grim prison years? "Give your spirit wings to soar over the walls."

She dozed again to be woken by the sound of footsteps on the stairs and a murmur of voices which she strained to hear.

'She's not an easy patient Sir, always restive. She's forever singing and calling out.'

There was a bark of male laughter, 'Well, I shall take that as a good omen. I would be more worried if she had become quiet.'

'It's yourself!' Màiri exclaimed in delight as Lachlan MacDonald ducked to enter the door, 'Mind you, I can't believe that you condemned me to a cell in a Temperance Hotel of all places. Have you got a bottle hidden about your person?'

'It's not an ideal refuge, I admit, but I was assured me that they would provide excellent nursing care.'

A contemptuous snort came from the bed.

'Not nursing of the standard you practised I'm sure but then I doubt if you're the best of patients.'

His angular face split into a grin as he excavated a bottle from the inside pocket of his overcoat. He sat on the hard chair beside the bed and was relieved to see some colour flow into her sagging, dingy face as she sucked at her drink. He could understand her stubborn wish to go her own way rather than follow the expected path. He too was considered perverse and a traitor to his class for supporting the rights of the crofters and for refusing to allow his sons to be toughened up at public school. Well, he had always followed his own judgement. Even as a young officer in the Behar Light Horse when he had insisted on learning enough of the men's tongue so that he could understand what they were saying among themselves. The other colonials were mystified by his efforts. Now he wondered if the Indian troops had resented his ability to eavesdrop, just as some of his tenants perhaps saw him as a spy even while they complimented him for his command of the Gaelic.

'Will you not have a drink yourself?' she asked.

'The doctor tells me I must ration myself severely if I am to keep the demon gout at bay, but I shall join you in spirit.'

'If not spirits,' she laughed, her chuckle turning into a gasp, 'A dram moistens the singing voice.'

'I shouldn't encourage you for they disapprove of your singing.'

'I need to cheer myself up. I do miss my cottage. Have you given it to anyone else yet?'

'No, I'm keeping it ready for your return.'

She looked at him quizzically, 'You can let someone else have it as long as it's someone I would approve of. I'm hanging on a shaky peg now.' She raised a hand to stop him protesting, 'The fox escaped a long time ago. He was a wild thing but he kept me company. So the house is empty now, as my body will soon be. I know my time is near as I've been having some strange dreams. I dreamt I was down yonder on the Scorrybreac shore, cutting seaweed with a sickle. As I touched some of the slithery stuff it turned into the red tresses of a poor drowned girl. I looked up and who did I see but the fairy washerwoman beating clothes with a rock in the Chracaig stream. The clothes couldn't belong to the young woman for she was already dead. So I knew she was washing my linen to warn me that my time was coming.'

He felt his heart race, uncertain how to keep pace with her flickering changes of mood, 'Surely it's a consolation for you that your words will live on?'

'Aye. I used to believe that the wheel would turn back to the old days and the glens fill up with folk again. Then when I came back to Skye I was overcome with grief at the shepherd's dogs barking at me when I walked to my old home. I don't know what will happen. When you try to move a wheel across rough ground you cannot predict where it will turn.'

'That's true but I believe there have been changes that can't be overturned. The crofters are no longer in mortal fear of being evicted.'

'And we've had some cèilidhs and sport along the way,' she chuckled, stifling a coughing fit, 'Fine speeches too, from Gaels and handsome young Irishmen.' She sighed, 'There have been plenty rogues and tricksters too, especially that scunner Ivory. What about that Mrs Gordon Baillie? She enchanted all the men with her wide shining eyes and flowing locks. Did she fool you too? I was always suspicious of her, of course.'

'She was convicted of fraud, I believe, a few years after disappearing from the island,' Lachlan said, 'But she left a fine sword with John MacPherson. She was no lady at all, only the daughter of a washerwoman from Dundee, I believe.'

'There's nothing wrong with that honest calling. I was a washerwoman myself. So was Michael Davitt. Imagine it! A one armed man beating clothes.'

He smiled, 'Then she became some kind of evangelist I believe and travelled abroad. And that man who was supposed to be her secretary was the father of one of her children and ...'

'They weren't even married!' she interrupted in a scandalised squawk, 'How are the mighty fallen. She richly deserved five years' hard labour, unlike poor Michael.'

'She certainly displayed plenty of dirty linen.'

Màiri laughed but the effort made her sink back, wheezing, on the pillow. He waited while she closed her eyes and, looking around the bleak room, he noticed one of her shoes pushed under the bed. It was a man's shoe, a solid brown brogue, the punched design still showing through the scarred leather. It listed over like a rotting boat abandoned on the shore. Tears began to moisten his eyes.

Suddenly her eyes snapped open again. He blinked and smiled at her. Her hands scrambled over the bedclothes, 'Where has my plaid gone? It's my best one, the one I designed for Professor Blackie.'

Lachlan rescued it from where it had slipped onto the floor.

'Do you remember the battle I had over the design of that plaid a few years ago? A fellow from Kingussie calling himself a tweed manufacturer proposed naming a new tartan of his own in honour of the Professor. I had to write a letter in The Clach's paper to put him straight on the matter. I told him how I had presented my tartan to the Professor some years ago and another one to you. I hope you've still got it?' She glowered at him.

'Yes, indeed. I well remember the occasion when you presented me with it. I arrived at that meeting in Glasgow absolutely frozen on a bitterly cold night. I feared that wearing the kilt and exposing my legs to the chill would invite the gout to attack me. I unwrapped your gift in front of the huge assembly of people who were there that night and very welcome it was too, spread on my frozen limbs.'

Màiri sighed, 'Do you know that the Professor wore that plaid every single day of his life until he died? Even then it decorated his coffin when he was carried to his last resting place. Anyway, I told yon manufacturer that he could buy the pattern from me. Not that he ever did.'

'Blackie was a good friend of the Gael but a very … um … theatrical gentleman.'

'"Blethering Blackie" he was called. Everyone knew him. He even appeared on slogans for the "Royal Drooko" brolly. "I walk the world a rain-tight fella …"'

'"Beneath the Joseph Wright umbrella,"' Lachlan completed, laughing, 'That's something the two of you have in common, a liking for umbrellas.'

She joined in until her laughter turning to coughing and spluttering. When she had recovered, her expression became serious, 'Since he died all his books seem to have been forgotten and people just remember the jokes about him. It's true he was a vain man but you have to put on a performance. People expect it.'

She whispered lines from one of her verses,

> Since vanity is a plant
> That satisfies the flesh,
> It clings to me as firmly
> As the lace to the shoe.

'Maighstir Ruaridh always said we shouldn't waste our time with vain frivolities of poetry and music as we pass through this vale of tears. What could I do though when I had so many verses spilling from my head?'

He heard the distress in her voice and took his time before replying, 'I can't believe that it is wrong to use a God-given talent. Your poems will live on because they inspire people. Professor Blackie on the other hand was a clever man but not a wise one. His poems were written to show off his cleverness, and they were written in English, an inferior language.'

'Are you saying he wasn't much of a bard?' Her tone was horrified.

'Yes, I am,' he chuckled.

She lay back and sighed. A peaceful silence settled between them. She seemed to have drifted into sleep but then she rallied again, 'Do you remember that time when your wee son came to visit me? He was fond of sitting at my feet and hearing my stories. One day, when he was with me, another lad came in to say that he'd seen a big important man coming up to the house in a horse and carriage, with a coachman carrying a big whip. Well of course I knew it was yourself come to find the wandering lamb. "Where's that wee imp?" you shouted, or maybe a worse word. I told him to hide under my skirts. "I haven't seen a sign of him," said I. But he spoilt my story by having to come out for air. He claimed he was half suffocated.'

'That wasn't me. It was another MacDonald I think' he said. Then he saw that her eyes had closed and that she really had fallen asleep this time. 'But it's a good tale nonetheless,' he whispered. His lips brushed her dried out cheek and he smoothed the coverlet over her work-worn hands. He tiptoed out of the room, squeezing the door shut behind him.

Alasdair Dubh: Black-haired Alexander

Bàn: Fair-haired

Banshee (Bean-shìth): Malevolent female fairy

Bealach a'chaoil rèidh: Narrow, even pass

Bean-ghlùine: Midwife

Beinn Buidhe na Creige: Rocky hill of the sunshine

Bide-a-wee: Live-in lover

Blàrach: Cow with a white spot on its face

Bodach: Old Man

The Braes: Group of villages about five miles from Portree

Bran: Dog belonging to Gaelic hero, Finn McCoul

Bugha Mòr: Valley of River Snizort

Bùrach: Mess, muddle

Cailleach: Old Woman

Caman: Shinty stick

Cèilidh: Evening of songs and story telling

Clachnacuddin (Clach na Cùdainn): Stone of the tub – a resting place and centre of gossip for washer women and water carriers in Inverness

Clann na Cloiche: Children of the Stone i.e. Inverness people

The Cuillin: Skye's mountain range

An Cumhang: The narrow pass on the way to the Braes

Dìleas: Faithful

An Dotair Bàn: The Fair Doctor, a factor for Lord MacDonald

Eilean a'Chèo: Island of Mists – a poetic name for the Isle of Skye

Fiann: Followers of Finn McCoul, mythical Gaelic hero

Fionn: Fair

Hielan man's umbrella: Railway Bridge in Argyll Street, Glasgow where Highlanders met

Isean: Chick – term of endearment

Maighstir: Master, Mr

Mo ghràidh: My love

Mointeach Mòr: Moorland near St. Columba's Loch, Portree

Murchadh na Fèilidh: Kilted Murdo

Murchadh Ruadh MacRath: Red-haired Murdo MacRae

Na Fir Chlis: The Northern Lights (lit. The Dancing People)

Piseag: Kitten

Sasannach: English person

Seumas an Sionnach: James the Fox

Sgitheanach: Native of Skye

Strupag: Snack, light meal

Tobar Iain Bhàin: Fair Iain's well

Trusair: Dirty fellow

ACKNOWLEDGEMENTS

I owe my first debt of gratitude to my grandparents, Seonaidh Bàn and Dolina MacRae, now deceased, who first awakened my love of Skye, but many other people have given me help along the way to producing this novel. Alyson Bailes, Rosemary Hagan and Jenny Manson read the first draft and made valuable suggestions that enabled me to chip away at its rough surface. I also made use of Hi-Arts, the excellent professional service for aspiring writers in the Highlands. The established writers Meg Bateman and Angus Nicolson were generous with their time and expertise.

On the research side the Archives staff in Portree were extremely helpful and well-informed as were the people in Portree and Inverness Libraries. I should like to give special thanks to Charles MacDonald who gave me free access to the papers of his great-grandfather, Lachlan MacDonald. Many people at Sabhal Mòr Ostaig, Oifis nan Fèisean and Lasair have enabled me to deepen my understanding of Gaelic language and culture. I owe thanks too to fellow members of The Skye Reading Room for their encouragement. Linda Henderson has been a shrewd and insightful editor, scraping away at the sediment and buffing up the final draft. My son Alan and his partner Laura have contributed much valued emotional and technical support. Finally, my long suffering husband Steve has been my computer expert, sniffer-out of inconsistencies, spell-checker and polisher of prose – all of this as well as enduring my grumpiness when things were not going well.